DEADWOOD
DEAD MEN

PRAISE FOR DEADWOOD DEAD MEN

"This novel is a riveting tale of suspense, love, and murder. It is set in the gold mining camp of Deadwood Gulch, Dakota Territory. Markley truly captures the soul of Deadwood in 1876—a lawless community of vagrants, miners, and merchants. This is a must-read for anyone who loves the stories of Deadwood's infamous past. Markley's work of fiction entertains the possibility of corruption and greed so deeply embedded in the legendary town—the reader will come away wondering if it's true."
> —Rose Speirs, Communications Director, Deadwood History

"The ending is captivating, completely different, and as wild as 1876 Deadwood was."
> —Mike Pellerzi, Lifelong Cowboy, Outdoorsman, and Guide

"A great story of true crimes—and true love—unfolds in Deadwood, in the days when it was a raucous mining town on the frontier. A fast-moving page-turner, this book brings the wild times back to life—murderers, gamblers, sporting ladies all play a part. Calamity Jane attends a play. A severed head is displayed in a restaurant. With a plot that keeps you guessing and scenes that will make you laugh out loud, this is a "must read.""
> —Nancy Plain, Three-Time Spur Award Winning Author

"*Deadwood Dead Men* is a lively recreation of the wild days of the West's most famous mining camp: True to the period without being archaic, addressing modern sensibilities without sacrificing historical authenticity. It's part rousing western, part detective story, and a thoughtful study of character, told with the pace of a thriller. I doubt there's another writer out there with the imagination to present the killing of Wild Bill Hickok as a whodunit."
> —Loren D. Estleman, Author of *The Confessions of Al Capone*

DEADWOOD
DEAD MEN

BILL MARKLEY

G

GOLDMINDS
NASHVILLE, TENNESSEE

Goldminds Publishing, Inc.
1050 Glenbrook Way, Suite 480
Hendersonville, TN 37075

Copyright © Bill Markley, 2013
Cover photo (hand/gun) © Ron McGinnis, www.ronmcginnis.com
Cover photo (historic Deadwood) Courtesy Deadwood History, Adams
Museum Collection, Deadwood, South Dakota
Cover design and interior design by Steven Law

ISBN: 978-1-930584-50-1

Library of Congress Catalog Number: 2011928604

PUBLISHER'S NOTE

This is a work of fiction. Names, characters, places, and incidents either are
a product of the author's imagination or are used fictitiously, and any
resemblance to actual persons, living or dead, events, or locales is entirely
coincidental.

Printed in the United States of America

www.goldmindspub.com

Dedicated to my mom, Gloria Markley, who taught me to love reading, and to my dad, Bill Markley, who taught me to love the West.

In extenuation I should point out that in many cases the lively lies and misconceptions which Deadwood's citizens cherished were more important in shaping Deadwood's history than truer more sober truths would have been, and I say, therefore, about my more suspicious tales, what an old-timer said to me after pouring a real stretcher into my gullible and receptive ear:

"If that ain't true, it ought to be!"

—Watson Parker, *Deadwood: The Golden Years*

CHAPTER ONE

Tuesday Evening, August 22, 1876—Jack Jones stared at his solitaire hand, the playing cards arranged in seven columns on top of an upended crate. Swilling the Old Crow whiskey, feeling the sweet burn, he forced the liquid down his throat.

The smell of unwashed bodies competed with tobacco and wood smoke, pinesap, and cheap liquor. Straightening his backbone and repositioning himself on the low stool, Jack shifted his gaze to the roomful of prospectors, ne'er-do-wells, loafers, and a sprinkling of sporting girls. They were all relatively new to Deadwood Gulch and they all had one thing in common—make money and make it fast.

Cigar and pipe smoke fogged Saloon Number 10's atmosphere. Guttering coal-oil lanterns attempted to dispel the August evening's gloom. Competing voices, hearty laughter, and raucous oaths all lubricated by rotgut whiskey strove to be heard above the others.

Jack felt the snout of his small hound dog press hard against his leg. Stonewall Jackson wanted out. "In a minute, fellow," Jack said, patting the dog's head. Stonewall sighed, circled beside the crate, and lay down with his jaw resting on Jack's boot.

One more hand of solitaire, Jack swore to himself, sweeping the cards into a pile and shuffling. *Maybe if I loiter here a little longer, I can find another good story to send the paper, something more than the latest pilgrim arriving in the gulch.*

Jack felt a slender arm snake around his shoulder. The scent of familiar perfume overpowered all odors.

A husky female voice whispered in his ear. "How's my favorite Jack Jones?"

"Why, Lil, I'm just fine and you're looking first-rate tonight," Jack said.

Lillian Rochelle wore one of the latest fashions, a pleated charcoal grey ankle-length skirt with a long, overlapping jacket bodice buttoned to the neck. A small matching riding hat was pinned to her golden hair.

"Got any news to spark the interest of my readers?" Jack asked. Stonewall's tail pounded vigorously against the floorboards.

"No knifings or beatings to speak of," Lil said, sliding onto Jack's lap and staring into his brown eyes. She reached around and gave him a long, slow kiss, her lips gently pressed to his.

"Now that is certainly newsworthy," Jack said, gazing into her twinkling blue eyes as he swept a stray strand of golden curls from her forehead.

Lil grabbed his hat brim, tugged it down sharply over his forehead, and stepping away, said with a smile, "Stop by later tonight if you're interested and I'll give you a full report of the comings and goings of Deadwood. Right now I've got to drum up a little business for the Deadwood Theater."

"I might have to take you up on that," he responded, stroking his close-cropped beard and grinning, as Lil pushed her way into the milling crowd. Jack resumed shuffling the cards.

Deadwood's been lively, he thought. *There's plenty of action. If I wait long enough something is bound to happen.*

Willing miners hoisted Lil's slim form up onto the bar as three loud strokes across a fiddle's catgut strings settled down the saloon's noise level.

"Boys! Boys!" Lil shouted. "Tonight Mr. John Langrishe promises you an extravaganza up the street at the Deadwood Theater. We bring you comedy, tragedy, and the latest songs and tunes from back East. As a little free treat, here's a song to whet your appetite."

"You're whettin' my appetite right now, little missy!" shouted a prospector, who was soundly pummeled by surrounding men as they shouted at him, "Shut up!"

Turning to the fiddle player below her, Lil said, "Proceed, Professor." The man slowly began the melody of *Dreary Black Hills* and after one run through Lil began with the haunting first verse:

"Kind friends, you must pity my horrible tale,
An object of pity, I'm looking quite stale,
I gave up my trade selling Wright's Patent Pills
To go hunting gold in the dreary Black Hills."

Then Lil broke into the chorus, and as many of the men knew the lines, they sang with her:

"Don't go away, stay at home if you can,
Stay away from that city, they call it Cheyenne,
For Old Sitting Bull or Comanche Bill
They will lift up your hair on the dreary Black Hills."

The Professor ended the tune, and Lil shouted, "Thank you, boys!" The saloon erupted with thunderous applause and shouts of "more!"

"Well, I suppose we can do one more verse. But after that you need to come to the show if you want to hear more. Professor!" The fiddler started up again and Lil joined in:

"Kind friend, to conclude my advice I'll unfold,
Don't go to the Black Hills a hunter for gold,
Railroad speculators their pockets you'll fill
By taking a trip to the dreary Black Hills."

The men shouted along with the chorus.

"Don't go away, stay at home if you can,
Stay away from that city, they call it Cheyenne,
For old Sitting Bull or Comanche Bill
They will take off your scalp on the dreary Black Hills."

The Professor ended with a flourish. The crowd shouted, clapped, and stomped their feet. Lil beamed, throwing kisses, as rough hands gently lifted her down to the floor, where she and the

3

Professor made their way through the crowd and out the door. The noise level remained high with excitement.

Jack uncorked the Old Crow bottle, refilled his glass, and resumed laying the cards down in a row of ascending stacks.

Look at these people, reckoning they're going to strike it rich, Jack thought. *New greenhorns arrive every day, thinking it'll be easy pickings. The good placer claims on Whitewood Creek are taken. Most of these men have nothing to do but spend what little money they have left and drift along somewhere else.*

A nasty, pungent, unwashed odor disturbed Jack's thoughts. Stonewall snorted from beside the crate.

"Captain Jones, ol' friend!"

Jack did not look up. Beside him stood a ragged, nondescript figure with an old Union army cap perched atop his head.

"Captain, may I sit down?" the grizzled-faced man said, eyeing the Old Crow bottle and pulling up a stool before Jack could deny his request.

"Captain Jones, can I have a sip of your Kentucky bourbon?" The derelict's breath was the stench of rotten meat. "I don't have any money, but I'm good for it."

"Bummer Dan, I'm sorry," Jack said, without looking up from his hand as he flipped the next set of three cards face up. "I've already grubstaked you for more than a bottle of whiskey. Got any news you can give me in trade?"

"No." Myer Baum, also known as Bummer Dan, scanned the crowd appearing nervous. "Please, just one good shot of whiskey."

"Why not take it up with Harry," Jack said, nodding toward Harry Young, Saloon Number 10's burly barkeep, who was having a boisterous exchange with a tipsy patron.

"That's a pinch of dust for a shot of whiskey," Young shouted. The miner spat a stream of brown tobacco juice in the general direction of a spittoon on the floor and pulled out his poke. Young snatched it from the miner's hand and opening it, thrust in his right-hand thumb and forefinger. His long fingernails grasped more than a standard pinch and placed the gold dust in the saloon's leather poke bag. He poured the miner a shot with his left hand as he ran his right hand through his greasy hair. Jack guessed that later that night when he would be alone, Young would carefully wash his hair, saving the water, and pan it to retrieve the gold flecks trapped by the grease in his hair.

"Harry won't grubstake me," Bummer Dan said as he unslung an old black-gummed haversack. He plunked it down on the crate, disturbing the order of Jack's well-laid cards. Bummer Dan had painted BD in large white letters on the haversack so he would always know it was his.

Bummer Dan rapidly glanced right and left. His eyes grew beady. *He looks like a rat guarding a piece of cheese,* Jack mused as he tried to figure out if he could salvage what was left of this solitaire hand.

Bummer Dan unfastened the haversack's keeper strap. "I showed this to Harry," he said as he fished through the sack's clutter. He removed a grape-sized object wrapped in a greasy cloth.

Making sure no one was close enough to see, and moving too close for Jack's comfort, Bummer Dan unfolded the cloth, revealing a gold nugget.

Jack tried to remain cool but his eyes widened.

"I told Harry I didn't have any coin or dust for a drink but I did have this. Harry said, sure, I could have a drink but he wanted to hold on to the nugget. I said no. Harry wanted to know if I had more where this came from. I said, 'I wouldn't tell you if I did.'"

Jack smiled. "Put that thing away before someone knocks you on the head. You're good for a drink with me."

Bummer Dan pulled out a dented tin cup from his haversack and Jack poured him a good, stiff drink. He downed the whiskey in two long gulps, smacked his lips, wiped his mouth with the back of his threadbare coat sleeve, and then grinned. "Whoa Emma! That was good, Captain Jones. Soon I'll be living the life of a gentleman, dining on oysters and sipping champagne."

Bummer Dan placed the wrapped gold nugget and tin cup back in his haversack. As he closed it he said, "When Harry asked if I had more nuggets where this came from, I said, 'That's for me to know since you won't give me any whiskey.' But I'll tell you, Captain Jones, I got more stashed in my shanty."

"Bummer Dan!" Jack hissed. "Don't be telling anyone else. You got to be careful."

"Aw, no one's gone to bother ol' Bummer Dan," he said, standing up and slinging the haversack over his head and resting it on his right hip. Giving Jack a jaunty salute, he turned and worked his way through the crowd to the front door and along with a breath of fresh cool air, he disappeared outside.

Jack looked down at his scattered cards. "Humph." *I didn't finish that hand. I owe it to myself to start over. But first, I deserve one more drink*, he thought and poured another glass.

Thunderous pounding came from the bar. The loud talk subsided.

"Attention! Shut up!" Harry Young shouted. The crowd grew quiet.

"I've been asked to tell how my good friend, Wild Bill Hickok, met his untimely death by Bill Sutherland, also known as Jack McCall. For all you greenhorns, I was the last person to talk with Wild Bill before he was shot right here in this very saloon almost three weeks ago, right at that table." Harry pointed to a circular table occupied by three card-playing prospectors and a professional gambler by the name of Johnny Varnes.

Here we go again, Jack thought. *How many times have I heard this? Each telling seems to change slightly.* He took a sip of whiskey and began shuffling the cards.

"Wild Bill and I had been friends for years, ever since Hays City, Kansas," Young began. "Seems like every town I moved to we'd run into each other. When Bill arrived in Deadwood back in June, the first place he stopped was right here, Saloon Number 10, as he was good friends with the owner, Carl Mann. Carl told Bill to use Saloon Number 10 as his headquarters, thinking Bill's fame would attract more customers. When Bill spied me behind the bar he said, 'Kid, here you are again, like the bad penny, but I'm awfully glad to see you.'"

"Git on with how Wild Bill got shot!" shouted someone hidden in the crowd.

Well said. Jack thought.

"Who said that?" Young growled, glaring in the direction of the shout. "Anyhow, Bill always sat with his back to the wall so no one could sneak up behind him. He told me he had a premonition he was going to get shot from behind. He always drank with his left hand, leaving his right hand ready to reach for his pistol if there was any sign of trouble. Speaking of his pistol, that reminds me of the time he was with General Custer outside Fort Hayes and shot six times at a telegraph pole, hitting it at a spot the size of your palm while ..."

"Git on with your damn story of Wild Bill's killing," shouted the same voice from the crowd. "I'm workin' up a thirst!"

Amen. Jack thought.

"Shut up, you!" Young shouted at his unseen nemesis. "As I was saying, on the night of August first and into the morning of August second, Bill was playing cards with Jack McCall, a worthless, cross-eyed son of a bitch. Never was sure which eye to look at when talking to him. Bill asked me to check the amount of gold in McCall's poke sack behind the bar. I weighed it and found it to be worth one hundred and seven dollars. Bill told McCall he had overplayed his hand by ten dollars. McCall said he would make good on it the next Saturday, but for the time being, he was broke. Bill gave him seventy-five cents for breakfast and said if he needed more to come see him.

"That afternoon, I was working behind the bar. Carl Mann, Charlie Rich, and Captain Massey were playing poker. Wild Bill and Colorado Charlie Utter walked in and the poker players invited Bill to join them. Bill asked Charlie Rich if he would move to the empty seat so he could sit with his back to the wall, but Captain Massey said Rich should not move, no one was going to sneak up on them. Bill reluctantly obliged him. The game got underway in earnest. Colorado Charlie left to eat his lunch. Bill was losing, and he asked me to get him fifty dollars of chips from the bar. I brought the chips over and gave them to him. Bill said, 'Massey, the old duffer, just broke me on that hand.' That's the last thing Bill ever said. That egg-sucking dog McCall snuck up behind Bill and shot him in the back of the head, shouting, 'Take that, you son of a bitch!'

"The bullet passed down through Bill's skull and out through his cheek to hit Massey on his wrist. Massey jumped up and ran out into the street, shouting Wild Bill had shot him. McCall pointed his pistol at us and we all ran out the door. McCall followed us into the street as a crowd started to gather. A horse was tied to the hitching rack, and McCall attempted to ride it out of town, but when he went to climb up into the saddle, it swung under the horse's belly. The cinch was loose and, in his haste, McCall didn't check to see if it was tight. McCall ran up the street, pointing his gun at people in the crowd. By now most everyone knew he had killed Bill. No one shot at him for fear of hitting others. McCall was finally grabbed from behind and disarmed. The mob was getting ready to hang him then and there. They were dragging him toward that good, stout ponderosa pine across the street and had a rope out. If it hadn't been for those crazy Mexicans Poncho and Carlos galloping into town dangling an Indian head and distracting the crowd, McCall would have been hung. Some of the businessmen persuaded the crowd that we should hold a proper trial, so that's what we did. Judge Kuykendall convened a miner's court. And you know what? The jury let that son of a bitch McCall go free. He claimed Bill had killed his brother. I didn't believe it, but the jury sure did. And that's how my good friend Wild Bill Hickok came to his end, right here in this very saloon and his murderer set free."

Saloon Number 10 was silent. Then three slow, loud handclaps sounded from the crowd along the far side of the bar.

"Haw! Haw! Haw! That's a tall tale if I ever heard one!" shouted a man in a colorful checked coat as he walked up to the pine-planked bar and leaned on it, glaring at Young. "And I don't think you were ever friends with Wild Bill, you liar!"

Jack looked up from his cards. The clapper was the gambler, Laughing Sam Hartman. Laughing Sam was known for his practical jokes that always amused him more than the fellow who had the joke pulled on him. Hartman was given the moniker Laughing Sam because of a scar on his right check that made him look like he had a perpetual smile on his face.

Young's left hand, the size of a small ham, shot out and clamped on Laughing Sam's throat. Young drew back his right hand balled into a fist, yanking Laughing Sam across the bar until their faces were inches apart.

"You dare mock me!" Young shouted in Laughing Sam's face as he squeezed tighter on his neck.

A gurgling noise erupted from Laughing Sam's mouth.

Young tossed him backwards, pulled out a pistol from under the bar, and aimed it at Laughing Sam's forehead. "Get out, you son of a bitch!" he roared. "Come back and I'll shoot you down like a dog."

Red faced, gasping for air, Laughing Sam staggered backwards.

"Next time you see me, it'll be the last thing you ever see," Laughing Sam swore.

He stormed from the bar, the man in his flamboyant coat cutting a swath through the miners, making a stark contrast against their drab clothing. Someone opened the door for him and with a cool blast of air, Laughing Sam was gone from Saloon Number 10.

Young broke the stunned silence. "Come on, boys! Drink up!"

"Humph," Jack grunted as he pulled out a small leather-bound notebook and pencil from the side pocket of his coat. Scribbling a few notes, he mumbled to himself, "Tuesday evening, August 22, 1876, minor ruckus at Saloon Number 10..."

Jack finished his solitaire hand, and then he tied up the deck with a string, put it in his coat pocket, downed the last of the whiskey in his glass, and corked the bottle.

Reaching in his vest pocket, he pulled out his Elgin watch and pressed the button to flip open the lid. The time was eight p.m. He returned the watch to its pocket, rubbing the Grand Army of the Republic fob between his thumb and forefinger.

"Stonewall," he said, nudging the dog with his foot. "Time for a little grub?"

Walking to the bar with Stonewall tagging by his side, Jack handed his bottle to Young for safekeeping under the bar.

Stonewall growled, baring his teeth at Young.

"What's wrong with that damn mutt of yours? Why does he only growl at me?"

"Don't know, Harry. He hasn't told me yet," Jack said with a grin.

"You won't be printing this little shouting incident in your paper now, would you?"

"Well, I'll be kind."

Young frowned, but said nothing.

Jack, with Stonewall trotting ahead of him, made his way through the crowd. To his left he passed the four men playing poker. Johnny Varnes, the professional gambler, with a pile of newly acquired chips stacked in front of him, glanced up at Jack, nodded with just the trace of a smirk, and went back to studying the eyes of the yokels losing to him.

Jack reached for the door and stepped outside onto the dry, rutted mud of the street. He breathed in the crisp, invigorating, evening air. Acrid campfire smoke punctuated the pine fragrance. Stonewall ran to the corner of the saloon building, sniffed, and hoisted his leg. A babble of tongues assaulted Jack's ears, everything from precise English accents to exotic Cantonese lingo. Miners, and those living off miners, filled Deadwood's Main Street this evening.

And why not? Jack asked himself. Jack knew that prospectors discovered gold here last December, and the camp did not start growing until this spring's thaw. Deadwood was the largest, fastest growing town in Dakota Territory, even if it was an illegal town within the Great Sioux Reservation. Everyone there wanted to make a buck during the Centennial Year of our country's founding. *Maybe*, Jack thought, *they will find enough gold to bring us out of our economic depression?*

Deadwood's buildings were a mix of log cabins and canvas tents, but newer buildings were being constructed of rough-hewn boards as sawyers had a ready supply of trees for lumber and there was an increasing demand for building material for homes, businesses, and mines.

Bawling teams of yoked oxen and oath-shouting bullwhackers alerted an excited crowd that a bull train—large, covered freight wagons loaded with tons of goods—had just arrived. People were trying to get a look at the latest goods that were stashed away in the wagons. Jack spied a young bullwhacker gawking at the sights of Deadwood.

"Howdy, young fella," Jack said. "First time to Deadwood?"

"Yes, sir," the young man said.

"My name's Jack Jones, reporter for the *Chicago Inter-Ocean* newspaper. Got a minute for a few questions?"

"Sure, Mr. Jones. By the way, my name's Pete Adams."

"What are you hauling, Pete?"

"Mostly food, dry goods, miners' supplies—picks, shovels, crowbars, and other hardware."

"Where did you come from?"

"We started from Fort Pierre on the Missouri River. About a two hundred and forty-mile trip in two weeks."

"I've been over the trail. Not much by way of human comfort out there."

"That's for sure, but fortunately it was uneventful. No problems with Indians or bandits."

Faint shouting started from the upper end of the gulch. The shout grew in volume as residents of Deadwood repeated it until people around Jack and Pete were shouting the phrase "Oh Joe!" and then others down the gulch picked up the shout of "Oh Joe!" It continued down the gulch as a wave. An earsplitting wolf howl broke through and overwhelmed the shout. The citizens of Deadwood laughed and went back to what they had been doing.

"What was all that?" Pete asked.

"It's a little Deadwood tradition. One night a few weeks ago, a prospector who had too much to drink fell into a pit. He was so drunk he couldn't climb out, and all night long he called 'Oh Joe!' for his partner to help him. So now, every evening, people will wait until someone begins the call up the gulch and then it travels as a wave all the way down. The wolf howl is an added touch by a prospector named Smokey Jones."

"That howl's enough to make my blood run cold!"

"Well, I'm off for my supper. Nice to meet you, Pete."

"Sure, Mr. Jones, likewise."

Jack turned away from the commotion surrounding the bull train's arrival and walked up Main Street, avoiding large rocks and tree stumps no one had bothered to remove, not to mention animal manure and garbage tossed into the street. The stench of a poorly constructed, not well-ventilated privy overrode all other smells for a brief moment.

Across the street, silhouettes of two men formed in the dim light that spilled out of a saloon. As they came into view, one had a distinctive checkered coat, and the other had a haversack slung over his shoulder. Laughing Sam and Bummer Dan appeared to be in deep conversation.

That's odd, thought Jack. *Didn't know those two were chummy.*

Jack continued up the street to Deadwood's imposing Grand Central Hotel, where he shared a room bunking with others for a buck a night. It was always hard to get to sleep with a room full of snoring, wheezing, foul-smelling strangers. Regardless, he knew it was the best place in town to room and eat three square meals.

Jack opened the Grand Central's front door and walked into a small lobby. Pine boards made up the walls, ceiling, and floor of the sparse lobby. To the left was a pine counter, and on the wall behind the counter hung a regulator clock. A balding, mustached Charlie Wagner , the proprietor, stood behind the counter. He had removed his coat and wore a white shirt, dark vest, and tie as he worked on his books.

"Good evening, Captain Jones," Wagner said, looking up from his work.

"How are you, Charlie?"

"Good, Captain."

"How's Aunt Lou's cooking tonight?"

"Same as always, mighty fine."

Jack walked past the counter, back the hallway, turned right, and entered the dining room. The warm fragrance of fresh baked biscuits greeted his nose, causing his mouth to water and his stomach to rumble. The dining room was not fancy, but functional, with rough plank floors and walls. Coal-oil lamps dispelled the darkness. Only a few customers sat at the tables. They were enjoying the food, one man wolfing it down as if he had not eaten in days.

A stern-faced, middle-aged black woman addressed Jack as she bustled out of the kitchen with a steaming bowl of new potatoes. "Are you going to stand there gawking, Captain Jones, or are you going to sit down so I can feed you?"

"Thanks, Aunt Lou," Jack replied to Lucretia Marchbanks. Her hair was pulled back into a bun. She wore a white blouse, and a pleated, charcoal-gray skirt. A long white apron protected her clothing.

Lou leaned down and scratched Stonewall behind the ear. "And I suppose this loafer hound of yours wants some table scraps too?"

Stonewall's tail wagged in anticipation of his nightly treat. Lou returned to the kitchen, followed by Stonewall.

Jack sat down at an empty table with a coal-oil lantern. He brought it closer to him. It would shed enough light for his purposes. He pulled out his notebook and reviewed his notes for the day. Lou appeared beside him with a satchel and a steaming mug of coffee. "Here's your writing paper, Captain."

"Thanks, Aunt Lou," Jack said, as he handed her his meal ticket. "I do appreciate you keeping my papers safe for me. Not sure they would remain untouched up in my room."

She punched the ticket and gave it back to him. "Lord knows what kind of men we have here from all over the countryside, if not the world."

Lou left for the kitchen as Jack began to write his report for the newspaper.

A few minutes later Lou returned with a plate of steaming roast beef, potatoes, gravy, and biscuits. "Move those papers so you can eat," she said. Jack complied and Lou placed the plate in front of him and handed him a napkin, knife, fork, and spoon.

"Got a little time for some table talk?" Jack asked.

Lou looked around the room at its few occupants well engaged with their meals, and said, "Certainly."

She pulled up a stool, sat down across the table from Jack, and sighed.

"How's business?" Jack asked.

"It's been brisk. So what do you have to write about today?"

"Not much. Harry Young threw Laughing Sam Hartman out of Saloon Number 10 and threatened to kill him if he came back."

"Um hum. What else you got?"

"Another bull train just arrived this evening, but neither of these will whet the interest of my Chicago readers, or even people living in Deadwood Gulch," Jack said, then shoveled a forkful of potatoes into his mouth.

"It surely is a shame what happened Sunday to Preacher Smith," Lou said, shaking her head.

"That was a shame, being ambushed by Indians... just outside of town."

"They say the Indians didn't scalp him because they saw he was a man of God."

"I don't know," Jack said. "Then there were the other three men killed by Indians the same day. I finished that story to send to my newspaper earlier today."

"Truly sad news."

"It certainly is."

"Aunt Lou!" a patron shouted. "Another cup of coffee when you get a chance."

"No rest for the weary!" Lou said, standing up and walking to the kitchen.

Jack dug into the beef and potatoes. Looking up from his meal, he saw a well-dressed customer standing in the dining room doorway.

"Judge Kuykendall!" Jack called out. "Care to join me, sir?"

The man looked over at Jack, nodded his head, and walked to his table. Jack stood and stuck out his right hand and Kuykendall took it with a firm grip. "I'm Jack Jones, reporter for the *Chicago Inter-Ocean* newspaper."

"I guess you already know I'm W. L. Kuykendall. I own a dry goods store over on Sherman Street."

"Have a seat, Judge."

"Please call me W. L.," Kuykendall said. "I see by your GAR watch fob you must have served for the Union."

"Yes, I was a captain for eight months, with the Pennsylvania 129th Volunteer Infantry," Jack said. "Saw a little action at

13

Fredericksburg and Chancellorsville. After being mustered out at the end and experiencing the stupidity of the generals who followed after McClellan was dismissed, I didn't re-enlist."

"I take it you're a fellow Democrat then?"

"No, but I thought Little Mac was a good general. Lincoln just wouldn't let him do his job. Did you serve in the war?"

"Yes, only I was on the opposite side. I'm from Missouri and served in the West. Started out a lieutenant, was captured, paroled, worked as a recruiter, and then served as a major. The war wiped me out financially so I headed to Colorado and other places in the West, working at sundry jobs and entered the legal field in Wyoming. Then I arrived in the Black Hills last winter."

Lou approached the table with two steaming mugs of coffee. "Judge, what will you have?"

"I'll have the same as Jack. It sure does look and smell good."

"Very well," she said.

"So W. L., what are your thoughts on the present situation of Deadwood and the Black Hills in general?"

"I would think you would agree with me that we need some form of government. Even though we are an illegal town, we need to have law and order. We need to hold elections and elect a mayor and town council."

"Do you think the federal government will send in troops to evict us as it's done in the past?"

"I don't think so. I believe we're here to stay. Think about it, General Crook is out there somewhere chasing Sitting Bull, Crazy Horse, and their brigands. The army can't afford the troops to evict us. Meanwhile, I know the federal government is working to buy the Black Hills from the Indians. Just think what opening up the Black Hills will do for the economy. The mining of gold is creating jobs to service the mining industry. Just look at what we have here, the Miners and Mechanics' Bank, hotels, a variety of stores, not to mention saloons. Why, J. J. Schlawig has even opened a brewery in town."

Lou returned with Kuykendall's plate of steaming beef, potatoes, and gravy.

"Thank you, Aunt Lou," Kuykendall said.

"But what about the rights of the Lakota, Cheyenne, and other tribes?" Jack asked. "The Fort Laramie Treaty created the Great Sioux Reservation strictly for their use."

"We can't let a few Indians hold up the progress of the country. Just think of what can happen. There are already farms and ranches starting up to supply food to Deadwood and other mining camps. We need the military to establish a fort nearby to protect the citizens. The stage lines should soon reach town, followed by the telegraph, then hopefully the railroad. This should all lead to building up the economy and help bring our nation out of its financial depression."

Lou walked past their table with a stack of dirty dishes. "Judge," she said, "eat your food or it's going to get cold."

"Thank you, Aunt Lou. I'll stop talking and eat."

They both concentrated on the food before them, eating in silence for a few minutes. Stonewall emerged from the kitchen, padded up to Jack, sat back on his haunches, and gave out a soft whine. "Stonewall, when I'm done," Jack said.

"Your dog's name is Stonewall?"

"Stonewall Jackson is the full name. There's a story to it."

"That's one I'd like to hear."

"I was working on a story about the Manassas, Virginia, countryside, and how it was recovering after the war and its first great battle. Walking along Bull Run Creek, I heard a pup crying. After searching the area, I found the pup. It was in the creek and it was trying to climb onto the bank. I fished him out and then went around to the nearby farmhouses, but no one would claim him. So I decided to keep him. I reckoned I needed to name him something significant. I thought of Moses since I rescued him from the water just as pharaoh's daughter had rescued Moses from the Nile, but I settled on Thomas 'Stonewall' Jackson, hero of the Battle of Bull Run."

Kuykendall chuckled. "That's quite a story."

After they finished eating, Jack dropped a chunk of gristle into Stonewall's mouth.

"Care to join me at the hotel bar for a liquor and cigar?" Kuykendall asked.

"Yes, I would be happy to do so." Jack said as they both stood from the table.

"I'd like to hear your take on the Jack McCall trial. I arrived in Deadwood after the murder and trial."

"Yes, quite a travesty of justice, if you ask me," Kuykendall said with a shake of his head. "There had been some talk among the more respectable element in the Gulch to hire Wild Bill as our lawman before he was gunned down. He would have made some of the more brazen criminals cower."

The two men walked across the hallway to the barroom. It was empty except for a few customers quietly talking at the bar. The atmosphere was a complete change from the boisterous Saloon Number 10.

"Brandy and a good cigar for my friend here and me," Kuykendall said to the bartender. After their drinks arrived, and they had the cigars well stoked, Kuykendall said, "Let me begin the sad tale of the McCall trial."

Kuykendall sipped his brandy and drew on the cigar before he began. "Wednesday, August second, I returned to Deadwood from some business I had conducted up in Lead when I met a friend who told me Wild Bill Hickok had been assassinated and the murderer had been caught. We ran down to Saloon Number 10, where a mob was congregating. A rope was found and the mob was about to string up Jack McCall, the murderer, when up the street galloped two Mexicans with the severed head of an Indian. The mob forgot about hanging McCall and cheered on the Mexicans with their trophy. Cooler heads took McCall away and placed him under guard in a storeroom."

"Yes, of course, there is no jail in town," Jack mused.

"Correct," Kuykendall said. "So a group of businessmen met in Langrishe's Deadwood Theater that night to establish a proper trial for McCall. To make a long story short, they elected me judge and others as court officers. The next day we held the trial at the Deadwood Theater. All officers of the court and the jury were armed with revolvers to ensure a fair trial. The theater was packed. The prisoner entered a plea of not guilty. The evidence showed McCall was a cowardly, cold-blooded killer, but he did tell a convincing tale that Hickok had killed his brother. The jury left to determine his fate. I believed the verdict would be death. We selected the same ponderosa pine across from Saloon Number 10 to hang McCall from that the mob had originally chosen and we made the hanging rope ready.

"The prisoner was led back into the theater when the jury was ready to pronounce its verdict. McCall was terrified. His teeth chattered and he shook the entire time. When the jury foreman read the verdict, I couldn't believe my ears. They acquitted McCall because he had avenged his brother's death! It was a travesty of justice!

"McCall was released. He loafed around town for a few days until his friends told him he had best leave before Hickok's friends decided to take matters into their own hands. I've heard rumor he's in Cheyenne these days."

"So you obviously don't agree with the verdict," Jack said.

"Absolutely not! It was a travesty of justice!"

Muffled shouts and the sounds of running boots on pine flooring made them turn their heads toward the hallway. A breathless man rushed in shouting, "There's been a killing at Saloon Number 10!"

Kuykendall and Jack quickly downed their brandies.

Jack turned to Lou, who stood there drying her hands with a dishtowel. "Aunt Lou, would you watch Stonewall while I head down to Saloon Number 10?"

"Certainly, he'll be no problem," she said, reaching down to hold the hound dog's collar.

"Thanks," Jack said and then followed Kuykendall into the lobby and out the door.

They hurried down the street, avoiding stumps, rocks, and other men making their way to see what had happened at Saloon Number 10. A crowd gathered at the saloon's entrance. Jack and Kuykendall pushed their way through to a small clearing in the forest of human bodies. Coal oil lanterns illuminated the scene.

Lil sat on the ground cradling the head of a lifeless body. Jack recognized Laughing Sam's flamboyant coat. *Harry must have made good on his threat*, Jack thought.

His eyes shifted to the man's face, illuminated by the lanterns' light. Comprehension flooded Jack's mind, then a flash of horror. The body was not Laughing Sam. It was Bummer Dan.

Deadwood Dead Men

CHAPTER TWO

೫ఎ⊂ß

Tuesday Night, August 22, 1876—"Lil," Jack said. There was no response. "Lil!"

She looked up at Jack as he spoke her name the second time, her eyes moist with tears. Jack sat on his heels in front of her, with Bummer Dan's body sprawled in the street.

"Lil, what happened?" Jack felt Bummer Dan's wrist for a pulse—nothing.

"Oh Jack!" Lil cried. "The Professor, and I had finished making our rounds and we were on our way back to the Deadwood Theater when we heard two shots, then we saw Bummer Dan stagger out Saloon Number 10's door and collapse. They say Harry shot him!"

"That's right," said the Professor who knelt at Bummer Dan's left side holding a lantern.

"What! Why?" Jack asked.

"I don't know," Lil said. "Bummer Dan never hurt anyone."

"This just doesn't make sense," Jack said. "And why is he wearing Laughing Sam's coat?"

"I heard two shots," said a man standing behind Jack. He turned and saw E. B. Farnum, who owned a store next to Saloon Number 10. He was talking to Tom Short, another storeowner from across the street. "I was closing my shop when I heard two shots," Farnum continued. "I ran out the door and heard someone say, 'I'm murdered!' It was this poor fellow here."

The crowd was becoming agitated. "Where's the son of a bitch who shot poor Bummer Dan?" a man shouted.

"He's still in the saloon," a grizzled old-timer said.

"Let's get him and string him up," a young well-dressed man shouted.

"Yes!" someone else said as more shouts came from the crowd.

"Find a rope," the young well-dressed man yelled.

The mob pressed toward Saloon Number 10's door.

"Careful boys, he's got a gun," a miner warned.

Jack stood as the crowd pressed around Lil and Bummer Dan's body. He moved with the mob into the saloon. Harry Young, pistol in hand, stood behind the bar. The crowd quieted down when the men saw his pistol.

"Harry," Farnum said. "Did you shoot that fellow, Bummer Dan?"

"Bummer Dan?" Young questioned. "I didn't shoot Bummer Dan. What are you talking about?"

"Someone shot and killed Bummer Dan in this saloon," Farnum said. "And folks say you did it."

"I didn't shoot him. But I did shoot at that no good son of a bitch Laughing Sam, who ran out of this place."

"That wasn't Laughing Sam. It was Bummer Dan," Farnum said. "It looks like he was wearing Laughing Sam's coat and hat."

"What?" Young appeared visibly stunned. "Bummer Dan walked in here wearing Laughing Sam's hat and coat? Why?" he asked.

"That don't matter none," the old-timer said. "What matters is you're going to pay for killing old Bummer Dan."

"If I'm the man you're looking for, I deliver myself up," Young said as he laid the gun on the top of the bar.

"Did you shoot your pistol twice?" Short asked.

"I did, and all I want is a fair trial. If I'm found guilty, I'm willing to suffer the consequences."

"Boys, bring him outside and let's give him a necktie party!" the young well-dressed man shouted. The crowd roared in agreement. Men grabbed Young, pinning his arms behind his back and leading him outside. The mob shouted, laughed, and cursed. Across the street stood a ponderosa pine with a substantial limb, which Jack McCall was rescued from being hung upon several weeks earlier. A stout miner tossed the rope over the limb. Another man fashioned a noose on one end of the rope. The crowd manhandled Harry toward the tree. Men roughly placed the rope around his neck and pulled up tight. Harry's eyes bulged and he gasped for breath.

The crack of a pistol shot rang out, ending the mayhem. Men grabbed their weapons. Jack instinctively reached for his Army Colt revolver, realizing he had left the gun with the Grand Central Hotel's proprietor for safekeeping.

"Thank you boys for your undivided attention," Johnny Varnes said, holding a smoking pistol in his hand, with his arm extended straight over his head. "Are we a passel of heathens or are we civilized men? You just can't hang a man without a trial. We need to have a legal way of doing things around here or else the federal government will never recognize Deadwood as a legitimate city. If we are not a legitimate city, your mining claims are not legitimate. Now let's hold a regular trial by jury."

The crowd was silent.

Varnes continued, "Why, is that you, Henry? Is that my brother Henry there with the rope around Harry Young's neck?"

"Yes, it's me," answered one of the men holding Young.

"Don't you think Ma would be ashamed at your actions tonight?"

Henry looked at the ground, not saying anything. The men around him glanced around.

From out of the dark, someone shouted "He's right!" and others joined in agreement. Henry removed the rope from around Young's neck, which Young slowly rubbed.

"Judge Kuykendall can preside," Varnes said.

"No!" Kuykendall said. "I'll not participate in another travesty of justice."

"Judge, please, we need a man of integrity," Varnes said.

"Find another judge. I'm done!" Kuykendall roared, pushing out of the crowd and stomping away from the scene.

"What about W. R. Keithley?" Varnes asked. "He can act as judge. Where is he?"

"I'm here," Keithley said, stepping forward into the lantern light. "I'll act as judge. Let's hold Harry for the night, meet tomorrow to establish the court, then pick a jury, and hold the trial."

The crowd shouted and cheered in agreement.

"Judge! Judge!" Tom Short shouted. "We can hold Harry in my fireproof building. It's about the safest place in town."

"All right then," Keithley said. "We'll need men to stand guard during the night."

Several men volunteered to take turns guarding the prisoner.

"Follow me up the street to my store," Short said as he pulled a ring of keys from his coat pocket. "We'll lock him in my storeroom." Young's face appeared more relaxed as a man on each side of him held his arms and led him up the street. Most of the mob followed along. Men talked about what they had seen and heard. Some shouted at Young that he would soon be returning to the tree to receive his justice.

Jack and Lil stood by Bummer Dan's body with a few others.

"Where's Laughing Sam?" Jack asked. "I'd like to talk to him."

"I haven't seen him," Lil said. Several men positioned themselves to lift Bummer Dan's limp body off the street.

"Wait a minute," Jack said. "Where's Bummer Dan's haversack? I don't see it slung on him." They rolled the body over. The haversack was not lying underneath.

"I never saw it on him," Lil said.

"You were with him the whole time after he was shot and never left sight of his body?" Jack asked.

"That's right."

"Humph, I wonder what he did with that haversack."

"Why?"

"Oh, just a little matter I might need to check on," Jack said, then turned to the men who were about to haul the body away. "Could you fellows check his pockets? I want to see if there is anything on him that would tell us how to contact his next of kin."

The men searched Bummer Dan's pockets but found nothing. They picked up his body and carried him off into the dark.

What did Bummer Dan do with that haversack? Jack thought. *And the gold?*

Out of the dark strode John Langrishe, the theater owner. He was a tall man, wearing a cape and a stovepipe hat that accentuated his height. An equally long nose adorned his face.

"Lillian—Professor," Langrishe said. "Due to the unfortunate circumstances of this evening, Deadwood's populace is in no mood for light entertainment, so I am canceling tonight's performance. We will resume tomorrow evening. I need to press on to tell the others. If you see any of the troupe, let them know," Langrishe tipped his hat to Lil. "Good night, Lillian, gents." He strode off into the darkness, his cape flowing behind.

Lil was now shaking. The reality of Bummer Dan's death had hit home. Jack put his arm around her. "Want to grab a cup of coffee?"

"Yes. I'd like that."

"We'll head up to the Grand Central Hotel, and see if Aunt Lou still has a pot on the stove."

"Lil," the Professor said, "I'll be heading home for the night. Here's the lantern. I can find my way in the dark. Goodnight."

"Thank you, Professor," Lil said. "I'll see you tomorrow."

Jack and Lil walked up the dark street, passing small groups of men discussing the murder and what would become of Young.

"Mr. Jones!" It was Pete Adams breaking away from one such talkative group. "Were you there? Were you at the scene of the murder?"

"No, Pete, I wasn't, but Lil here saw Bummer Dan stagger into the street and die. Lil, this is Pete Adams, and, Pete, this is Lillian Rochelle."

"I'm pleased to meet you, miss."

"Likewise."

"Sorry to hear you had to be present for such an awful event, Miss Rochelle."

"Thank you, Mr. Adams."

"Pete, we're headed up the street for some coffee, if you're interested in joining us," Jack said.

"I'd like that, Mr. Jones."

"And it's Jack. Just call me Jack."

"Sure thing, Jack."

"Jack, what do you think of Johnny Varnes firing his gun and calming down the crowd?" Lil asked. "That certainly seems out of character, doesn't it?"

Jack chuckled. "You mean after his little gunplay a few days back?"

"Yes."

"What gunplay are you talking about?" Pete asked.

"Four days ago, Johnny Varnes and another gambler named Charlie Storms got into an argument over a card game. They decided to settle the dispute by dueling on Gold Street. Varnes has a Whistler double-action English pistol that..."

"What's a double-action?" Lil asked.

"A double-action means you don't have to pull the pistol hammer back to cock the gun," Pete answered. "By pulling the trigger back, it self-cocks the gun and then fires. After pulling the trigger, it's ready to fire again."

"I never knew there was such a gun," Lil said.

"The British have had double-action guns since the '50s and used them in the Crimean War," Jack said. "They haven't caught on yet here in the United States because they're a little temperamental and aren't as reliable as the single-action Colt."

"Jack, please continue with the Varnes and Storms gunfight," Pete prompted.

"Varnes and Storms squared off in Gold Street at 6:00 p.m. and began shooting at each other," Jack said. "One of Varnes's bullets hit an innocent bystander, Joe Ludwig, in the thigh while he was standing in the Wertheimer and Company store. Varnes ducked behind a wagon as he fired at Storms, who remained standing exposed in the street. Several of Storms's shots from his Colt pistol hit the wagon Varnes was hiding behind. When Varnes was out of bullets, he shouted to Storms he was giving up and threw up his hands." Jack chuckled, then continued. "When Storms heard this he shouted back, 'Go get a better gun. You can't hit a barn door with that one.' At this point, their friends intervened. They sat down to a few drinks and were soon on friendly terms."

Pete laughed. "That would have been some fight to see."

The three of them reached the Grand Central Hotel and entered. Charlie Wagner was behind the counter.

"Does Aunt Lou still have coffee on?" Jack asked.

"She surely does," Wagner answered. "Horrible news about Bummer Dan. Any idea why Harry Young shot him?"

"Harry claims he didn't know it was Bummer Dan," Jack said. "He told the mob he thought he had shot Laughing Sam."

"We need some law and order around here," Wagner said shaking his head.

"That we do," Jack agreed.

The three entered the dining room. Stonewall ran up to Lil whining, his whole body wiggling in happiness. Lil scratched him behind the ears. He moved on to Pete, sniffed him, and timidly allowed Pete to roughly rub his head. He greeted Jack last, panting and wagging his tail.

The room was empty except for Lou, who was mopping the floor, and one of her helpers, who was clearing tables.

"Ah, I see you brought guests back with you, Captain Jones," Lou said.

"Good evening, Aunt Lou," Lil said.

"How are you, Miss Lil?"

"A little rattled after seeing Bummer Dan die."

"Bummer Dan killed! So that's what all the commotion's about. Well, just sit down here, honey, and I'll get you some coffee and add some nice cream and sugar to it."

"Thank you."

"And who is this fine young gentleman?"

"I'm Pete Adams, ma'am," Pete said.

"Nice to meet you, Mr. Pete Adams, have a seat," Lou said and left to get the coffee pot and mugs.

They sat at a clean table. Lou returned with the pot, poured coffee into four mugs, and joined them at the table. Lil was visibly shaken. Her hands trembled when picking up the coffee mug and raising it to her lips.

I need to ask Lil again about Bummer Dan's haversack, Jack thought. *But she's shaken. I'll wait until she is better composed. What happened to that haversack and more importantly that gold nugget?*

"Miss Rochelle, please tell me about yourself and how you come to be out here on the frontier?" Pete asked.

Lil took another sip of coffee, sat the mug on the table, and stared at it for a moment.

"Well I'm from a small farm in Iowa," she said, looking up straight into Pete's blue eyes. "Ma and Pa didn't have much. It was a hard go. I'm the oldest of eight children. It was difficult for Pa and Ma to try to keep that many mouths fed. I just always loved singing whenever I did chores and especially when we went to church down the road.

"One day Uncle Jack Langrishe showed up for a visit. He's my ma's older brother. After supper, while he and Pa were smoking cigars on the front porch, and Ma and me were in the kitchen washing the dishes, I started to sing. Uncle Jack stopped his talk with Pa and walked into the kitchen behind Ma and me listening, without us knowing he's there. When I was done, he clapped his hands and shouted 'bravo.' He said I had a magnificent voice and he wanted me to join his troupe. We would see the world, and I would have the opportunity to become rich and famous. I told him I would think about it .

"That night I talked with Ma. She said I was old enough that I could choose to do whatever I thought best and Pa had no problem with it. I lay in bed with my little sisters snuggled in all around me. I couldn't sleep. I kept thinking, 'This may be my one chance to see the world.' The next morning I said 'Yes! I will do this.' But I told Uncle Jack I wanted a portion of my earnings to be sent to Ma and Pa and he said that could be arranged. I was so happy I spun in circles laughing, as my sisters jumped and squealed for joy."

Jack could see Lil was smiling, forgetting for a moment the tragedy she had just witnessed.

"So how did you come to the Black Hills, Miss Rochelle?" Pete asked.

"Uncle Jack taught me the finer points of singing, how to read music, dancing, and acting. We traveled throughout the West, mostly mining camps. We were in a Colorado mining camp when word reached us of the bonanza in Deadwood Gulch. Uncle Jack said we need to go where the money is, so here we are!" Lil ended with a flourish of her uplifted hand and laughed. "And what is your story, Mr. Adams?"

"Please, Miss Rochelle, call me Pete."

"Sure, Pete, and please call me Lil. Now, tell us your story."

"Here's a coincidence for you, I'm from an Iowa farmstead too. My story is about the same as yours, Miss Lil, with the depression, a poor harvest, and my mother and father needing to feed lots of mouths. With one added horrible twist—a plague of locusts just like you read about in the Bible! Hoards of locusts invaded our farm this spring. They covered everything and then ate it. When they were done and they moved on, there were no crops left in the fields. They stripped the leaves off the trees and even ate the bark.

"I left the farm to strike out on my own. I got a job working as a bullwhacker with the wagon train that just came to Deadwood. The boss told me I could return with him, or if I wanted to stay here, he would pay me off in greenbacks. So after seeing Deadwood Gulch, I think there's plenty here a young man like me can work at and make my pile. So I told him to pay me off."

"Which trail did you come in on?" Lou asked.

"The Fort Pierre to Deadwood Trail," Pete answered. "It was lonely but beautiful out there. Stark scenery, no people."

"No people? You didn't see any Indians?" Lou asked.

"Not one."

"Most of them are probably trying to get back to the agencies and claim they weren't involved in the fight at the Little Big Horn," Jack said.

"That might be so, Mr. Jones," Pete responded. "It was tough work on the trail handling those oxen, but at times when you looked off into the distance—it was as if you were looking into eternity. When we reached Pino Springs, I thought it was like an oasis right out of the Arabian Nights stories I read as a boy, the swift babbling stream, the trees, and lush vegetation. I remember when we climbed that steep hill west of Pino Springs and I could look back from whence we had traversed, I looked into that distance eastward that seemed to disappear with the curvature of the earth and thought, 'There's no turning back now. I am so far away. Will I ever see my mother and father again? Will I ever see my brothers and sisters? My boyhood chums?' It seems such a long way to get home again."

"What did you think when you first saw what the Sioux call Paha Sapa, Hills Black?" Jack asked. "For my part I was taken with their dark, foreboding beauty, stretching across the western horizon as if an island in a vast sea of prairie."

"When I first saw the Black Hills," Pete said, "the first thing that went through my mind was 'I got to go over there and see that!'" The rest of them chuckled. Pete's discourse made Jack think of home and loved ones left behind, and as he forced himself free from his introspection, he could see the others had also turned inward with their own thoughts of home and family.

"And then," Pete continued, as Jack realized Pete felt free and comfortable to express his deepest innermost thoughts and to express those thoughts to complete strangers. "And then, the night sky. Have you seen that sky?"

Everyone murmured a soft yes.

"The night sky was vast and inexpressible—the deep dark of the night. The sweet smell of the sage. The munching, breathing, rustling sounds of the cattle. The howls of the coyotes on the distant ridges. But above all was the night sky, and the myriad of stars—so many it was hard to make out the constellations that my granddad had pointed out to me when I was little. The Milky Way stretched from horizon to horizon! It seemed I could reach out and touch it. I just laid on my back, watching with awe and wonder. The world seemed insignificant, the night sky was everything."

Jack looked at Lou and Lil. They were enthralled with Pete's discourse on the heavens.

"Humph," Jack cleared his throat. "I agree. You are very perceptive for someone your age. How did you develop this?"

"I don't know," Pete said. "I've always been fascinated with God's world—plants, animals, people. I'm enthralled with life. I want to experience as much of it as I can."

"Well said, Pete," Lil responded.

"I agree," Lou added.

"But I am sorry," Pete said. "I dwell too much on myself. Aunt Lou, what is your story, if I may ask."

"It's a different story than any of your lives have been," Lou responded. "Are you sure you want to hear it?"

"Yes," they all replied.

"All right then, I was born a slave, a slave owned by my white uncle, Martin Marchbanks. Think about that. Not only did someone own me, but it was my own uncle. Don't get me wrong, they treated me very well, but you have no idea what it is like to have no control over your own life. You have to get permission to do anything out of the ordinary.

"To begin with, I was born March 25, 1833, near Algood, Tennessee. I was the oldest of eleven children so I had to help Momma with the younger ones. As I grew older, I was trained to help with housekeeping and to help in the kitchen. That's where I learned to cook.

"I got to go west during the California Gold Rush. One of Mr. Marchbanks's daughters insisted on going to California, and I went along as her traveling companion. I got to see gold fever strike sane men and realized it's where the money is. So when the War Between the States was over and I was free, I left the Marchbanks and struck out for Colorado, cooking my way from mining camp to mining camp until now, and here I am! And I'm happy to be here. Everyone appreciates my cooking!"

"They sure do," Jack responded.

"Captain, tell us a little about yourself," Lou said.

"Not much to tell," Jack said. "I was born and raised on a farm in eastern Pennsylvania, and I got a good public school education. I joined a Pennsylvania volunteer regiment during the war, and my neighbors and relatives in our company elected me captain. I saw a little fighting and then got out when my enlistment was up. I tried my hand at farming, but didn't care for it, headed west and got a job reporting for the *Chicago Inter-Ocean* newspaper, and I've been reporting from various locations ever since.

He looked across the table at Lil. She was smiling and appeared calm.

"Lil, do you mind if we talk about Bummer Dan?"

"Go ahead," Lil said. "I feel I can talk about it now."

"Captain Jones?" Lou asked. "Can you start from the beginning for me?"

"And me," Pete added.

"Well, there's not much to tell," Jack said. "Laughing Sam and Harry Young had a little ruckus in Saloon Number 10 tonight. Harry threw Laughing Sam out of the saloon and said if he ever came back, he would kill him. Earlier I had a talk with Bummer Dan, and he left the saloon before Laughing Sam. When I walked out of Saloon Number 10 to come here for supper, I saw Laughing Sam and Bummer Dan talking together across the street. After supper, I heard there was a shooting. I returned to Saloon Number 10 where I saw Lil holding Bummer Dan's body. He was wearing Laughing Sam's hat and coat, which to me is very odd. The crowd apprehended Harry Young for shooting Bummer Dan, but Harry claims he thought he shot Laughing Sam and not Bummer Dan. That's all I know. Lil, does that sound right to you?"

"Yes."

"Lil, is there any more to this story you can shed light on?"

"No."

"Did you see Laughing Sam at any time after the shooting?"

"No."

"Bummer Dan always kept his haversack close to him. When I examined his body, the haversack was not on him. Did anyone take his haversack off of him, before I got there?"

"No. I was one of the first people to reach him when he fell to the ground. As I told you before, there was no haversack on him. Why are you so concerned about a haversack?"

"There is something of importance to Bummer Dan in that haversack. I would like to find it, try to find out if he had any family, and send them his possessions."

"I see," Lil said.

"I need to find Laughing Sam," Jack said, more for himself than the others. "He might be able to help me locate the haversack."

"That Laughing Sam is a bad character," Lou said.

"Why do you say that?" Jack asked.

"I hear he did something bad to that working girl, Tid Bit."

"What did he do?"

"Not sure. You'll have to ask Tid Bit or her friend, Calamity Jane."

Calamity Jane Cannery. Jack thought. *Well, I suppose I can track her down and hear a few of her tall tales.* "You think Calamity Jane or Tid Bit might be able to tell me where Laughing Sam is?"

"I don't know, but it might be as good a start as any other," Lou said.

Jack pulled out his Elgin watch and saw the time was approaching midnight. "I suppose that will have to wait until tomorrow. It's almost tomorrow."

"I must get back to the theater," Lil said. "Uncle Jack and Auntie must be worried sick that I'm out so late."

"I'll escort you back, Lil," Jack said.

"Let me pay for the coffee," Pete said as he pulled a leather wallet stuffed with greenbacks out of his coat's inner pocket.

"No, no, no!" Lou said. "This coffee is on the house. And put those bills away, young man, or some ne'er-do-well will surely take them from you."

"I agree with Aunt Lou, Pete," Jack said, then laughed. "You must be a member of the Greenback Party!"

"No sir!" Pete said. "It's just that my boss paid me in greenbacks."

"First thing tomorrow," Jack said, "put most of those greenbacks in the bank for safekeeping before anyone finds out you have them. Banknotes and hard cash are scarce commodities around these parts."

"Thanks for the advice," Pete said. "I've never been partial to banks after what I saw they did to neighbors who were in dire straights, what with poor crops and the depression."

"Suit yourself," Jack said. "Where are you sleeping tonight?"

"Oh, the boss said I can continue to bed down with the bull train until they return to Fort Pierre, which will probably be in a day or two," Pete answered.

They all pushed back from the table and stood up.

"Good night to you all," Lou said. "I still have some cleaning to do, and I need to prepare for tomorrow's breakfast. No rest for the weary."

Jack lit Lil's lantern as the threesome, followed by the dog, left the hotel and stepped out into the street. Directly across the street from the Grand Central Hotel stood the Deadwood Theater. The Grand Central and the Deadwood Theater were the largest buildings in town. The theater was still far from complete, having an unfinished floor and canvas for a roof.

"It was nice to meet you both," Pete said. "I hope I can count you as my first new friends in Deadwood."

"Of course, Pete!" Lil said as she reached on tiptoes to give him a kiss on the cheek. Jack stretched out his hand and gave Pete a firm handshake, "You bet, Pete. Friends indeed! See you tomorrow."

Pete disappeared into the night.

"Lil, are you feeling better?" Jack asked.

"Yes, Jack. Thank you for everything tonight," Lil said, as she again stretched upward on tiptoes to kiss Jack, not on the cheek, but a full kiss on his mouth. Jack, still holding the lantern in his right hand, circled Lil's waist with his left arm. He held her like that for what seemed to him only a second, but wanting it to last an eternity.

A loud theatrical cough brought them back into awareness of their surroundings. In front of them stood Uncle Jack Langrishe, holding a lantern and wearing a nightshirt and sleeping cap.

"Lil, it's late," Langrishe said. "It's time to leave Captain Jones to his own devices. We need our sleep so we can rehearse the new acts tomorrow. Good night, Captain."

"Good night, sir. Good night, Lil," Jack said as he handed her the lantern.

She flashed a smile at him. "Until tomorrow, Captain!" Lil patted Stonewall and left arm-in-arm with her uncle.

Jack watched them disappear into the darkened theater to their sleeping quarters. He continued to stare into the darkness long after they had left. *I think I'm beginning to grow fond of that girl.* He realized he was still smiling. He looked up into the night sky. The brighter stars were visible, despite a waxing quarter moon. Images of his beloved wife, Mary, and his child, Sarah, flooded his mind. The smile vanished. Sadness gripped his heart.

He turned and walked slowly back toward the hotel in the darkness of the street, and in the even deeper darkness of his soul.

CHAPTER THREE

ℰᴑᏣᎡ

Wednesday Morning, August 23, 1876—Jack Jones stepped through the Grand Central Hotel's front door onto the porch. He breathed in the cool, crisp air, stretched his arms upwards, and yawned. Stonewall emerged by his side following suit, stretching out his hind legs and yawning. Aunt Lou had just finished stuffing breakfast into man and beast. The sun peeked over Hebrew Hill in front of Jack, briefly blinding him. Jack had finished writing his dispatch describing last night's shooting. He planned to send it and a second dispatch concerning the recent murder of Preacher Smith to his editor via express.

Loud shouts punctuated the murmur of hundreds of human voices. Someone slowly plunked a banjo. A continuous racket of rockers and sluice boxes, sawing wood, hammering nails, pickaxes striking rock and shovels scooping gravel overrode the tinkling, gurgling music of Whitewood Creek, attempting to flow through its course as prospectors working their placer claims constantly changed and diverted its waters to assist their search for gold flecks. Small arrastra mills grinding rock on rock added to the mix of sounds. A pistol shot rang out far up the gulch, then another and another in steady succession. "Someone must be doing a little target practice," Jack said to his hound.

A team of oxen headed south, pulling an empty, rattling freight wagon. Several men wearing slouch hats and work clothes rode on the wagon. One of them spied Jack, then waved his arms over his head.

"Mr. Jones!" Pete shouted. "I mean Captain! I mean Jack! Good morning to you, sir!"

"Pete, good morning to you!" Jack shouted back. "Where are you off to?"

"We're headed up to Lead!" Pete shouted. "I got a day job loading ore into wagons. They plan to haul the ore to the smelter in Omaha. I'll be back when the loading is done!"

"Good! Track me down when you get back. I'd like your report on the hard rock mining in Lead!" Jack shouted.

"Yes, sir! I surely will do that!" Pete shouted as the wagon rolled up the road.

Jack pulled out his pocket watch and flipped open the lid. The time was ten minutes after eight o'clock. He always synchronized his watch with the Grand Central's regulator clock. After all, the Grand Central was where he could find his three square meals.

"Well, Stonewall, let's see if we can find Colorado Charlie and send out these dispatches," Jack said. He stepped into Main Street, joining the throng of miners and those living off the miners. He and Stonewall walked three doors down to the Lee & Brown Store on the corner of Main and Gold Streets. A shingle with Pioneer Pony Express burned into it hung below the building's main sign. Sitting on a stump, dressed in beaded buckskin, the always dapper Colorado Charlie Utter was using a rag to rub grease into the headstall of a newly fashioned bridle. Charlie looked up from his work as Jack approached. Stonewall ran up to him and licked his hand.

"Well, good morning, Stonewall," Charlie said, rubbing the hound behind his ears. "And how are you today, Captain Jones?" he said, standing up.

"Good, Charlie. Have a little business for you if you're interested," Jack said, grasping Charlie's outstretched hand.

"Always interested in a little business, Captain. What do you have for me this time?"

"Two dispatches for my newspaper. One concerns the death of Preacher Smith and the second concerns last night's murder of Bummer Dan."

"That sure is a shame about old Bummer Dan. Why the heck do you think Harry Young had to go and shoot him?"

"I'm not sure. Harry claimed he didn't mean to kill him. He thought he was shooting at Laughing Sam."

"Why would Harry think he was shooting at Laughing Sam?"

"Well, that is the strange thing about this case," Jack said. "Bummer Dan was wearing Laughing Sam's hat and checkered coat. So I can imagine in the dim light of Saloon Number 10, it might be easy for Harry to mistake him for being Laughing Sam, especially when he was wearing Laughing Sam's clothes."

"Is there bad blood between Harry Young and Laughing Sam?" Charlie asked.

"I don't know, but I did see a confrontation between them last night. Maybe their feuding was going on before that."

"I couldn't tell you," Charlie said. "I don't know much about those characters. Although, Wild Bill knew Young from before Deadwood and thought well of him."

"The killing of Preacher Smith is an even sadder tale," Jack said.

"That it is. It's such a shame the Injuns had to go and kill him. He certainly was a man of God. What's your understanding of what happened? I was out of town making my express run to Fort Laramie and back, so I missed all the excitement."

"As I understand it, Preacher Smith as usual was preaching on the street, standing on a crate and had a good crowd. During the sermon, Calamity Jane grabbed his hat and used it to collect the offering and shamed many to contribute more than they would have been accustomed to give," Jack said.

"That Calamity Jane, she is something else!" Charlie said, breaking into a grin.

"She surely is," Jack agreed. "Anyway, after the take, they counted it and the combination of dust, coin, chips, and markers added up to roughly two hundred and fifty dollars. Not bad for less than an hour's work."

"Not bad at all," Charlie said. "Maybe I should go into the preaching business."

"After that, Preacher Smith headed north out of town to preach at Crook City. Not more than a couple miles north of town, Indians gunned him down. There are some peculiar facts about this killing of Preacher Smith. The Indians shot him through the heart with a lead bullet. They did not scalp or otherwise mutilate him and they took his money, including the markers."

"Interesting that the Injuns would take his money, but even more interesting that they would take markers. Maybe they had a use for them—use them as padding or to start a fire."

"Humph, yes," Jack pondered. "I hear they found nothing that belonged to the good preacher on that brave they killed near him. You would think, if the Indian was the killer, he would have had some sort of trophy on him to cerebrate the kill."

"You know, if my pard Wild Bill was still around, this horseshit would soon come to an end."

"How so?" Jack asked.

"Some of the more well-to-do businessmen in town were fixin' to hire him as the town lawman, even though we don't really have laws and rules. Wild Bill would have done a good job of knocking heads together and running off those who would want to rob and steal," Charlie said, shaking his head and looking down past his beaded moccasins to the mud and filth in the street .

"This is all well and good to speculate, but I better be getting back to business," Colorado Charlie continued. "I assume your Chicago newspaper will pay for the dispatches in the usual manner?"

"Yes, that's correct," Jack said. "By the way, you haven't seen Laughing Sam this morning have you?"

"I've seen neither hide nor hair of him."

"Well if you do, tell him I'd like to talk with him about the shooting last night."

"I bet if nothing else, you'll see him during the trial," Charlie said.

"That's right. Jury selection should take place tomorrow and maybe the trial later that day."

The tone of the street noise rose in volume and intensity. Jack and Colorado Charlie turned to see what all the commotion was. Two muscular Cantonese men walked up the street, one behind the other. Each carried a staff in his right hand, and a stout pole rested on their left shoulders. Over the pole lay a woven mat to screen the sun. Below the pole and suspended between the two men by bamboo rods was a platform and backrest. This sight alone would cause people to stop, stare, and comment, but the person the men carried was the one who caused the stir.

A young Cantonese woman sat upon the platform, her limbs and feet tucked under her. Richly embroidered red silk robes flowed down, covering her entire body. A white silk sash gathered the woven silks together at her slim waist. One delicate hand held a fan decorated with painted flowers and birds, which masked the lower half of her face. Combs held her black hair in place, arranged like a frame around her pale face. The fan accentuated her dark brown eyes. The men who had a glimpse of the upper half of her face appeared mesmerized. The few soiled doves who were out this time of day scowled and whispered. The woman was stunning.

As the two men approached Charlie and Jack, the Asian beauty spoke a sharp command, stopping them. Her dark eyes danced with amusement. She lowered the fan below her face. She was smiling.

Colorado Charlie and Jack snatched the hats off their heads and stammered together, "Good morning, ma'am!"

Nodding her head slightly to them, slowly and distinctly she said, "Good morning, gentlemen." Laughing, she raised the fan to cover her mouth. Speaking a command in Cantonese to the two men, they proceeded on their way. Charlie and Jack stared after the woman, until she and her escort were lost from their sight in the humanity and cattle filling the street. Both men realizing they still held their hats in their hands, quickly returned them to their heads.

"Was she staring at you?" Charlie asked.

"No, I think she was admiring your flowing golden locks," Jack said.

"I don't know," Charlie replied.

"Do you know anything about her?" Jack asked.

"Not much. I hear she's very wealthy, and I would say, looks and acts the part. If she is rich, why is she here? Who would want to come to this God-forsaken place if they could live anywhere they want? She's bought three lots where Sherman Street runs into Main and she is having workmen construct three buildings on those lots."

"Humph, well back to the business at hand, can you tell me where..."

"Wait a minute," Charlie interrupted. "I forgot, I have a message for you that arrived yesterday!" He bounded through the Lee & Brown's door and soon emerged, handing an envelope to Jack. Ripping it open, he quickly scanned the message. It was a letter from his editor. He read it slower the second time.

July 31, 1876
Chicago, Illinois

Dear Jones,

We have not heard for some time from Macmillan who, as you know, has been with General George Crook since May. We want you to leave Deadwood, find Crook posthaste, and determine the army's disposition. Find out what it has accomplished, as well as the status of the hostiles, after which you will send a complete report to us. Hire a guide if necessary and transportation. Buy any supplies you may need to procure. We authorize you to have all items billed to the *InterOcean*. There is no time to lose.

Your Obedient Servant,
Obadiah Green

"Humph! Who's the obedient servant here?" Jack said to himself.

"What do you mean?" Charlie asked.

"My editor thinks I need to chase after Crook and find out what has happened to him and his army. Seems they have disappeared off the face of the earth."

"Weren't you with Crook earlier this year?"

"Yes, I was with him up until after the fight on the Rosebud. I left after Crook decided to try his hand at fly-fishing for trout in the Big Horn Mountains instead of continuing to pursue the Sioux and Cheyenne. Maybe if he hadn't dawdled, he could have put pressure on the hostiles, pushing them into General Terry and Custer's hands. Things might have been very different and Custer and his men might still be with us."

"It was a bad deal," Charlie agreed.

"When does the express leave for Fort Laramie?" Jack asked.

"I'll be sending a rider south in two days."

"So I have two days, not more than three, to report on the outcome of Young's trial, get my supplies together, and find a scout who can possibly locate a missing army that could be anywhere in Dakota Territory," Jack calculated. *And try to figure out what happened to Bummer Dan's gold,* Jack told himself.

"Charlie, hand me back one of those dispatches, would you?"

Charlie gave Jack one of the brown-papered packages. Jack produced a pencil from his coat pocket and began to write on the package:

Dear Obadiah,

I will attempt to find Crook, but after you read about the recent murder here in Deadwood, you should agree with me that the trial of the murderer is significant and should help the *InterOcean's* circulation. I'll send my report after the trial and then hit the trail for Crook, his army, and the hostiles.

Your Obedient Servant,
Jack Jones

Jack grinned as he wrote "Your Obedient Servant."

"As I was about to ask earlier, I know you're good friends with Calamity Jane..."

"I sure am good friends with her!" Charlie responded as he winked.

"Can you tell me where she is?"

"Well, she's likely to be found just about anywhere, but she has been frequenting Al Swearengen's Cricket Saloon an awful lot. She's been earning money there as a dance hall girl. If she's not there, she might be tending those fellas what came down with smallpox at the pest house outside of town. She claims she's immune to smallpox, and maybe so. She tends to them every day and stays healthy as a horse. And if you can't find her at those places, come by my camp in the evening. She stops over every now and then."

"Thanks for the tip, Charlie. One last question, since I now have to chase after Crook, any idea on a good scout who might be able to help me find Crook and keep my scalp at the same time?"

"Well, right off the top of my head, no pun intended, you might try California Joe Milner. He knows the Hills and surrounding territory better than any other white man. He rode into town with Wild Bill and me. He's hard to find though. The more flush merchants hired him to scout about the territory for hostiles and warn the town in case of attack. Seems the good merchants are skittish until the army can round up the hostiles and take them back to their agencies."

"If California Joe's in town, where would I find him?"

"You could find him at just about any watering hole, but half the time he'll stop by my camp and freeload off my whiskey. I'll let him know you're looking for him. You're staying at the Grand Central Hotel, right?"

"Right," Jack said. "I'm not sure what he looks like."

"He's a blue-eyed man mountain standing over six feet tall, wearing the largest sombrero I've ever seen," Charlie said. "He's an ugly cuss, although if he cleaned up some he'd probably be presentable. He wears buckskins, but not as clean as mine. His red, bushy beard and long hair are all matted, greasy, and unkept, and he's quite the talker."

"Thanks, Charlie, I appreciate it," Jack said. "I better move along. I think I'll nose about the *Black Hills Pioneer* office to see if they'll share any news, and I need to stop in at the livery stable and see if they have any news on my horse with the Montana Herd out on Centennial Prairie. I'm concerned about him after the Indian raid on the herd Sunday. I'm hoping he's not listed among the missing."

"I hear the Injuns are still poking around the herd, trying to steal a horse or two more," Charlie said. "People are saying the Injuns ran off two hundred horses. I usually keep a few mules and horses out there, but during the day of the raid, all mine were away being used. Hope your horse is safe."

"Thanks, Charlie," Jack said. "Come on, Stonewall."

Jack decided to first check on his horse and then visit the newspaper shop. Jack and the dog turned left, walking west on Gold Street toward the stable situated flush against the steep gulch wall. Several horses stood motionless in a small corral, except for their tails swishing at flies. The sign over the building's door read "Montana Feed, Livery, and Stable." Jack pushed open the door and walked into the main part of the building. Inside it was cool and dark. Aromas of hay, horse manure, and sawdust mixed and competed to overwhelm each other. A row of stalls ran along the right-hand side of the building. Several horses standing in the stalls chomping on hay looked up. A horse in the closest stall nickered a welcome. Jack walked over to the horse, put out his hand for the horse to smell, then stroked the horse's forehead, and as Jack rubbed behind the horse's ear, he said, "And what's your name?"

"His name is Paco," a voice with a distinct French accent said from the haymow. A white-haired black man stopped forking hay and asked, "Can I help you, monsieur?"

"I want to check on my horse with the Montana Herd out at the Centennial Prairie," Jack said.

The man approached closer and Jack could see he had led a rough life. Long scars ran across the man's arms and one ran diagonally across the left side of his face. Stonewall ran up to him. The man bent down to let the dog lick his hand and then the man stroked the top of Stonewall's head.

"I must look in the book to see about your horse," the man said as he walked to a roughly fashioned counter and opened a large ledger book.

"Your name please, monsieur?" the man asked.

"Jack Jones."

The man flipped through a few pages, running his finger down each page.

"Ah yes! Here it is, a bay gelding with blaze on his forehead, one white sock on the right foreleg, and a five-inch scar on his left shoulder."

"That's correct."

"I have no entries beside the horse. The men are still gathering the horses together. Many ran off during the Indian raid. It may be a few days until they have an accurate count and we will know if your horse is with the missing or the found."

"That's fine," Jack said. "Thank you. By the way, we have not officially met. As you know, my name is Jack Jones and if I may ask, what is yours?"

"But of course, my name is Hannibal Morris, but you can call me what everyone else does, Old Frenchy."

"And you can call me Jack."

"Very good, Monsieur Jack."

"So you are from France or Louisiana?"

"Ha! Ha! No, *mon ami*. I am from French Guiana."

"I see. If I may be so bold as to ask, how did you come by those scars?"

"Ah yes. I was born a slave in 1819. My first master was cruel. I ran away when I was sixteen years old. My goal was to join the maroons and…"

"Wait a minute, Old Frenchy. What are maroons?"

"Ah yes. The maroons are escaped slaves who live beyond the settlements and plantations, out in the jungle. They live as free men. And that is what I wanted to be. But I was caught and I was whipped in front of the other slaves to show what would happen to them if they tried to escape. I was sold to another master and again tried to escape. Again, I was caught, flogged, and sold. Five times, I was sold. Finally, my last master brought me to New Orleans with him. The American War Between the States started and when General Butler captured New Orleans, I walked away from my master and never looked back. I've been a free man ever since. I am one of the first to reach Deadwood and I have a good job here at the livery stable. I love this country! Ha-ha!"

"What a story, Old Frenchy! I am glad to make your acquaintance."

"And what is your story, if I may ask?"

"Not much to tell, Old Frenchy. I'm employed as a newspaper reporter for the *Chicago Inter-Ocean*. And I'm writing a story on last night's murder of Bummer Dan by Harry Young."

"That is a sad story," Old Frenchy said, a broad smile vanishing from his face.

"As part of my story, I want to interview Laughing Sam Hartman. You don't happen to know where I could find him do you?"

"Ah, *mon ami*, I do not know the man."

"How about Calamity Jane?"

Old Frenchy broke into a grin. "Who can say with her? She is like the wind. Here one moment, gone the next."

"My final questions, do you know California Joe and if so, have you seen him in town?"

"*Oui*, I know him, and no, I have not seen him, monsieur."

"Well, I thought I would ask. Thank you for telling me your story. I'll see you around town."

"Thank you, my new friend. *Bonjour*."

Jack and Stonewall left the building and walked a few steps to the south on West Main Alley to the new building housing the *Black Hills Pioneer*. It was sandwiched between two buildings used by women of loose virtue. Jack entered the front office. The overpowering smell of printers ink permeated the air. There appeared to be no one around. Outdated newspapers cluttered the room, and a stack of the latest editions leaned against the wall by the door. A newly constructed pine table served as the editor's desk and a stump served as the editor's chair. Papers and bills were strewn in disarray and in heaps on the table. Clangs of metal on metal punctuated by swear words came from the back room.

"Halloo!" Jack shouted. "Anyone about back there? Hide your stories! It's the opposition!" The backroom door flew open. A stout, smooth-shaven man wearing a printer's apron over his clothes stood in the doorway. Begrimed with printer's ink, A.W. Merrick strode into the front room.

"Oh, it's only you, Jones," Merrick said, peering over his spectacles.

"And I'm happy to see you too, A.W. What's news today?"

"Why should I share my hard-earned information with you?"

"Why not? We both have different readerships. We might as well collaborate."

Merrick removed his spectacles, stared at Jack, and grinned. "Care for a shot of whiskey?"

Jack glanced at the regulator clock on the wall behind Merrick's head. The clock's pendulum was swinging with its methodical tick-tock as its hands indicated 10:30 a.m. He took out his pocket watch. It read 10:00 a.m., which he believed was the more accurate time.

"Humph, why not?" Jack said.

Merrick turned and entered the backroom, returning a minute later with a half-full whiskey bottle and two battered tin cups. He poured an inch of the amber-colored fluid into each, gave Jack a cup, and held his up to Jack's.

"A toast to our successful endeavors!" Merrick said.

"To our successful endeavors!" Jack responded. They clanked their cups together and downed the whiskey. Merrick smacked his lips, and Jack exclaimed, "Oh Emma!" They both laughed.

"Now down to business," Merrick said. "What are you working on?"

"The main story is the murder of Bummer Dan," Jack said, "And any follow up there might be to the killing of Preacher Smith."

"Those aren't the real stories! The real story is the growth of this town, and lack of government. If we had good sound government, we could put an end to most of these murders. We could put an end to the disease running rampant through this town. We could put an end to the sharp practices that are gouging our good citizens. Oh Emma! Just look at the streets! Sure, we have the town platted, of sorts, but the streets are filled with filth. Why hell, the damn stumps and boulders are still protruding up from the mud that will suck the boots right off your feet and swallow small children. We need good government and the rest falls in place!"

"Well said, sir, but I still need to follow up on these other stories."

"By all means, then go ahead, but I still think you are missing the real story! The town continues to grow and is slowly becoming civilized, whether people want it to or not. Why, just last week Judge Joe Miller's family arrived in town. Others are thinking of sending for their families once the army escorts the Indians back to their agencies." Merrick took a breath. "And then, Jones, just think, once the Indians are no longer a menace, the stage lines have promised they will start regular runs to Deadwood, and the telegraph will follow. We will not have to rely on Utter and his ilk to find out what is happening in the rest of the world, and to let the world know of our progress. Why, someday I can envision a railroad running to Deadwood. That's progress. That's the real story."

"I agree with you, but I need to report on these killings too," Jack said. "What is your take on the murder of Preacher Smith?"

"A tragedy," Merrick said shaking his head. "A horrible tragedy. Smith was our only semblance of a minister here in town. Look at the Chinese. They are in the process of building their own house of worship on lower Main Street. I think they call it a Joss House, and we can't even keep a damn preacher alive!"

"Why do you think the Indians would have killed Smith? An unarmed, peaceful man, neither scalping nor mutilating him, and they took only his money and markers."

"How do you know Indians did it?"

"Who else would do such a thing?" Jack asked.

"Anyone would. Just think, he was carrying quite a lot of money. Just about everyone in town would have known that. Who's to say that someone didn't follow him? They could have approached him acting friendly to get close enough to have a clear shot at his heart, snuffing out his life, and taking his money. Dead men tell no tales!"

"An interesting theory," Jack said.

"Indians would have taken more than just money."

"Humph. What about Harry Young shooting Bummer Dan? What do you think was going on there?"

"Rumor has it that Young and that so-called Laughing Sam Hartman had been having an ongoing dispute, but over what, I have no idea. For some odd reason known only to Bummer Dan, who is now deceased, and Laughing Sam, Bummer Dan was wearing Laughing Sam's hat and coat. Young claimed he thought he was shooting Laughing Sam, not Bummer Dan, a lethal case of mistaken identity."

"Speaking of Laughing Sam, I'd like to talk with him about what happened last night," Jack said. "Any idea where I might find him?"

"If I knew where he was, I'd be there right now getting his story for the paper. I've sent a few hounds out trying to track him down with no luck. Maybe he left town, giving Bummer Dan his hat and coat as parting gifts."

"I hadn't thought of that," Jack said. "Maybe he was so intimidated by Harry Young last night that he thought the best thing to do would be to leave town and head off to another mining camp. But hopefully we'll see him testify at the trial."

"Yes, if he shows up. But I wouldn't count on it," Merrick said.

"Why do you say that?"

"Maybe he thinks he would be implicated in poor Bummer Dan's death. Even if Bummer Dan wearing his hat and coat could be construed as a practical joke, it ended in the death of Bummer Dan. And Laughing Sam could be held accountable for that."

"Another interesting thought," Jack mused.

"Will you join me in another morning libation?" Merrick said as he picked up the bottle and began to pour himself another shot into his cup.

"Thanks, A.W., but I better hold off this time. I'll take you up on that offer later."

"Suit yourself," Merrick said as he downed the whiskey.

"You don't happen to know where Calamity Jane would be? I heard she might be at the Cricket Saloon."

"No, I don't know where she is, but the Cricket would be a good place to look for that harpy. Why do you need to see her, if I may ask?"

"Since neither of us can find Laughing Sam, Calamity Jane just might be able to direct me to him."

"Good luck to you, Jones."

Jack left Merrick to his ink and whiskey. With Stonewall zigzagging back and forth in front of him, checking out the latest smells along the way, Jack returned to Main Street. He headed north down the street filled with the continuous mass of humanity, bellowing oxen, and sharp-tongued bullwhackers. He arrived at the Cricket Saloon and was about to enter when behind him, he heard an unmistakable female voice roaring curses, and when he turned to look, was amused at the whirlwind presence as she surged through the mass of humanity. "Captain Jones!"

CHAPTER FOUR
ဢဢ

Wednesday Late Morning, August 23, 1876—"Captain Jones!" Calamity Jane Canary shouted, pushing one miner who was too slow to get out of her way.

"Move, ya old son of a bitch!" she shouted, giving the miner a swift kick in the rump and showing her man's work boot beneath her ankle-length, lavender, day-dress with purple piping. She wore a knotted purple scarf around her neck, and a broad-brimmed man's hat rode atop her red head. Her face was plain, but pleasant. Her figure was boyish. She lunged at Jack, who laughed as he caught her.

"Captain Jones, I haven't seen ya since we left that damn old goat Crook, trying to find those bastard Sioux along the Big Horns! How ya been doin'?" she asked, holding on to him as if he was the last man in the world.

"Well, Calamity, I've been doing just fine. I've been reporting on a few stories here in Deadwood."

"Why haven't I seen ya?"

"I don't know. I guess our paths just didn't cross until now."

"Where's that real son of a bitch? That hound of yours."

"He's snooping around somewhere. He'll come back and find us. What have you been up to?"

"Just about anything I can do to keep my body and soul together, Captain. I'm currently employed by that son of a bitch Al Swearengen, to dance with hard-luck bastards in the Cricket Saloon, but I'm my own gal. He don't own me. I work for me and pay him a percentage, and I help out lookin' after his new girls. Break 'em in, so they're ready to be rode hard by these horny bastards who can't make a living anywhere else." In a lower voice, she added, "Not sure how much longer I'll be partnering with Swearengen. He's rough on those girls. He's even blackened his own wife's eye a time or two and will farm her out if the price is right. But that bastard weasel knows better than to aggravate me and my friends. If he touches any of us he'll wind up a gelding, if ya know what I mean." She grinned. "So what brings ya to the Cricket?"

"You."

"Aw, didn't know ya got soft and are now sweet on me?" She stood back from Jack, but held on to him at arm's length.

"Sorry, just trying to do my job and track down a man. I thought if anybody knows where he is, you're that person."

"That's for certain. Come on into the Cricket where it's a little cooler. We can sit down and have a whiskey for old time's sake."

"Sounds like a fine idea," Jack said.

They walked toward the door to Jack's right when Stonewall ran up to Calamity, his tail wagging and a soft whine coming from his throat. He jumped on her as she bent over and cooed, massaging his floppy ears. "How's my favorite little hound dog, Stonewall? Let's go inside and find ya some grub, ya little son of a bitch. Come to think of it, I haven't had a bite to eat and, Captain, ya look like a damn scarecrow. Don't they feed ya around these parts?"

"Actually I'm being fed quite well by Aunt Lou."

"That woman sure can cook!"

Jack noticed a bulging haversack slung over Calamity's shoulder. "What have you been up to with that haversack?"

"Everyone knows a smallpox epidemic has hit town, and being a reporter, I'm sure ya know that them's that's got it are forced out of town and quarantined to an isolated shanty to live or die. Well, I'm not going to let those damn sons of bitches die by themselves. I can't get smallpox, so I go out and take care of them. No one else will."

"That is a commendable act you're doing, Calamity."

"Aw, it ain't nothin'. It just needs bein' done. Come on into the Cricket. Let's stop this jawing in the sun and get inside where it's cool."

Calamity Jane was right. It was cool inside the Cricket Saloon. Jack's eyes took a few seconds to adjust to the dim light. A rough-hewn stage ran along the right wall with a bar far to the back. A few tables and stools had been placed in front of the stage. Three women wearing wraps sat at a table near the front of the building. The rest of the room was empty except for a man behind the bar.

"Captain Jones," Calamity said, "let me introduce ya to my friends."

"Starting on the left, this here's Kitty Arnold, next to her is my old friend from France, California, Montana, Colorado, and a hell of a lot of other places, Eleanor Dumont, also known as Madame Mustache. Don't let the name fool ya, her mustache ain't that bad. And last, but not least, Tid Bit."

She waved a hand at Jack. "And ladies, this here's an old friend of mine from when I was with Crook's boys out in the wilds of Wyoming, Captain Jack Jones, who is, among other things, a reporter for a fancy back-East newspaper and a right nice gent."

The three women acknowledged Jack with smiles. The blond-haired Madame Moustache, older than the other women, held out the back of her hand for Jack to kiss, which he did. Tid Bit was embroidering a dress laid across her lap. Jack could see he had interrupted their conversation.

"Looks like you all are busy here," Jack said. "Maybe I should come back later."

"Nonsense," Kitty said. "Please pull up a stool and join us."

"If you insist."

"We insist," Madame Mustache said. Stonewall made the rounds of the three women, becoming an immediate hit.

"Hey you!" the man at the bar shouted. "We don't allow no dogs in here! Get that mutt out of here!"

"Johnny!" Calamity Jane shouted. "The dog is my guest and if I says he stays, he stays. Got that?"

The man scowled but did not say anything. He went back to polishing glasses with a dirty rag.

"Captain, what say ya to that whiskey?" Calamity said.

"Sure thing, Calamity. Let me buy you ladies all a drink,"

"Johnny!" Calamity shouted. "A bottle of whiskey. The good stuff. And five glasses." The man slowly finished his polishing and then rummaged under the bar for a bottle of the good stuff.

"Who's the barkeep?" Jack asked softly to Calamity, who was sitting to his right.

"That son of a bitch's name is Johnny Burns," she said, in a not so soft a voice. "He's Al's boy," and to the bar she yelled, "Hurry it up, you slow-moving horse's ass."

Burns leisurely walked to the table, then setting down the bottle and glasses, he said, "And I love you too, Calamity."

"Aw shucks, ain't he nice. Ha! Ha! Johnny, ya know I don't mean nothing by it."

"I know, Calamity."

"Now leave us alone, you castrated bastard, I mean, sweet Johnny," Calamity said, with a mischievous grin.

Jack uncorked the bottle and poured five glasses to the brim.

"Oh, thank you, Captain!" Kitty said.

"A toast," Jack said, hoisting his glass. "Here's to four of the finest women in Deadwood!" This was answered by a chorus of thank yous and the clinking of five glasses. Shots were downed, lips were smacked, a cough or two, and smiles around.

"Captain Jones is here on business," Calamity proclaimed.

"And what might that be?" Madame Mustache asked.

"Murder and mayhem," Jack responded with a smile.

"Oh, poor Preacher Smith. It was so horrible," Tid Bit said.

"It surely was," Kitty agreed.

"Captain, we were the ones what laid out poor Preacher Smith's body for burial," Calamity said.

"We removed his coat and shirt," Madame Mustache said. "Tried to wash out the blood stains, but didn't get it all. Tid Bit mended the gunshot hole as best she could."

"We washed the blood off his body," Kitty said. "Then we washed his hands and face, put his shirt and coat back on him, combed his hair, and brushed the dirt from his beard. All ready for burial. That new fellow, Seth Bullock, said the prayers over the grave. Seems like a nice man."

"Don't think I've met him yet," Jack said.

"He and a fellow by the name of Sol Star just arrived from Montana. They're setting up an emporium," Calamity said.

I'll have to stop by their establishment and see what supplies they have on hand for my trip to catch Crook, Jack thought and then said, "I need to take a few notes."

"Is this an interview?' Calamity asked. "Will we make it in your Eastern paper?"

"I'm not guaranteeing anything," Jack replied. "You never know about editors, what they will keep, and what they will toss out. Sometimes it depends on how much space they have to work with. But I'll give it a try and let's see what happens."

Jack fished his notebook and a pencil out of his coat pocket, and opening to a blank page, started to write, saying, "Tell me again, how many wounds there were?"

"We already done told ya, it was only one," Calamity said. "One lead bullet to the heart."

"No other wounds, cuts, marks, powder burns?"

"Wait a minute," Kitty said. "Come to think of it, there were powder burns on his shirt. Weren't there, girls?"

"That's right!" Calamity agreed as Jack continued to write.

"One bullet wound to the heart. Powder burns to the shirt," Jack said as he looked up from his writing, poured himself another shot, and then remembered to pour whiskey into his table companions' glasses.

"You're a right proper gentleman, Captain Jones!" Calamity said lifting her glass.

"Hear! hear!" the other women agreed.

"Thank you all. Now back to the business at hand. You say there was no mutilation, and nothing else was taken..."

"Except those Injuns took his Sunday church collection!" Tid Bit said.

"There was a right tidy sum," Calamity said. "I should know, I counted it for him."

"How much?" Jack asked.

"That poke was worth near two hundred and fifty dollars in dust, coin, chips, and markers. Quite a take, if ya ask me," Calamity said.

"You should have seen how Preacher Smith earned his keep that day!" Kitty said.

"Calamity Jane took up the offering for him," Madame Mustache said.

"I take it you weren't there, Captain?" Tid Bit asked.

"Sorry, ma'am."

"Well, it was quite beautiful, if you ask me," she responded.

"Tell me," Jack said.

"As you may know, Preacher Smith always did his preachin' on the street," Tid Bit said. "This time he found an old crate, stood on top of it, and proclaimed the Lord's Word to those heathen in the street who stopped to listen, remembering their upbringing and their home folks. Although some knotheads were too interested in their damn faro games to even look up or listen. Preacher Smith's words moved Calamity to run up to his crate. He had removed his hat before the Lord and held it in his hand. Calamity snatched it from him and used it as an offering plate. She interrupted his sermon long enough to shout 'Ya sinners, dig down in your pokes, now. This old fellow looks as though he were broke, and I want to collect two hundred dollars for him!' She pestered each of those fellows in the crowd. Wouldn't let them alone until they threw something in the hat. She even forced herself on the fellows playing faro, stopped their games until they paid up!"

They all laughed except Calamity Jane, her face somber and wooden. Tears began to stream down her face, as she said, "Ain't it too bad, that the only man who comes to this God-forsaken town to tell us how to live, has to be killed by Injuns!"

Tid Bit put her arm around Calamity and hugged her. Calamity pushed away and wiped her eyes with her bandanna.

"Humph," Jack cleared his throat. He was uncomfortable seeing a blubbering Calamity Jane, who was always bluster and show.

"But there was an Indian lurking there who probably killed Preacher Smith. That same Indian killed Lou Mason before he himself was killed by Texas Jack. Isn't that correct?" Jack asked.

"That's right," Madame Mustache said.

"Did that Indian have the two hundred and fifty dollars on him?" Jack asked.

"Good question. No one ever saw any money. No one ever asked about the money until now. Maybe Texas Jack would know," Madame Mustache said.

Jack wrote: "Track down Texas Jack, ask about money."

"That Texas Jack, he's one crazy bastard," Calamity said. She appeared to have recovered her composure. "I'm not sure that Injun was the one that killed Preacher Smith anyways."

"Why do you say that?" Jack asked.

"Because the fellas that were at the site of Preacher Smith's killing said that Injun was slowly riding up to them making the sign of peace, and our half-brained bastards started shooting at him. Shoot first, ask questions later. Then that simpleton, Lou

Mason, has to go and try to flush the Injun out of the brush and gets himself gut shot and bleeds out. Oh, Emma!"

"Then Texas Jack kills the Indian and doesn't satisfy himself with just lifting the scalp," Madame Mustache said. "He chops off the whole head. How revolting!"

"Well, it ain't that bad!" Calamity said. "Remember the day, my best friend, Wild Bill, the man I love, was shot by the weasel-faced, cross-eyed bastard Bill Sutherland or Jack McCall or whatever that egg-sucking dog's name is? That day was the day that Mex, Poncho, I think is his name, anyway he and his sidekick, I forget his name, ride into town with this head of this Injun chief. We're all happy 'cause what with Custer and his boys getting themselves killed and my Wild Bill being ass-assonated, I needed a little fun. So, me and Harry Young, poor Harry being locked up like that, anyway me and Harry and half the town, we tag along with Poncho and his sidekick and buy celebratory drinks from establishment to establishment. The town was whoopin' it up. All the while, here I am, forgettin' about my Wild Bill being dead. Anyhow, we had a gay old time traipsing through the town with that chief's head in tow. Someone got the bright idea to run the chief's head up the town's old Fourth of July flagpole, which we did. Then we all danced around it like a maypole only it was more like an Injun war dance. We was jumpin', hollering, and yelling. It was great fun. Not sure whatever happened to that chief's head. It was starting to get a little rank."

"Yes, but what about Texas Jack?" Jack asked.

"Oh well, he raced into town with his own Injun head tied to his saddle, flopping around. Folks thought it was disgusting and he paraded it from saloon to saloon, until that Bullock fellow—he and his compadres have styled themselves as a self-appointed sanitary commission—said it was unhealthy. Just last night they took it away from Texas Jack right here in this establishment, dug a hole outback of here and buried it."

A faint sweet scent drifted in from behind Jack.

"Don't say?" a deep female voice drawled behind him.

"Why, pull up a stool, Dirty Em!" Calamity said and to the bar she shouted, "Johnny, bring another glass for Dirty Em here!" and turning to Jack she said, "Captain, this here's one of our best friends, Dirty Em. Dirty Em, this gent is Captain Jack Jones, reporter for a big paper back East. He's gonna make us all famous!"

"We'll see. Nice to meet you, Em," Jack responded as he stood, turned, and tipped his hat to a stunning brunette standing behind him. She nodded her head, a cigar clenched between her teeth. She wore a red paisley evening dress, revealing her limbs and a bit of cleavage. Dirty Em slowly dragged a stool to the table and sat down as Jack returned to his seat. She was young, but she had a haggard, hangdog look, with dark circles under her brown eyes. She held in her left hand a bundle of ten cigars tied together with a string, which she plunked down on top of the table.

"Whatcha got there, Dirty Em?" Calamity asked.

"The fellow I was with last night didn't have as much money on him as he had claimed. I insisted on full payment, so he offered these cigars in partial payment. I can't smoke them all myself so here, each of you have one."

They all thanked Dirty Em as she distributed the cigars. Everyone pulled out knives of various shapes and sizes and cut off the tapered smoking ends. They all struck their lucifers on the rough pine table, they held the flames to the ends sticking out of their mouths and were soon puffing and enjoying the cigar fragrance and taste.

"Can't understand why someone would want to smoke one of those newfangled little cigars they call a cigarette?" Calamity said. The others nodded in concurrence.

There was a lull in the conversation as everyone enjoyed the cigars.

"Anyone know where I can find California Joe Milner?" Jack asked.

"Hell no!" Kitty spat.

"He is a most disgusting animal!" Madame Moustache said.

"You'll know when he's around," Calamity said.

"How so?" Jack asked.

"Because ya'll be able to smell his stench a mile away, even upwind!" Calamity shouted over the laughter of the other women.

Changing topics, Calamity said, "Captain Jones, you may not know this, but you're sitting with an illustrious passel of beauties here."

"How so?" Jack asked with a smile.

"We're all just about the first women that came in to this here town and I can tell you, none too soon. Lots of these here billy goats looked like they ain't seen a woman for years. Like they've been stranded with that Franklin expedition up in the Arctic for years and were running out of food or something. We were about as popular as cats in a barn full of coonhounds." Changing course, Calamity said, "Why, that makes me think we need some food, and we need it now! I'm as hungry as a bastard weasel in a hen house!" Calamity shouted, "Johnny! We need some of that stew and hard bread!"

Burns looked up from reading the latest edition of the *Black Hills Pioneer* spread out on the bar and scowled at Calamity.

"In a minute," he responded.

"Bring seven plates!"

"Seven? There's only six of you."

"I need seven! I'm not forgettin' my favorite hound here," Calamity said as she rubbed one of Stonewall's ears. Burns muttered to himself as he disappeared out back to where a cast-iron pot sat on a wood fire. Burns brought the pot and set it on the table, then he ladled beef stew onto seven tin plates. He took the pot back out to the fire and returned with six spoons and a package of hard bread.

"Thank you, Johnny dear," Calamity said.

"You're welcome," Burns said. Conversation ceased as the six humans and one dog wolfed down stew. Customers entering the Cricket headed straight to the bar to wet their whistles. Jack gnawed a cracker and finished his stew. Pushing his plate toward the center of the table, he stoked his cigar with a few puffs. He watched the women each finish their meals, then stack their plates on top of his. Leaning back and blowing a stream of smoke toward the ceiling, he moved to the topic he was most interested in.

"Anyone see Laughing Sam?" They all stared at him, frowning in disbelief. Tid Bit gasped, frozen mid-stitch. Calamity Jane, pushing back from the table, stood, knocking over her stool. Stepping back from Jack, she shouted, "What business do ya have with that horse's ass son of a bitch?" The tip of the cigar clenched between her teeth glowed bright red. Jack, wide-eyed and open-mouthed at their reaction, was at a loss for words.

"I said, what business do ya have with that horse's ass!" Calamity repeated.

Jack found his tongue, "I want to ask him what he knows about Bummer Dan's murder."

"What's to ask?" Calamity said. "Harry Young plugged two lead bullets into that old fart Bummer Dan. Case closed."

"That horrible man!" Tid Bit said.

"Who? Bummer Dan?" Jack asked.

"No! Laughing Sam!" Tid Bit said.

"I'm confused," Jack said. "All I want to do is ask Laughing Sam a few questions about what was going on last night when Bummer Dan was killed."

"No good was what was going on, if you ask me," Dirty Em said as the rest of the women nodded their heads in agreement.

"Calamity, sit down," Jack said. "Please."

She picked up the overturned stool, brought it back to the table and sat down.

"I want to find out why Bummer Dan walked into Saloon Number 10 wearing Laughing Sam's hat and coat," Jack continued. "And I want to know why I saw the two of them talking in the street about an hour before the shooting."

"Why, ya silly ass! Ya really don't know?" Calamity said. "Why, that bastard Laughing Sam and that rat-faced Bummer Dan were in cahoots together. They ran a crooked faro game. They were partners—partners in crime, thick as thieves— the worst type."

For the second time within the course of a minute, Jack was stunned and at a loss for words.

"I–I–humph, Bummer Dan and Laughing Sam partners?" Jack said.

"That's right, Captain," Madame Mustache said.

"Laughing Sam is a very bad man," Tid Bit said. She still had not resumed her embroidery project.

"The worst," Kitty agreed.

"Why do you say so?" Jack asked. "There's plenty of men in this town running crooked games of chance."

"Let me tell ya a little story, Captain. But I think it's one ya ain't gonna print in your paper," Calamity said.

"I'm listening," Jack said, picking up the whiskey bottle and pouring them all another healthy shot.

"Laughing Sam was smitten by Tid Bit here," Calamity started. Tid Bit smiled and looked down at the dress she had resumed working on. "Laughing Sam agreed to pay Tid Bit two ounces of gold dust to be with him for the night. The next morning, he gave her a poke bag, saying there was two ounces of gold dust in it. Laughing Sam told Tid Bit she needed to give him the bag back after she took the dust back to our camp. When she arrived in camp that morning, Tid Bit asked me to take care of her gold dust. When I looked at it I saw it weren't gold dust."

Tid Bit took up the narrative. "Calamity says to me 'Tid Bit, you poor little red-headed devil. That ain't gold dust, it's just brass filings and black sand.' I started to cry."

"I told Tid Bit to shut up," Calamity said. "We'd fix that son of a bitch, Laughing Sam."

"About eight o'clock that evening," Tid Bit continued. "Me and Calamity visited Colorado Charlie Utter's camp. I told Charlie and his friend, White Eye Anderson, what Laughing Sam did to me."

Calamity continued, "I says to Colorado Charlie, 'Charlie, I need to borrow your two ivory-handled six-shooters,' and he obliged me. Tid Bit and I marched over to the Senate Saloon, followed by Colorado Charlie and old White Eye. As you know, the Senate is always crowded. It's a busy place filled with all sorts trying their damnedest to lose all their money. That's where Bummer Dan and Laughing Sam had their crooked faro operation set up. Well, I've got Charlie's ivory-handled pistols in each hand and march right up to Laughing Sam's layout. His weasel partner, Bummer Dan, is standing there too, and in my loudest voice, I shout to the crowd. 'Listen up, you sons of bitches!' That got their attention. I also might have fired off a shot straight up towards the ceiling. I dunno. Anyway, I told the crowd what that sorry horse's ass had done to poor Tid Bit. There were lots of angry fellas, let me tell ya."

"I never heard a man get such a cussing as Calamity gave Laughing Sam," Tid Bit said. "She held those pistols pointed right at his nose and said he owed me two twenty dollar gold pieces for my pain and humiliation. He quickly found two twenty dollar gold pieces and handed them over to me."

"So now ya know why we could care less about what happened to Bummer Dan," Calamity said. "And if the same thing happens to Laughing Sam, I say good riddance!"

"Hear, hear!" chimed in the women.

"I understand now why you were upset," Jack said. "But I'm still trying to piece this story together. Why would Bummer Dan be wearing Laughing Sam's hat and coat?"

"I have no idea," Kitty said and the others nodded their heads in agreement.

"Have any of you seen Laughing Sam today?"

"Not me," Dirty Em said, and the others agreed.

"Let me try a different approach," Jack said. "Do any of you know where Laughing Sam lives?"

"No!" Tid Bit said and the rest shook their heads in agreement. "He moved to a different location after he cheated me. He must have been afraid Calamity or me might try to do something more to him."

"How about Bummer Dan? Anybody know where his place is?" Again, they all shook their heads no.

"Let's try a different tack," Jack said. "Any idea why Harry Young and Laughing Sam disliked each other?"

"I'm just supposing," Kitty said. "But us girls all came to Deadwood Gulch together with Wild Bill and Colorado Charlie. Harry Young worshipped Wild Bill and so a friend of Bill's was a friend of Harry's. So when Laughing Sam cheated Tid Bit, that set Harry on the warpath against Laughing Sam, and the bad blood between them just got worse and worse."

"Poor Harry," Tid Bit said, not looking up from her embroidering.

Jack was rapidly scribbling in his notebook. "Humph, this is all very interesting," he said.

"It still don't amount to more than a pile of steaming horse shit," Calamity said. "Harry Young pulled out a pistol and shot that rat-faced fart dead. Where's the rope? Let's get this deed done and proceed on."

"Calamity Jane Canary! No!" Tid Bit looked up from her work, fuming at Calamity.

"Well, just sayin'," Calamity said. "Sorry, Tid Bit. I just get carried away sometimes."

"Bear with me," Jack said. "This is what we know. Laughing Sam and Bummer Dan are partners. Laughing Sam and Harry Young are enemies over Laughing Sam cheating Tid Bit, who is a friend of Harry Young."

"He was very kind to me," Tid Bit interjected.

"Who was kind to you?" Kitty said.

"Harry."

"Last night," Jack continued, trying to regain control of the conversation, "Harry Young throws Laughing Sam out of Saloon Number 10 and tells him if he comes back in, he will shoot him dead. A couple hours after that, Bummer Dan, wearing Laughing Sam's hat and coat walks in and Harry shoots him. Am I missing anything?"

"No, Captain," said Calamity. "Except good riddance to Bummer Dan and it can't be too soon for that horse's ass Laughing Sam."

Jack was still scribbling notes when up walked a middle-aged man with black thinning hair, a moustache, and a slight paunch.

"Why, Al, how do ya do today?" Calamity said.

"Fine, Martha, and how are you?"

"Fine, just fine."

"And who's this gent who seems hell bent to out write Sam Clemens?"

"This be the honorable Captain Jack Jones, with one of them big Eastern newspapers out of Chicago," Calamity said. "And Captain Jones, this is Al Swearengen, owner of the Cricket Saloon." Jack stood and shook hands with Swearengen.

"Glad to make your acquaintance," Swearengen said.

"Likewise," Jack said and sat back down.

"Shouldn't you ladies be paying attention to our fine customers over there, belly up to the bar, most likely in need of female companionship?"

"Go to hell, Al," Calamity said. "We'll go to work when we damn well please. We ain't your little hussies you can hit and push around. Remember our arrangement, we're independent business women, and we pay you a percentage of the take for using your pus-covered hell hole of an establishment."

"Yes, yes, of course. I was just trying to encourage you to make a little money for yourselves and to throw me a measly shekel or two."

"You might say, they're all entertaining me," Jack said.

Turning from Calamity, Swearengen said to Jack, "And what brings you to our fair establishment, if I might ask?"

"I'm trying to track down Laughing Sam Hartman. I want to ask him a few questions about the murder of Bummer Dan last night."

"Wouldn't it be better to ask Harry Young those questions, seeing as how he's the one who pulled the trigger—twice?"

"I'd like to know why Bummer Dan was wearing Laughing Sam's hat and coat."

"That I couldn't tell you, and I haven't seen Laughing Sam at all."

"Do you know where either of them live?"

"No, can't help you there either."

"Al, we were talking about Preacher Smith," Kitty said. "Don't you think it's strange the Indian didn't scalp the preacher, took only his money, and Texas Jack didn't find any of the preacher's money on him?"

"Maybe it wasn't an Indian that did kill poor Preacher Smith, but some no-good white man," Tid Bit said.

"That's horse shit!" Swearengen responded. "We all know it was the work of those damn heathen devils and not white men."

"Just saying," Tid Bit responded and went back to her embroidery.

"Jones, what do you think? I plan to tear down this rattrap and rebuild the Cricket Saloon into a proper theater, with a long stage for shows that will be real extravaganzas. I'll have a long bar where men can easily order their libations, and I'll have some discrete, curtained areas where the ladies can entertain their beaus. It will be a gem of a saloon, in fact that's what I will call it—The Gem Saloon. What do you think?"

"That sure does sound like something else," Jack said.

"Huh? Oh, thanks," Swearengen said. "I need to see about some new girls who just arrived. Make sure they know the ropes." He left and the women began to snicker. "He don't have much rope to show them hussies," Kitty said.

"I'm going to have to get moving to see if I can track down Laughing Sam," Jack said and then in a louder voice to reach Burns at the bar, "Johnny, I'm ready to pay up for the whiskey and the grub for the entire table here."

"Sure, boss!" Burns responded and walked toward the table.

"You don't have to do that," Dirty Em said.

"No, I insist," Jack replied, holding out a ten-dollar gold piece. "Will that cover it?"

"It sure will, Captain Jones!" Burns replied.

"By the way, have you seen Laughing Sam? Or for that matter, California Joe?"

"Ain't seen neither of them fellows," Burns said as he snatched the coin out of Jack's hand and pocketed it. Scooping up the dirty plates, he left toward the back door.

"Well, ladies, it's been a pleasure. Tid Bit, may I ask what you are embroidering?"

"You surely may, Captain," she responded and stood up. "It's my continuing project. I've been sewing on my dress the names of all the men who have spent the night with me. The higher the name placed on my dress, the more favored they are. My most favorite I place near my heart. The ones I despise, I embroider them on my dress's derriere. See where Laughing Sam is?" Jack looked at the dress and saw prominently displayed on the area of the derriere: "Laughing Sam Hartman."

"This way I can sit on him whenever I want!"

Jack laughed, tipped his hat, turned, and walked out the door into the street, followed by Stonewall. The mass of humanity and oxen continued moving about the street, each to his own purpose.

CHAPTER FIVE
ᔕᓫᓫᓫᓫᔕ

Wednesday Afternoon, August 23, 1876—What do I know about this murder? Jack thought. *Young and Hartman are feuding to the point that Young threatens to kill Hartman if he returns to Saloon Number 10. I see Hartman and Bummer Dan conversing on the street. They are partners in running a faro game. Hartman is known for pulling dirty tricks. Bummer Dan walks into Saloon Number 10 wearing Hartman's hat and coat. Young shoots and kills Bummer Dan. Young claims he thought he was shooting at Hartman. So what about the haversack and gold? Bummer Dan had it at the time I saw him and Hartman on the street, and Bummer Dan did not have it on him when he was killed. So...maybe Bummer Dan gave it to Hartman for safekeeping. Another reason to find Laughing Sam Hartman.*

Across the street from the Cricket Saloon stood Saloon Number 10. *Maybe I'll find some answers there.* Jack, with Stonewall trailing, walked across the street and entered the saloon. His eyes readjusted to the dim light. A few patrons stood at the bar. Johnny Varnes was sitting in the same spot he had been last night. No one else was at Varnes's table, so he was occupying his time with a hand of solitaire. Jack walked up to the table opposite Varnes and said, "Mind if I join you, Johnny?"

Varnes looked up. "Not at all, Jones, looking to start a little game of chance?"

"No thanks," Jack said as he pulled up a stool. "Just trying to find some information to round out my dispatches to the paper on the Bummer Dan murder."

Anson Tipple, the bartender, called from the bar "Captain Jones, would you care for your bottle?"

"I surely would."

Varnes swept up his cards and shuffled them, saying "That was some doings last night, wasn't it?"

"It surely was."

Tipple set Jack's Old Crow whiskey bottle and a relatively clean glass on the table. "Anson, while you're here, let me ask you both a few quick questions, if you don't mind. Have you seen Laughing Sam or do you know where I can find him?"

"I haven't seen him," Varnes said.

"Nor I," Tipple said. "And I have no idea where he might be. You could ask at the Senate Saloon where he runs his faro game."

"I have no idea where he hangs his hat either," Varnes said. "Why are you interested in Laughing Sam?"

"I want to know why Bummer Dan was wearing Laughing Sam's clothes. Don't you think that's peculiar?"

"It is," Tipple said. "Harry had no problem with old Bummer Dan. It was Laughing Sam he was worried about. Between the three of us, I know for a fact, that Laughing Sam had threatened to hurt Harry these past two weeks. So it's no wonder Harry was jumpy when he saw Bummer Dan wearing Laughing Sam's clothes walking toward him. I'm sure he thought it was Laughing Sam coming back to do him harm, so he pulls out his pistol and fires. That's what I think. I've got to get back to my other customers."

"Wait. Before you go, have either of you seen California Joe? I need to see if he's interested in a job."

"Haven't seen him, but if I do, I'll tell him you're looking for him," Tipple said as he turned and walked back to the bar.

"I haven't seen California Joe either," Varnes said, staring at his cards as he shuffled, "It is peculiar about Bummer Dan wearing Laughing Sam's clothes. Old Bummer Dan didn't dress very well. Maybe Laughing Sam had a smidgen of compassion and just so happened to give him his hat and coat as a gift that night. As I say it aloud, it sounds farfetched, but who knows, maybe that is the case. I can see why you want to talk to him. It would certainly add to your story to know that fact."

Jack poured Old Crow into his glass and swirling it before taking a drink, said more to himself than Varnes, "I just can't figure out what happened to that haversack."

"Haversack? What are you talking about?" Varnes asked. Jack realized he was probably revealing too much information, but the cat was out of the bag and maybe Varnes could shed some light.

"The haversack is not a major concern, but as you know I was here last night before the shooting. I had left for supper before that happened. You might have noticed Bummer Dan was also in here earlier in the evening."

"Yes, I remember seeing him."

"He was wearing that old haversack with BD painted on the side. When Harry shot him, he did not have the haversack on him. I just thought it might have items in it that we could send to any family he might have."

"I see. That is commendable of you. Maybe if you find Laughing Sam, he can tell you where it is."

"Right," Jack said as he took another drink of his whiskey. *Slow down with these drinks*, he thought. *It is still early in the day, and I need to change the topic away from the haversack with Varnes.* "Last night, that was a fine thing you did, Johnny, breaking up that necktie party."

"Thank you, Jones. It just was the right thing to do. We do need to have law and order around here. I know that new fellow, Seth Bullock, and others are trying to do the right thing with setting up their Sanitary Commission to nip in the bud our smallpox epidemic."

Jack nodded in agreement and drained the last of his whiskey down his throat.

"Just think, the absolute absence of government," Varnes continued. "We have the federal government, but where is it? If the army showed up, they would probably try to evict us from Deadwood just as Crook did to us down in Custer last year this time. So look for absolutely no help from them. Then there's the Dakota Territory government in Yankton. Hell, they don't even know where we are. No county government and no town government. No taxmen, no police, no courts really. Oh yes, we'll have a trial here today or tomorrow, but is it legal? There are those who would say not. So if you think about it, we the people here in Deadwood, we are the government, and when we need to do something as our small society, we will form a Sanitary Commission or a judge, jury, and court. Then just as Cincinnatus did, they will disband themselves when they have fulfilled their job—not like elsewhere, where once you form a government or pass a law it's there to stay for good or bad."

"If I understand what you are saying, here in Deadwood it is man in nature without government," Jack said. "The Creator has endowed us with an inherent knowledge of good and evil and we come together as a society to care for each other, or to right a wrong, and then dissolve that temporary governmental function until needed again."

"Right you are, Jones. Isn't it wonderful here? We can do as we please as long as we don't harm someone else. Men can play any game of chance they want, drink all night if they'd like. Smoke the Chinaman's opium, spend the evening with a beautiful woman if you have the money, and above all, make money any way you can and not have the government official there with his hand in your pocket."

"Well said, sir! But I must be on my way," Jack said, standing up. "I need to try to find these men and attend the jury selection tomorrow."

"I too plan to sit in and watch the jury selection. It should be interesting."

"Until then," Jack said, shaking Varnes's hand, then returning his bottle and empty glass to the bar.

Back out on Main Street, Jack walked up the street toward the Senate Saloon. To Jack's left, nailed over the door of a newly constructed log building was a sign with a five-pointed star. "Sol" was painted on one side of the star and "Star" on the other side. Below that was painted "& Bullock" and under that "Wholesale and Retail." Another sign on the door read "Open."

"Humph," Jack grunted. "Stonewall, stay out here. I think I'll see what goods they have to outfit my trip. Maybe they know where those two fellows are that I'm looking for."

Stonewall was engaged in sniffing new smells. Jack knocked on the door. "Come in!" a voice boomed from within. Jack pushed the door open. The log building was one large room filled with rough shelves, tables, and stands displaying mining supplies, hardware, clothing, canned goods, sacks of flour, groceries, and sundry items. There was tinware, ironware, even a few pieces of glassware. Crates stood in the middle of the floor, with their lids pried open and packing material and the contents either still inside or piled on the floor. A short man stood behind the counter writing in a ledger book and a taller man was stacking canned goods on a shelf.

"Good morning, or I should say good afternoon now," the man behind the counter said. "What can we do for you?" Jack detected a faint German accent.

"Good afternoon, my name is Jack Jones, reporter for the *Chicago Inter-Ocean.* I'm looking for supplies to outfit me and another person on a month-long trip. I'm also fishing for a little information, so I hope I might find both here."

"You've come to the right place, sir," said the man stocking shelves. He stuck out his right hand and said, "The name's Bullock, Seth Bullock, and this here's my partner, Sol Star. We just arrived in Deadwood the first week of August. Business has been booming!"

Jack then shook hands with Star, saying, "Glad to make your acquaintance too."

"So what can we help you with, Mr. Jones?" Star asked.

"Please call me Jack."

"Not a problem, Jack, and please call us, Sol and Seth."

"My editor has tasked me with tracking down General Crook and his army and reporting back on their situation. I understand they could be almost anywhere to the north of the Hills between the Little Big Horn and the Missouri River. So, I think I'll need supplies for two people for a month. I'd need a complete outfit—food, equipment, boxes of ammunition for a Winchester 73 and an Army Colt 1873. I plan on taking two horses, along with two rented mules from the livery."

"We should be able to accommodate you," Bullock said.

"Thank you, which leads me to my next question. My thought is to hire California Joe as my guide. Have either of you seen him?"

"I know who he is, but I've not seen him," Star said.

"The same with me," Bullock said. "When do you plan to leave, so we know how much time we have to put together your items?"

"It depends on when I find California Joe and whether he is willing to guide me. If he is not, I'll have to find another competent guide, and that might take some time, but my goal is to leave town this Sunday, August 27th."

"That should give us enough time," Star said. "How about if we compile a list of foodstuffs and gear we think you may need? Stop back tomorrow and you can add and subtract from the list."

"I like that idea. Please proceed with it," Jack said. "Now I'd like to change subjects, if that's all right with you?"

"Yes," they said in unison.

"I'm sure you know about the murder of Bummer Dan last night."

"Yes," Bullock said.

"I'm looking for Laughing Sam Hartman. I'd like to ask him a few questions about what was going on that night."

"I haven't seen him," Star said.

"I haven't seen him either," Bullock said. "I can understand why you would like to talk with him. People tell me there was bad blood between Young and Hartman. Each threatened at various times to kill the other. I hear Bummer Dan Baum was wearing Hartman's hat and coat when Young shot and killed him. Something is not quite right with that. Mischief is afoot, if you ask me. There is no reason Baum should have been wearing Hartman's clothes into Saloon Number 10, a situation he would have known was dangerous. Hartman and Baum were partners. Don't you think Baum knew it would be dangerous to impersonate Hartman in Saloon Number 10, just after Young threatens to kill Hartman if he steps back in the saloon? Those two were up to something no good and whatever it was it went wrong—dead wrong."

"That's very perceptive, Seth," Sol said.

"Yes it is," Jack agreed.

"I was a sheriff in Helena, Montana, before I came here," Bullock said. "And I'm still interested in homicide and bringing the perpetrators to justice."

"It seems most everyone I've talked to has concerns about the latest murders and is of the opinion we need to establish law and order in this town," Jack said.

"They are correct. Deadwood needs law and order, but the trick is that we have no legal basis to establish a legitimate government. This is still land owned and controlled by the Sioux Indians. It's theirs and not ours until the federal government either buys it from them or forces them to give it up and sign a new treaty. Until then, the army could come in at any time and evict us just as they were doing with all those miners on French Creek."

"But it's so bad that someone can literally commit murder in this town and get away with it," Jack said. "Look at that fellow Jack McCall shooting Wild Bill and the jury letting him off."

"That was before my time," Bullock said. "I think I might have made a citizen's arrest and hauled McCall off to the Dakota Territory prison in Yankton."

"I've heard he's been seen in Cheyenne," Star said.

"What's your theory as to what happened with Preacher Smith?" Jack asked.

"Most people say the Indians got him," Star answered.

"And I'm not so sure about that," Bullock said.

"How so?" Jack asked.

"There's lots that don't add up," Bullock said. "First of all, I had the opportunity to examine the body. If you don't know, some of the businessmen in town formed a Sanitary Commission after the outbreak of smallpox. Sol and I joined the commission when we arrived in Deadwood. We built a pest house outside of town to house those infected with smallpox, and we sent off to Cheyenne for vaccine."

"I met Calamity Jane Canary on her way back from taking care of the patients in the pest house this morning," Jack said.

"Martha Canary is quite the nurse. She is one of the few people willing to provide assistance," Bullock said.

"She claims she is immune to smallpox," Sol added.

"The commission is the only semblance of any kind of government we have in town," Bullock said. "One of our self-appointed duties has been to develop a cemetery, which is now called Ingleside, on the east edge of town."

"Just think," Star added. "The town needed one place to bury bodies, otherwise they were starting to be planted anywhere people wanted to dig a hole in town. The same goes for privies. There's no control. Someone builds a privy along Whitewood Creek and the next person takes his water just downstream. No wonder people are getting sick!"

"When Preacher Smith was killed," Bullock continued, "it was the duty of the commission to inter the body. As you know, Indians also killed Lou Mason and two other individuals that day. I had the coffins opened so we could make sure Smith was buried in the grave assigned to him in our ledger book, Mason was buried in the grave assigned to him and so on with the others. My previous job as sheriff in Montana has whetted my curiosity so I couldn't help but take a few moments to examine Preacher Smith's body. There was only one gunshot wound and that was to the heart. Calamity Jane and her friends had sewn the bullet hole through the shirt and tried to wash it, but it appeared to me that there were powder burns on the shirt. There was no mutilation of the body. His Bible, his sermon notes, all personal effects were found on his person except for that morning's offering, which I was informed was close to two hundred and fifty dollars. Mischief is afoot here, if you ask me."

"But I hear that Texas Jack said there were Indians about when he and Mason came upon Preacher Smith's body," Jack said.

"That's right," Bullock said. "But when questioned, Texas Jack said there was only one Indian on horseback, who slowly approached making the sign of peace. Mason and Texas Jack both shot at the Indian, wounding him and knocking him off his horse. The Indian was able to crawl into the brush. Mason approached the hiding spot and was gut shot by the Indian. After which Texas Jack was able to get the drop on the Indian, kill him, and cut off his head. We have all had evidence of this, as he paraded the head up and down Main Street until we took his gory trophy away from him, declaring it unsanitary and burying it."

"It had become a little ripe," Star mused.

"And as we know, shortly after dispatching the Indian, Mason died," Bullock continued. "So we know the Indian killed Mason, but do we know the Indian actually was the one to kill Smith."

"Why, is there doubt in your mind?" Jack asked.

"Number one, remember there was no scalping or other mutilation of Preacher Smith's body. Number two, nothing was taken from Preacher Smith's body other than the money. I suppose the Indian knew what money is and would know to use it to trade for items he would need back at his agency. But then we come to number three—if the Indian knew the purpose of money and took it, why was it not discovered on the Indian's body?"

"Right!" Star said. "And if this Indian was the one who murdered Preacher Smith, why would he openly approach two armed men as he tried to show peaceful intent?"

"I suppose he might have tried some treachery on Texas Jack and Mason," Bullock said, "Or maybe some other Indian murdered Preacher Smith and this poor fellow just happened to be in the wrong place at the wrong time. But my theory based on this evidence is that Indians did not murder Preacher Smith, but a white man murdered him. Here's my scenario. Preacher Smith is walking to Crook City. He meets a white man along the trail. They exchange pleasantries, the man gets close to the preacher, pulls out a pistol and shoots him at point blank range, killing him and stealing his money. Texas Jack and Mason come upon the scene of the murder, they see the Indian, jump to the conclusion that the Indian must have killed Preacher Smith and commence shooting at him. It's great cover for whoever committed the murder. No one will look for him because they think the Indian did it and he's dead."

"That certainly sounds plausible," Jack said.

"I agree!" Star added.

"So in conclusion," Bullock said. "We closed the coffin lids and placed the bodies in their graves. Preacher Smith was Methodist. We searched the gulch high and low for a Methodist prayer book or order of service but could find none. The only thing we did find was the Episcopal Book of Common Prayer, which I read. We sang a hymn, I said a closing prayer, and we were done."

"Not bad for a Gentile," Star said. Jack had a quizzical look on his face.

"Oh, if you didn't figure it out, Jack, Mr. Star is of the Hebrew persuasion, late of Bavaria," Bullock said.

"Oh, that explains the star on your sign," Jack said.

"Actually the star on the sign is not the Star of David. That has six points. This one has only five points," Star said, grinning.

"Deadwood certainly is an international town, if you ask me," Bullock said. "Not only is my partner here originally from Bavaria, but I'm from Canada, and there are probably people here representing nations from every continent."

"I've learned much here this afternoon," Jack said. "I thank you gentlemen for agreeing to provision me and for the thought-provoking information. I'm going to have to be on my way. I still want to track down Laughing Sam and California Joe, if I can today. I think I'll see if they are in the Senate Saloon."

"Well, Jack, I don't want to tell you what to do with your business, but since you are here and you are on your way to the Senate Saloon, maybe you should stop in Tom Short's store and see if you can get any additional information out of Harry Young," Bullock said.

"I like that idea very much," Jack said. "I think I'll take you up on that and visit him."

"Don't forget to stop back tomorrow and we'll have your list of supplies together for you," Star said.

Closing the door behind him, Jack stepped out into the bright sunshine. The temperature had continued to climb. It hadn't rained for a few days and the constant beating of the ground by wheel, man, and beast churned dust into the air. Jack gave a short, soft whistle and Stonewall, who had been snooping about the side of the building, came bounding up to Jack, who rubbed the hound behind his ears.

"Let's go see Harry Young," Jack said. "Humph, on second thought, you stay out here in the street and rummage around, since you're not fond of Mister Harry Young."

It was not much of a walk to Tom Short's store, built on the same side of the street as Star & Bullock's. Short's building was probably the most substantial building in town, being of brick manufacture from the new brickworks located at the north edge of town. Short's emporium sold crockery, furniture, hardware, tools, and more.

Jack stepped through the open door and saw Tom Short sitting in his rocking chair, while a customer stood discussing the price and attributes of the tools he had on hand. Short was the proud owner of the only rocking chair in Deadwood, and he kept it for his exclusive use. Turning at the sound of Jack's entrance, Short said, "Captain Jones! It's nice to see you. Can I interest you in a nice pickax, shovel, or sluice box?"

"Not today, sir," Jack said.

"But I can guess what you're interested in seeing," Short said with a smile.

"And what would that be?"

"Why, our prisoner of course!" Short answered rocking back and forth in his chair.

"What a fine idea. I'll take you up on that," Jack said grinning.

"Old George! Let the good Captain Jones in to see our guest!" Short shouted to an old bewhiskered codger who sat on a stool, his back resting against the closed storeroom door and a double-barreled shotgun propped up against the wall within easy reach.

"What?" Old George said, looking up from his project. He had been intently whittling the end of a stick into a sharp point.

"I said," Short shouted, "let Captain Jones into the storeroom!"

"Why didn't you say so? Don't be mumbling! You got to speak up!" Old George shouted back. He stood up and attempted to spit his chew into a nearby spittoon, but some of it did not make it past his tobacco-stained chin whiskers. Pushing away the stool with his foot and opening the door, Old George shouted into the room, "Harry, you got a visitor!"

There were no windows. A solitary coal-oil lamp sitting on top of a crate provided feeble light. Jack entered the room and Old George slammed the door behind him.

"Good day, Captain Jones," came Harry's voice from a dark corner of the room. "At least I think it's day."

"It is, Harry. It's..." Jack pulled out his pocket watch and held its face up to the lamp, "It's half past one in the afternoon."

"Thank you, Captain."

"How are you holding up, Harry?"

"Fine."

Jack heard rustling sounds and Young appeared in the light.

"Do you care to talk about what happened last night?" Jack asked.

"Yes, I have nothing to hide," Young said as he dragged a crate over to the one with the lamp.

"Have a seat," he said as he pulled up a second crate across from Jack and sat on it.

"Do you mind if I take notes?" Jack asked.

"Not at all," Young said. Jack brought out his notebook and pencil and leaned closer to the coal-oil lamp.

"So what happened last night? I saw the incident between you and Laughing Sam, when you threw him out of the saloon. I don't know if you saw him, but earlier that night Bummer Dan was in Saloon Number 10," Jack said, then he thought, *Let's see what he says about Bummer Dan.*

"I saw that old weasel, too. He wanted free drinks from me. He had a good-sized nugget he showed me that he thought would be good for many drinks. I was glad to accommodate him, but I told him I would have to hold the nugget as collateral or something else of value, which I'm sure he doesn't have. He said no, that he would not let me hold it for safekeeping and I told him fine, then get out, no drinks for you. I saw he came over to where you were sitting and he must have connived a drink out of you."

"That he did," Jack said with a chuckle. "So tell me what happened later. I wasn't there. I had left to grab my supper."

"Yes, I remember you brought your bottle back to the bar. We talked, and then you left. Later that evening, I was washing and drying glasses behind the bar toward the back of the building where the light is dim. Anson Tipple was working up at the front. I looked up from the tub and I saw someone who I thought was Laughing Sam walking toward me. Laughing Sam had been making threats against me for some time, and when I saw the hat and the checkered coat, I thought it was Laughing Sam come to do me in. I had a pistol and before he could get any closer, I pulled it up from behind the bar and shot once, pulled the hammer back, cocking it again and shot him a second time because he was still advancing toward me. He then turned, ran out of the saloon along with everyone else. That was the last I saw of him. The way he was moving, I thought sure I missed Laughing Sam, and I prepared for him to come back and try to attack me again."

"Wait a minute, Harry, I need to catch up with my notes," Jack said. When he was done writing Jack said, "So then what happened?"

"Well, those fellows came back to me and said I had shot Bummer Dan. I said no, I had shot at Laughing Sam. It was only when they were hauling me outside and people were wanting to string me up did I realize I had shot the wrong man. I am truly sorry for that. If I am to die, my only wish would be that I had shot and killed that bastard Laughing Sam Hartman."

"What happened? Why the bad blood between you and Hartman?"

"Hartman has a mean streak in him. I've become very much in love with one of the working girls in town here. Hartman used her poorly and I told him as much. She is such a sweet beautiful girl."

Jack looked up from his note taking. "You're talking about Tid Bit, aren't you?"

Young's eyes widened. "How did you know?"

"Just an educated guess," Jack answered.

"She has a special dress where she embroiders the names of those she cares about and even those she don't, only lower down."

"I know, she showed me the dress as she was working on it this morning as we sat with her friends and talked about last night's happenings," Jack said.

"She's placed my name close to her heart," Young said.

"Humph, well you'll be happy to know that she has placed Hartman's name on her bottom."

"Ha! Ha! That's the first thing that's made me laugh since this whole mess started," Young said. "It angers me that Hartman is still out there walking the streets."

"No one has seen Hartman since last night. Any idea where he might be?"

"Have you tried the Senate Saloon?"

"That's my next stop to look for him. So after Hartman tried to swindle Tid Bit, what happened?"

"I confronted Hartman, told him he was a lowdown skunk and then I put my fist into his face. The boys pulled me off him before I could do any real damage. Hartman swore he was going to get even. I heard from several people that Hartman told them that he planned to hurt me real bad. I tried to ignore it, but he tried to aggravate me whenever he saw me. You saw what he did last night."

"Yes, I did see him in action. Now, changing focus a bit, I keep asking myself, why did he give Bummer Dan his clothes, and why did Bummer Dan wear them into Saloon Number 10, knowing he was entering a bad situation?"

"Those two were always up to no good, always bamboozling someone. There must have been some flimflam going on, but I'm not the one to ask that. Hartman is the one to find and ask."

"What do you know about the status of your trial?" Jack asked.

"From what I've heard from Tom Short and a few visitors, some of the more influential businessmen are trying to form a court. It's been difficult so far. They're saying the jury selection won't begin until tomorrow. I have three good men who will represent me—Mr. McCutchen, Mr. Miller, and Colonel May."

Jack finished writing and said, "Anything else you can tell me that might help me understand what happened?"

"No. If you have to write this for your paper, please let your readers know I was scared. I thought Hartman was coming to shoot me, and I shot in self-defense."

" I'll do that. Thanks, Harry." They shook hands and Jack walked to the door.

"Old George, let me out," Jack said, banging on the door. There was no response. "Old George!" Jack banged louder. An uncontrollable, claustrophobic wave swept through Jack.

"Ha! Ha! The second thing today for me to laugh at," Young said.

"Yes," Jack said, then yelled, "Old George! Open this damn door!" as he continued his pounding. The door swung open.

"Oh, you want out?" Old George shouted.

"Yes! Thank you!" Jack shouted and stepped into the main room.

"Get what you came for?" Short asked, smiling as he rocked back and forth.

"Yes, as much as I could. Say, by the way, you haven't seen Laughing Sam or California Joe, have you?"

"Sorry, can't help you there."

"Thanks again," Jack said and left the building, stepping into the busy street and bright sun. It was a short walk up the street to the Senate Saloon.

Stonewall took off after another dog. Jack lost sight of him, as the dogs wrestled and chased each other. Good thing, a sign on the door of the Senate read, No Dogs Allowed. The saloon was filling with men, priming themselves for the next day's jury selection. The general gist of the conversations Jack overheard was divided on whether Harry should hang or walk. Jack approached the bar. The barkeep was busy pouring shots of whiskey.

"Excuse me," Jack said, "I just need to ask a few quick questions."

"And people in hell need ice water," the barkeep said as he walked off to deliver the whiskey. He soon returned and leaned forward, his elbows on the bar.

"Go ahead," the barkeep said.

"Thanks. Is this where Laughing Sam runs his faro game?"

"Yes. Why do you want to know?"

"I'm a reporter for the *Chicago Inter-Ocean* and I'm writing a story about the shooting last night. I'd like to talk to Laughing Sam to add to my story."

"I haven't seen him since last night."

"Do you happen to know where he lives or where Bummer Dan lived?"

"Sorry, can't help you there either."

"A different set of questions. Do you know who California Joe is and if so, have you seen him?"

"I know him, but haven't seen him."

"Thank you, much obliged," Jack said as he turned from the bar, and left the Senate for the street. That was a dead end. One thing was certain. It looked to Jack like Laughing Sam was lying low for now. Jack scanned the street for Stonewall but did not see him. He gave a low whistle, and Stonewall came bounding around the corner. "Ha! There are you are, fellow!"

Standing as a rock in the middle of the flow of humanity dividing and passing around him was one of the strangest human beings Jack had ever met—Fat Jack. Fat Jack stood over six feet tall and wore a tall stovepipe hat, giving the perception that he was even taller. His girth was the opposite of his name. Fat Jack was thin as a rail. His face gaunt as if his skin was stretched over a skull. His threadbare frock coat hung limp on his scarecrow body. In each upheld hand, he held a pair of cotton socks. In his hatband was tucked a sheet of paper that read "Socks 15 Cents." He sang out at the top of his lungs, "S-Socks! Socks for S-Sale! Who wants a p-pair!"

If anyone knows where I can find Laughing Sam or California Joe, or where Bummer Dan lived, I bet it's Fat Jack, Jack thought.

"Fat Jack! How are you doing this fine afternoon?" Jack asked.

"F-Fine, Captain. H-How are you?" Fat Jack replied.

"Good! I'm wondering if you could help me? Have you seen California Joe? Or Laughing Sam? I'm also wondering if you could tell me where Bummer Dan lived?"

"D-Don't, d-don't you need a pair of s-socks?" Fat Jack said holding out the two pairs of socks.

"Humph, I suppose," Jack said, digging out coins equaling thirty cents and handing them to Fat Jack, who pocketed the coins and pushed the two pairs of socks on Jack.

"A-Ain't seen C-California Joe for some d-days. And I a-ain't seen Laughing S-Sam since yesterday."

Jack was disgusted, and he was wondering how he was going to wrestle his money back from Fat Jack.

"B-But I do know where B-Bummer Dan lived. He lived a-across Whitewood C-Creek in the c-camp over there. C-cross over the new bridge, t-turn left, wander through the camps about a h-hundred yards n-north. He had a l-little shanty there and h-had his name on a sh-shingle."

"Much obliged, Fat Jack!"

"Th-th-thank you c-captain. I must be off!" With that Fat Jack fished the coins out of his pocket and raced toward the nearest outdoor faro game.

"Well, this certainly is good news, Stonewall!" Jack said, looking down at his dog. "Let's go find Bummer Dan's shanty."

Banjo and fiddle music started up in front of the Deadwood Theater. As Jack walked toward the theater, the sound of a tambourine added to the musical mix. The tune was a rousing rendition of "Rose of Alabama." Two longhaired, bearded banjo players, one being Banjo Dick Brown, and the Professor stroking his fiddle, sat on stools with their backs to the Deadwood Theater, and a beaming Lil stood beside them, tapping her foot and maintaining the tune's beat with her tambourine. She wore a powder blue ankle-length riding habit, with a small matching hat pinned to her hair. The men broke into the song's lyrics:

Away from Mississippi's vale
With my ol' hat there for a sail
I crossed upon a cotton bale
To Rose of Alabama
I landed on the far sand bank
I sat upon the hollow plank
And there I made the banjo twank
For Rose of Alabama
Oh brown Rosie
Rose of Alabama
Sweet tobacco posey
Is my Rose of Alabama
Sweet tobacco posey
Is my Rose of Alabama.

The men sang several verses. A small crowd of men gathered round, tapping their feet and clapping their hands. Some joined in when they knew the words. Stonewall, with tail a-wagging, ran up to Lil. She searched the crowd until she spotted Jack, waved and broke into a big smile.

The musicians ended the song with a final flourish. John Langrishe, wearing his top hat and cape, and flourishing a cane in his right hand, stepped forward with arms upraised, "Citizens of Deadwood," he shouted. "This is just a sample of the musical delights and fine theatrical entertainment awaiting you this evening within the Deadwood Theater. We have the finest musicians and actors this side of Denver. It's a first-class male-and-female comedy company. Doors open at 9:30 p.m. and the festivities begin at 10:30. Tonight, we bring you that timeless drama, *The Streets of New York*! And now, maestros, please continue!" Langrishe stepped away with a flourish of his cape as the musicians began a fast-paced "Soldier's Joy."

Lil set her tambourine down by Banjo Dick and ran to Jack, throwing herself into his arms as the men closest to them hooted and whistled at them.

"Jack! Oh, Jack! I can't believe it's only been a few hours but I feel like I haven't seen you for days!" Lil said, ignoring the onlookers.

"I'm extremely happy to see you too, Lil," Jack said. They finished their embrace but held on to each other at arms' length.

"Jack, will you be able to attend the show tonight? I very much hope you can make it."

"I wouldn't miss it for the world, Lil."

"What have you been up to?" Lil asked.

"Yes, do tell us," said one of the nosey lookers-on. Jack glared at him and said to Lil, "Care to take a short walk with me?"

"I would love to," she said, taking his arm. They moved slowly up the street, finding a less crowded lane to walk and talk.

"I've been trying to track down Laughing Sam," Jack said.

"I assume no luck, since you used the word 'trying,'" she responded.

"That's right. It seems that no one has seen him since last night. The other interesting piece of information is that Laughing Sam and Bummer Dan were partners in a faro game."

"I didn't know that," Lil said. Neither spoke for a long distance. "Surely Laughing Sam will show for the trial to testify," Lil said. "After all, you would think he would want justice for his friend."

"Yes, you would think so," Jack agreed. "One good piece of information—I learned where Bummer Dan lived. I was actually on my way to visit his shanty to see if his haversack is there when I ran into your performance."

Lil stopped dead in the street, turned and stared at Jack. "What is so important with this haversack? You are obsessed with it. What has it got to do with anything?"

Jack looked up in the sky, then looked around them, and grabbed her arm, continuing to walk on.

"All right, I'll tell you, but don't say anything to anyone until I get this figured out. Do you agree?"

"Agreed."

"Last night after you left Saloon Number 10, Bummer Dan stopped by where I was playing cards. He showed me a large gold nugget he had come by and kept it wrapped up in his haversack. That's why I'm interested in the haversack. I want to find the gold nugget and send it or a note with the value of the nugget to his next of kin, if I can figure out who that would be. The other tantalizing part of this story is that Bummer Dan said he had more gold stashed away. That's why I want to talk to Laughing Sam, to see if he knows what happened to the haversack, since Bummer Dan was wearing Laughing Sam's clothes last night. I also want to look through Bummer Dan's shanty. Maybe the haversack is there and just maybe that's where Bummer Dan kept his additional wealth."

"I see, it all makes sense," Lil said. "Last night, Aunt Lou said she had heard that Laughing Sam had done some underhanded things to one of the working girls. If she is correct, then maybe Laughing Sam took Bummer Dan's gold from the haversack when he saw that his friend was dead. He took the gold and left town, not caring that there would be justice served for his murdered friend. That's why no one's seen him."

"Maybe so, Lil."

"Jack, I need to get back to the theater. We have practice for the play later this afternoon."

"Certainly," Jack said and they turned to retrace their steps to the theater. "There's something else I need to tell you, Lil," Jack said.

"What, Jack?" She said, turning towards him with a soft smile on her lips. He blushed and looked toward his feet.

"I...Well, I need to tell you I am very fond of you, Lil," Jack said.

"Jack, I am very fond of you. I want to be with you all the time."

"I know, Lil, it's just that I have some things I need to work out. It has nothing to do with you and all to do with me," Jack said.

"Can you talk to me about it?"

"I don't think so. No, not now."

They walked on in silence. He had a firm grip on her arm.

"There's something else I need to tell you," Jack said, releasing his grip as she again stopped.

"What is it, Jack?"

"I have to leave in a few days. My editor is sending me out to find General Crook and his army."

Lil frowned and her face turned white as she stared into Jack's eyes.

"You have to leave in a few days? You have to find General Crook? But it's dangerous out there. The Indians are still on the warpath. How do you even know where to find Crook? Will you be coming back if and when you do find him?"

"All good points and questions. First, I am coming back and I do want to find you here when I come back. Second, I know it's dangerous. I want to contact a man who might be able to help me locate Crook and keep the Sioux from locating me. The man's name is California Joe. I need to find and hire him, but I haven't seen him yet."

They continued to walk down the street. Lil placed her hand in the crook of Jack's arm.

"All right, Captain," she said. "I suppose I can wait until you come back. But, you better do so. Who is going to look after that mangy hound of yours?"

"I hadn't thought of that," Jack said. "I suppose he could tag along. He made it this far with me."

"Think about it. I would be willing to take care of him, if you think it would be dangerous for him on your trip," she said. "And it would be another reason for you to return," she continued with a smile.

"I'll think about it," Jack said.

They had returned to the front of the theater. The musicians and their crowd had left. The street was teeming with people. Lil and Jack were close, gazing into each other's eyes. "I had best be getting back to practice," Lil said. A commotion further out in the street drew their attention away from each other.

"I says that horse of yours can't outrun a three-legged donkey!" shouted a man with a Texan drawl who was mounted on horseback. He hurled his verbal challenge at a Mexican, also on horseback. A little further behind him was another Mexican, also mounted.

"Ah, Señor, I have seen you ride, and if your horse reached a fast trot he would shake you off," the first Mexican said.

"Hooh, ha, hah!" the second Mexican laughed. The taunts drew a crowd of interested bystanders.

Deadwood Dead Men

"I wonder who those men are?" Lil asked.

"I don't know," Jack answered, then realized he had seen the man doing the challenging before, but where?

A bewhiskered miner standing near Lil and Jack said, "Why, that feller on the horse with the fancy silver bridle is Texas Jack. He's the one who kilt that Injun that kilt Lou Mason and Preacher Smith, and then chopped off the Injun's head. Didn't ya see him when he galloped into town with that there head tied by the hair to his saddle, just a floppin' along? It was quite the sight."

"Who are the other two fellows?" Jack asked the miner.

"The feller in the front doin' most of the talkin', that's Poncho Mores. The feller behind him laughin', that's his partner Carlos. Them's the two what kilt that Injun and galloped through town waving that Injun's head about when the crowd was going to hang that young feller what kilt Wild Bill. Seems to me there's developin' a little competition betwixt them fellers! I'm surprised them two Mexicans are in town. They're supposed to be out patrollin' with old California Joe."

"Thank you, sir, this information is most useful!" Jack said. *I'll have to ask them if California Joe is in town*, Jack thought, and then realized, *I know where I've seen Texas Jack before. He was the other man with Varnes's brother who had the rope around Harry Young's neck last night!*

The bantering back and forth between Texas Jack and Carlos and Poncho continued.

"Let us put it to a test," Poncho said.

"You mean a race?" Texas Jack asked.

"*Si!* A race!" shouted Carlos from the rear.

"There's going to be a race!" shouted someone from the crowd.

"Who's racing?" another shouted. The buzz in the crowd increased.

"All right!" Texas Jack said. "We'll race here in Main Street. We can start down past the Cricket Saloon and right here between the Deadwood Theater and Grand Central Hotel can be the finish line. What are the stakes?"

"Oh, Señor Texas Jack, I must have that beautiful silver inlaid bridle with the silver conches, if you please," Poncho said.

Texas Jack was silent.

"Come on, Texas Jack!" a voice from the crowd shouted. "It's a sure bet you will win!"

"All right!" Texas Jack said. "What are you putting up against my bridle?"

"Ah, Señor Texas Jack, I will put up fifty Yankee dollars in gold that Carlos and I have saved when we collected it on that poor, unfortunate Indian's head two weeks ago."

"Carlos, show the man our money," Poncho said. Carlos produced a possible bag decorated with black, white, red, and yellow beads, forming beautiful patterns in the Lakota tradition. He dug into the bag and produced two twenty-dollar and one ten-dollar gold coins, holding them high for all to see.

Texas Jack took a minute to ponder the wager. "It's a deal," he said, reaching across the saddle and shaking Poncho's outstretched hand. The crowd laughed and shouted. Men were frantically making and taking bets with each other on who would win the match. Carlos began to put the coins back into his possible bag.

"Hold it right there, Carlos!" Texas Jack shouted over the crowd noise. "Not that I don't trust you, but I think a disinterested third party should be holding those coins."

"What about the silver bridle?" Poncho said.

"You can see where it is at all times since it will be in front of you the entire race," Texas Jack said. "If you win the race—which you won't—you can take it off my horse right then and there."

"*Si*, I agree! I will take it off your horse when I win," Poncho answered. "Now let me find someone to hold the Yankee dollars."

"I'll h-hold them for y-you!" Fat Jack shouted.

"No thank you, Señor Fat Jack," Poncho shouted back. "You would only lose my money at the nearest faro game!" The crowd roared with laughter and Fat Jack grinned in agreement. It did not take Poncho long to scan the crowd and find the one he wanted to hold the coins. He backed his horse and stopped alongside Carlos, who handed him the three coins. He clicked to his horse, who moved forward until they came to Lil. Poncho spoke a gentle "Whoa," and his horse stopped in front of Lil.

"My beautiful *señorita*," Poncho said, sweeping his sombrero from his head and holding it over his heart. "Would you be so gracious as to hold these gambling stakes for me until I redeem them from you at the end of the race against this poor, miserable Texas Jack?"

Lil smiled and gave a short curtsey. "I would indeed be honored to hold your golden coins for you, sir," she replied in her best theatrical voice. Poncho deposited the coins into her upturned palm, replaced his sombrero on top of this head, clicked to his horse, and returned to Texas Jack.

"*Amigo*," he said to Texas Jack. "Let us clear the street and begin our race!" The two of them, followed by Carlos, began to walk their horses down the street to clear the humanity away. The crowds needed little encouragement. Men were always looking for something new to entertain them or some event to wager upon. Three bull trains were in the street, but the bullwhackers drove their oxen closer to the buildings to help create a wider lane. It was almost as if an invisible force swept the men out of the center of the street and onto the sidelines as the three riders made their way down the street, far beyond the Cricket Saloon.

"Oh, this is so exciting, Jack!" Lil said.

"It surely is," Jack said as he watched the two distant riders and their mounts line up for the start of the race. Carlos and his horse were off to the side. Carlos held a pistol in his left hand, pointed straight up over his head.

"That's interesting," Jack said to himself aloud.

"What's interesting?" Lil asked.

"Just that Carlos is left-handed. See, he holds his pistol in his left hand."

"He ain't left-handed," the bewhiskered miner who was still standing near the couple interjected. "Carlos told me he injured his right hand years ago. His fingers are too stiff and weak to pull a trigger, so he learned to shoot left handed."

"Thank you, sir," Jack said.

The man spat and said, "You're welcome."

Jack saw smoke spew from Carlos's pistol and the delayed report of the pistol shot reached Jack's ears. The two riders took off at a full gallop. The entire town of Deadwood erupted in cheers and shouts. Texas Jack was jabbing his large Chihuahua spurs into his horse as he whipped him on the rump with his quirt. Poncho was leaning forward giving his horse his head. The horses and riders were neck and neck. Poncho's horse appeared to enjoy the challenge and began to pick up the pace, pulling slightly ahead of Texas Jack's horse. Texas Jack spurred harder, furiously whipping with the quirt. Poncho leaned further forward and spoke to his horse, who leapt ahead of Texas Jack's horse. The rapid pounding of the hooves grew louder and louder as the two charging animals raced at breakneck speed toward the finish line. Poncho's horse stretched a full length ahead of Texas Jack's horse as they flew across the finish line.

The crowd erupted in a roar. Individual reactions were mixed. The winners shouted their happiness, while the losers grumbled as they handed over their money and gold dust. A laughing Carlos astride his horse trotted up behind the contestants as the crowd surged forward, surrounding the three riders. Poncho, smiling from ear to ear, reached out his hand to shake hands with Texas Jack, who only sneered, "My horse stumbled at the start, otherwise I would have won."

"That may be so, *amigo*, however, I am the winner today!" Poncho said as he dismounted and took the bridle off his horse. Then, turning to Texas Jack's horse, he removed the silver bridle, replacing it with his bridle and adjusting and placing the silver one on his own horse. The crowd shouted, hooted, and laughed. Once Poncho had mounted his horse, he laughed, pulled out a pistol, and shot into the air. Swinging around, he rode up to Lil and stopped.

"*Señorita, gracias* for watching our money," he said as she handed him the coins.

"It was my pleasure, sir!"

Poncho tipped his sombrero.

"Carlos! *Amigo!* Let us ride!" With their spurs jangling, the two of them trotted their horses back down Main Street to the shouted approval of the crowd. The street took some time to return to normal, as men retold the race they had just watched to each other.

"How exciting, Jack!" Lil said.

"It surely was," Jack said, as he noticed a scowling Texas Jack watching the jubilant Mexicans trot down the street. Texas Jack swore to himself, reined his horse in the opposite direction, and left at a slow lope, scattering the onlookers in his way. Someone lit off a string of firecrackers, creating a staccato of small, popping explosions.

"I best be getting back to play practice," Lil said. "Don't forget, the play is at half-past ten tonight."

"I won't forget. I'll be there," Jack promised. They embraced and kissed to the hoots and catcalls of onlookers. Lil and Jack broke away from each other, smiling. Lil waved to the surrounding men and said in a loud voice, "You can see more of that type of action on stage tonight, boys!" To which they all hooted and hollered again. Lil vanished into the theater.

Jack looked at his pocket watch. It was now 4:00 p.m. Time was getting away from him. He headed up the street, with Stonewall by his side. He didn't have far to walk until he came to Lee Street, where he turned left at the General Custer House Hotel. At the rear of the hotel was the newly constructed Lee Street Bridge, which crossed Whitewood Creek. Some well-meaning citizens of Deadwood had taken it upon themselves to construct the bridge, making it easier for people to cross over the creek without getting wet.

Jack stopped in the middle of the bridge to gaze at Whitewood Creek as it flowed north. Hundreds of men were in the water and on the banks, shoveling and sifting sands and gravel, diverting water into sluice boxes and rockers, and panning. The pools and riffles were gone. Men had channelized the stream and diverted its flow for their purposes. Humanity in motion, relentless in its pursuit of gold, and water in motion, relentless in its pursuit of the sea. Both man and nature creating a constant murmur in their quest.

Jack turned back to the business at hand, crossing the bridge into the camps that many in town called home. The camps were laid out in a haphazard way. Since there was no town government, people set up camp wherever they felt inclined to do so. There was some semblance of streets out of necessity, so people could pass through to get to their tents or shanties. There were a few log cabins and no clapboard houses. Those who could afford it lived in tents. Those who could not lived in shanties or shebangs made of scraps of wood, canvas, and boughs. Men stood guard at their dwelling places while their partners were at the creek, panning and sluicing. The camps held a hodgepodge of men from every walk of life, every race, and most religions—some without religion. Jack turned to the left, proceeding north as Fat Jack had told him. Some of the men had campfires stoked, and cast-iron pots and skillets hung over the fires in preparation for their evening suppers. A smoky haze hung over the camps. The sounds of chopping wood and the low hum of countless voices filled the air.

Jack slowly made his way through the tents and hovels for about one hundred yards, as Fat Jack had directed. He did not see the Bummer Dan sign at first, but on his second scan, he saw it—a cockeyed shingle with Bummer Dan painted in white. The lower portion of the one-room building was constructed of logs. The top part was a canvas tent. The surrounding dwellings were of similar construction, nothing of permanence.

No one was visible in this part of the camp. Bummer Dan's tent flap was untied. Jack pulled it back and looked within. The only items resembling furniture were a few blankets, strewn on top of a bed of pine boughs, and a crate for a table. Bummer Dan's few possessions were strewn about haphazardly. "Humph," Jack grunted. "Either Bummer Dan lived like a pig or someone has ransacked this place." Stonewall entered and sniffed about. Jack followed him in, dropping the tent flap behind him. He noted a few items of clothing hanging on a wooden peg, as well as pots and pans, a box of hard bread, but other than that, nothing. The haversack and its gold were nowhere to be seen. "Bummer Dan said he had more gold stashed somewhere. His shanty would be the logical place to hide it, since he lives right here and could keep an eye on it better," Jack said aloud. He began looking through the clothes on the peg to see if there was anything in the pockets. Some items of clothing were scattered on the floor. He searched those and found nothing. Not only was he looking for the haversack and gold, but he was hoping to find information on Bummer Dan's family so he could at least inform them of his death, if not send them the gold.

Jack looked through the blankets. It appeared that someone had scattered the pine boughs, looking to see if there was anything there, or if there was disturbed earth, where Bummer Dan might have buried his gold. Jack looked in the cracker box. It was empty. He moved the crate and saw disturbed earth. He picked up an old, battered tin cup. Dropping to his knees with his back to the tent flap, he began scooping out the disturbed dirt, using the cup. Stonewall enthusiastically joined in the action, sending dirt flying behind him.

Jack heard the movement of canvas. The inside light increased, and then came the click of a cocking pistol.

"Hold it right there, mister!" commanded a man's voice behind Jack.

CHAPTER SIX
ഇൗൾ

Wednesday Late Afternoon, August 23, 1876—"Stand up!" the voice commanded. "Raise your hands over your head." Jack complied. The voice had a slight British accent. "I have a pistol aimed at your head. If you try anything foolish I will pull the trigger. Do you understand?"

"Yes," Jack answered. Stonewall continued digging, sending dirt flying behind him.

"I want you to slowly turn towards me."

Jack complied. He could not distinguish the man silhouetted by the outside light.

"So you return to complete your robbery of Bummer Dan," the silhouetted man said.

"I don't know what you're talking about," Jack responded.

"You were here last night searching through Bummer Dan's possessions and my friends and I chased you away."

"You have me mistaken for someone else. I wasn't here last night. If you need proof, we can go visit the Grand Central Hotel or the Deadwood Theater, where my friends can tell you I was with them most of the evening."

"Step out of the tent into the sun where I can see you better," the man ordered. As Jack slowly proceeded toward the front of the tent, the man dropped the flap, stood back to the side and behind Jack as he emerged outside with his hands still raised.

"Turn around," the man ordered. As Jack complied, he was surprised to see that the man who had the drop on him was Chinese. The man appeared to be in his mid-thirties. He was dressed as any miner in Deadwood but wore his hair in a long braid. Atop his head was a broad-brimmed hat and in his hand he held a Navy Colt, which was leveled at Jack's forehead.

"Very slowly, unbutton your coat with your left hand and hold it open so I can see if you are armed," the man ordered. Jack complied, revealing that he was unarmed.

"Tell me again why you are here?" the man said.

"I'm following up on my investigation of the Bummer Dan shooting. I'm a reporter for the *Chicago Inter-Ocean*. I knew Bummer Dan and I came here hoping I could find more information on him, if there is any information on his family, and if there is anything here that could be sent to his family."

"How do I know what you tell me is true?"

"Let me show you my card," Jack said as he slowly reached with his left hand into his coat pocket. The man continued to aim his pistol at Jack's forehead. Jack slowly removed his card and held it out to the man. The man took it with his left hand and held it up to his eyes. "This reads you are John Jones with the *Chicago Inter-Ocean* newspaper. All right, Mister John Jones. I will trust you a little more. Maybe your story is true," the man said as he handed back the card. He brought the gun down to waist level, pointed it away from Jack, and slowly eased the hammer back from the fully cocked position.

Stonewall chose at that instant to finish his digging and bolt out of the tent. Seeing the man, he ran up to him with tail wagging, expecting the man to pet him. The man obliged the dog.

"May I put my hands down now?" Jack asked.

"Yes, Mister Jones, you may," the man said as he continued to pet Stonewall. The man was now smiling. "What is the name of your dog?" the man asked.

"Stonewall Jackson."

"Stone Wall Jack Son, that is a strange name."

"You have me at a disadvantage, sir," Jack said. "You know my name, who I work for, and even my dog's name, but I do not know yours."

The man stood straight. "Ah yes," he said and bowed. "My name is Fee Lee Wong," He straightened up and extended his hand. Jack shook it.

"Pleased to make your acquaintance, Mr. Wong."

"Please, John Jones, call me Fee Lee."

"Sure, Fee Lee, and please call me Jack."

"Yes, Jack it is, then," Wong said. "Jack, tell me again why you are here."

"Last night as you must know, Bummer Dan was shot and killed by Harry Young in Saloon Number 10. Bummer Dan was wearing his partner's coat and hat at the time he was shot. His partner was Laughing Sam Hartman."

"Yes, I know who they are. I live two houses to the south of Bummer Dan and Laughing Sam lives two houses to the north of Bummer Dan."

"That's very good news to know. I'm gathering information for my newspaper story, so I'll need to ask you a few questions, if you don't mind. I'd also like to see if Laughing Sam is home and question him."

"That is good with me. Let us first go to my home where we can sit and be more comfortable as we talk. I was in the process of brewing tea when you so rudely interrupted me. Would you care to join me for a cup?"

"Yes, that's fine with me," Jack said. Wong led the way as Jack and Stonewall followed behind. Wong came to a lower-half log and upper-half canvas one-room house. A blanket served as the door. Wong held the blanket to the side, bowed and motioned Jack to enter, which he and the dog did.

The canvas allowed enough light inside for Jack to see that the one-room dwelling was tidy and clean. The floor was smoothed timber, on top of which lay a rug. A sleeping mat was rolled to the side. A small cast-iron stove with a pipe leading up and out of the tent sat at the rear of the dwelling. A wood fire blazed within the stove and on top stood a kettle with roiling water within. A small cabinet held porcelain dishes and a large crate contained a variety of packages displaying Chinese writing. In the center of the room sat a large crate that served as a table. Two small stools stood on either side of it.

Wong motioned for Jack to sit at the crate. Wong opened a sack grabbing a handful of dried tea leaves. He removed the kettle lid and dropped the leaves into the boiling water. Wong took two porcelain teacups from the cabinet and placed them on the crate in front of Jack. He went back to the stove and waited for the water to return to a boil. Wong took a small towel and used it to protect his hand as he removed the kettle. Holding a spoon by the spout to keep the tea leaves from coming out, he poured tea into the two cups and placed the kettle on a flat rock by the stove. He sat down opposite Jack and raised the cup with both hands, saying, "To your health." Jack picked up his teacup and imitated Wong saying, "And to your health."

They both took a sip. Jack was not much of a tea drinker. He was partial to coffee, but this had a very good flavor.

"This is excellent tea," Jack said.

"Thank you, Jack. As you might imagine, it is very hard to get good tea in America. And especially hard to get tea here in Deadwood. I have to send a special order for it."

They sat in silence sipping the tea.

"Do you care for more tea?" Wong asked.

"Yes," Jack replied. After Wong refilled their cups and returned to his seat, they took a few more sips in silence.

"Fee Lee, may I ask you a few questions?"

"Yes, go ahead."

"I'm curious how have you come to speak English so good and how did you come to be in Deadwood?"

"Ah yes, you ask two questions that intertwine, and if you have time, I can tell you my story."

"Yes, I would like to hear it."

"I speak English because of the English!" Wong said with a laugh. "I am from Canton in China's Guangdong Province. The British have had an interest in Guangdong for years. They have become involved in all aspects of business in that region of China, including smuggling illegal drugs—opium. When the Emperor tried to stop it, the British government went to war with China to continue the opium trade. A little opium for medicinal purposes is good, but many of my countrymen cannot use too much of it or they become hopelessly addicted. For years the Emperor's government has been trying to lessen its effect in China, as well as here in America."

Wong took another sip of tea.

"As for me, my father believed that to do well in business, I should learn the language of the English, so he enrolled me in a missionary school not only to learn the Christian religion, but also to read and write English. Chinese from Guangdong have been coming to America ever since gold was discovered in *gum shan* and so..."

"Wait a minute," Jack interrupted. "What's *gum shan?*"

"Oh excuse me for the lapse! Ha-ha! *Gum shan* is Cantonese for Gold Mountain, the name we gave California. The early reports that came in letters to Guangdong from men who went to California said there was so much gold that people were picking up gold nuggets off the ground. Of course, it was not true, but it started the Chinese gold rush for California. When we were old enough, my brother and I asked my father for his permission to travel to California to seek our fortune. At that time, Guangdong was a poor place for a young man to find work. The British banks were calling in their loans, there was discontent, and the Emperor sent troops in to put down the rebellion. It was a good time to leave."

Wong drained the rest of his tea, rose, and brought back the kettle, refilling their cups.

"How did you decide to come to Deadwood?" Jack asked as Wong returned to his stool.

"My brother and I worked at many jobs in California— placer mining, railroading, laundry, and cooking. It seems I have tried my hand at many jobs. When news first reached California about the gold strike in Deadwood Gulch, I wanted to come here and see if I could make my fortune. My brother had had enough in California and decided to return home. With the modest amount he had earned, he could live in comfort for the rest of his life, but I wanted more."

Wong took a sip of tea and continued. "I found a small group of Americans who were heading to Deadwood. They needed a cook. I said, 'I can cook!' They sampled my cooking and hired me on the spot. We traveled by train to Cheyenne and then started our journey north along the trail to Fort Laramie and into the Black Hills. One evening, a group of men attacked us. We never found out if they were Indians or white men. They fired into our camp most of the night. I stood with the others, firing rifles and pistols at our attackers. By morning, they were gone. When we reached Deadwood Gulch, we staked claims along Whitewood Creek and drew lots for who got what claim. One of the men did not want to share with the 'heathen Chinaman' but the others voted him down and said if I could equally help defend them along the trail, I equally would share in the rewards. I received two placer claims, which have turned out to be good producers, so much so that I have hired some of my countrymen to work them for me. My goal is to open a store to sell Asian goods to my countrymen, make my fortune, and return to Guangdong to live in luxury. In the meantime, I think I can be of use to the Cantonese community and the white community. A bridge, if you will, as I am the only person in Deadwood who I know who can speak both languages fluently. I am not bragging. I am only stating the fact."

"That's not bragging, Fee Lee. It's commendable of you to be of service to everyone," Jack said. "One question I have," Jack continued. "This morning I encountered one of the most beautiful women I have ever seen, being carried by two men. Who is she?"

"Her name is Di Lee."

"Can you tell me more about her?"

"She is from Guangdong, the same as me. She is young and single, but she is not a courtesan. She has the means to live independent of any man."

"What is she doing in Deadwood?"

"I cannot say."

Jack was not sure of that answer, but let the subject drop.

"Tell me again what you were doing in Bummer Dan's home?" Wong asked.

"Three things actually," Jack began. "First, I wanted to see if there would be any additional information there that could tell me why Bummer Dan was wearing Laughing Sam's clothes. Second, I wanted to see if there was any information on his relatives, where they live, and if there was anything in the shanty of importance that I could send to them. Third, and most important, is that Bummer Dan had gold on him that I would like to find and send to his family, if possible."

"I see," Wong said and thought for a moment before saying, "And what if you find this gold, but you do not find any information on his family, then what will you do with his gold?"

"Good question. I hadn't thought of that," said Jack. "I suppose I could give it to the poor or maybe to the Sanitary Commission. They could use it to improve the town."

"Equally good answers, Jack," Wong said smiling, and then continued, "How do you know Bummer Dan had gold?"

"Last night, I was in Saloon Number 10 and Bummer Dan showed me a large nugget of gold he kept wrapped in cloth and close to him in his haversack. He told me he had hidden more gold. When he was shot and killed, he did not have the haversack or the gold on his body."

"I see," Wong said. "You believe Bummer Dan may have returned his haversack to his home with the gold in it, or that he hid the gold in or near his home with the rest of it for safe-keeping."

"Yes, or maybe Laughing Sam is holding it for him."

"Or maybe after Bummer Dan was killed, Laughing Sam decided to keep the gold for himself. Maybe he knew Bummer Dan had more gold hidden at his home."

"That's a possibility," Jack said. "The only other person who I know who knew about Bummer Dan's gold is Harry Young. Bummer Dan showed him the gold nugget and hinted that he had more, but Harry has been sitting in Tom Short's storeroom this whole time."

"This is very interesting," Wong said. "Let us go back to Bummer Dan's home and see if we can locate information on his family and possibly the gold."

"Good idea," Jack said as they both stood. "And thank you for the tea. I enjoyed it."

"The pleasure is all mine," Wong said.

When they returned to Bummer Dan's shanty the sun had disappeared behind the western ridge and it was dark inside. Wong found a coal-oil lamp, struck a lucifer, which flared in the gloom, and then lit the lamp's wick. The two of them looked through Bummer Dan's meager belongings as Stonewall decided to tackle the hole again, enjoying tossing up a stream of dirt. They checked every item, looking for any letters from home or scraps of paper. But there were none. They searched every nook and cranny, finding nothing. They examined the floor but found no indication of any abnormal surface disturbance that would indicate someone had dug a hole and covered it up—other than the hole Stonewall was working on.

The dog growled. Both men turned and saw that the hound had something in his teeth that he was tugging on. Stonewall tore loose a small leather bag from its obstruction and shook it rapidly from side to side. "Hey, what have you there, Stonewall?" Jack said as he removed the bag from the hound's jaws. Examining it under the lantern light, they discovered it was an empty leather poke bag.

"Carefully turn it inside out," Wong suggested. "Maybe we can find out what was in it." Jack slowly worked at doing just that as Wong held the lantern close. Nothing. And then, a small golden gleam, and then another. There were several flecks of gold the size of pinheads.

"Well, would you look at that!" Jack said.

"It appears Bummer Dan hid his gold in this sack and someone removed it," Wong said.

"I agree," Jack said. "Thinking back on last night, from the time I saw Bummer Dan on the street with Laughing Sam until when he was killed at ten o'clock, less than two hours passed. I suppose he could have returned to his shanty, dug up his gold, returned to town to borrow Laughing Sam's clothes, and walk into Saloon Number 10 to be shot and killed."

"That still leaves the question, where is his gold, since no one found it on his body," Wong said. "It is more likely that whoever I scared away from his home last night was the person who took the gold."

"What time was that, Fee Lee?"

"I do not know, Jack. I do not own a timepiece."

"Humph," Jack grunted. "It seems to me that if I could find Laughing Sam and talk with him, some of this mystery might clear itself."

"What do you want to do with this gold?" Wong said.

"We have found no evidence of family to send it to. I have no need of it. Do you know of any poor who it could help?"

"I do, and I will give it to them," Wong said with a smile. "Let us look outside. Perhaps there is something out there we overlooked."

They searched the outside walls of the shanty and again in every conceivable place that might be a hidey-hole.

"I think we found the one and only spot where Bummer Dan hid his valuables," Jack said.

"I believe you are correct, Jack. Let us go and see if Mister Laughing Sam Hartman is home."

Men were returning to their cabins, shanties, and shelters. Fragrances of cooking food filled the air. Lanterns glowed in dwellings, and men stood in the streets conversing over the murder, horse race, and other events of the day.

As Wong and Jack approached Laughing Sam's shanty, it appeared dark and unoccupied, like the shanties on either side of it. Reaching the front door, they heard something being knocked over and falling, clattering to the ground. Two squirrels scampered out the open door. Stonewall gave chase, but he was no match for their speed. Jack and Wong looked at each other and laughed. Wong still held Bummer Dan's lantern in his hand.

"Halloo inside the house!" Jack said. His answer was silence. "Well, let's go inside," he said. The lantern revealed a single, simple room, similar to Bummer Dan's, only this one appeared to be in order except for a box of hard bread the squirrels had been feasting on before they were rudely interrupted.

"It doesn't appear that anyone has gone through Laughing Sam's belongings," Wong said.

"Except those squirrels," Jack responded. "I'd hazard a guess he has not been back to his shanty since last night."

"I agree," Wong said. The two men stepped outside the hovel. The twilight was rapidly fading into the blackness of night.

"So where does this leave us?" Jack said.

"We know last night, probably after Bummer Dan was killed, someone entered his home to search his belongings and found the hole where he buried his gold, took it, and covered up the hole to hide what he had done," Wong said.

"We know Laughing Sam has not been seen since before the murder," Jack added. "We know Bummer Dan probably did not tell many people about his gold. Harry Young knew, and I would say that most likely Laughing Sam knew as well."

"And it appears Laughing Sam has not been to his home since last night," Wong continued.

"Unless we're missing something, I think Laughing Sam is the one who dug up Bummer Dan's gold," Jack concluded. "I doubt Laughing Sam will show up in court tomorrow. I doubt we'll see him again in Deadwood."

"I think you are right," Wong said and then changing topics, "Can I interest you in more tea, some rice, and a bit of pork?"

"Thanks, Fee Lee, but I have supper waiting for me at the Grand Central Hotel and I promised a young lady I would attend the theater and watch her performance this evening. But I would like to come back for more tea tomorrow evening so we can further discuss this murder and you can further my education in Cantonese culture."

"I would be happy to do that. How about tomorrow evening when the sun is disappearing over the ridge? I will delight your tongue with more Chinese tea."

"Agreed!" Jack said.

"Jack, take this lantern with you. I have one and Bummer Dan will have no need of it anymore."

"Thanks, Fee Lee," Jack said as he and Stonewall left their new friend and began to pick their way through the shantytown toward the Lee Street Bridge.

Walking through the hodgepodge of dwellings, Jack heard the faint strains of a tune and voices singing. A banjo, fiddle, and spoons accompanied men's voices. As he approached, he recognized the old Irish tune *Devilish Mary*. He had not heard it for years. It was their song.

> *It's tararinktum, tararinktum ,*
> *Tararinktum ready!*
> *Meanest girl I ever did meet and her name was Devilish Mary!*

Jack thought back to that hot August night of his youth in Pennsylvania. Friends had invited his family to a barn dance. There were people from all over Schuylkill County, many he had never met before. Even some Pennsylvania Dutch were there. He never did figure out until he was older why they called these Germans by the name Dutch. One German girl caught his eye, and he was sure he had caught her looking at him a time or two. He asked a few acquaintances who she was, but they had no idea. She hung back with the Dutch crowd and it seemed that all their boys were constantly getting the nod from her to dance with her.

> *Well, I went down to London town,*
> *They called it Londonderry,*
> *An' there I spied a purty little gal,*
> *They called her Devilish Mary.*

The chief fiddler called out to the crowd that the next dance would be the hat dance. With this dance, Jack was bound and determined to get close to the girl and meet her. Two lines of people formed facing each other, one line all men and the other line all women. Three chairs were set up at the front of the two lines. The chief fiddler selected a man, a boy, and a girl to sit in the chairs. He placed the girl in the middle chair, with each of the males to the right and left of her. The chief fiddler handed the girl a top hat, which she placed on her lap. The chief fiddler returned to his position with the other musicians and started up the tune for the dance. It was "Devilish Mary."

We got to courtin' very fast
An' got in the devil of a hurry;
We made up the match that very day
An' got married the very next Thursday.

The girl sitting in the middle looked at the man on the right and the boy on the left, then handed the hat to the man on the right and sashayed off with the boy on the left, down between the two lines of men and women until they reached the end and joined the lines. The man moved to the middle chair and waited for the next two women to sit on each side of him. Then he had the chance to choose with whom he would dance down between the two lines of people clapping and moving to the rhythm. Jack calculated where he needed to be in line to be able to sit at the same time the beautiful German girl would be sitting. He weaved out of the line and then back in again, excusing himself to the males he squeezed between. It worked! She was sitting in the middle and he was sitting to her left. She looked at him, smiled, then handed him the hat and danced away laughing with the German boy on her right. A dismayed Jack moved to the center chair, gave the hat to the woman on his left, who appeared to be twice his age, and danced down between the lines with a girl taller than him.

We hadn't been married but about three weeks
Till she looked as mad as the devil,
An' ever' time I said a word
She hit me with the shovel.

The German girl looked at Jack, smiled, and then gave a wink as they proceeded to the head of the lines. Again, he worked his positioning so he was sitting with her in the middle. The girl placed the top hat on her head and grinned. She looked at Jack, then looked at the other man, then back at Jack and gave the hat to the man sitting on the other side of her. She grabbed Jack's hands and they danced between the lines of fellow dancers. Her smile made Jack the happiest he had ever been in his entire life. When they reached the end of the line, the song ended, and they still held both their hands and stared into each other's eyes.

"What's your name?" Jack asked.

"Maria Schultz. But you can call me Mary—possibly Devilish Mary!" And they both laughed. "Come, let's step outside for a breath of fresh air," she said. Outside the barn, Mary looked up into the sky and said, "Look! It's a waxing moon. Maybe it's a sign?" And she smiled at him.

We hadn't been married but about four weeks
Till I told her it was best we parted;
She didn't say nary a word to me,
But she gathered up her duds an' started.

Jack was smiling, thinking of the good times this song brought back. Then the lump built in his throat. The smile disappeared from his lips. He felt as though a hand gripped his heart, and tears welled in his eyes. He moved quickly away as the chorus concluded:

It's tararinktum, tararinktum,
Tararinktum ready!
Meanest girl I ever did meet and her name was Devilish Mary!

As man and dog crossed the bridge over Whitewood Creek, the nightly ritual of "Oh Joe!" began back in the camps and washed like a wave of voices down the narrow gulch. Jack, with Stonewall by his side, entered the Grand Central Hotel. The regulator clock above the front desk showed the time as fifteen minutes to nine.

"Good evening, Captain Jones," Charlie Wagner said.

"Good evening, Charlie," Jack replied.

"It's been an eventful twenty-four hours, has it not?"

"That it has been," Jack replied and handed Wagner the lamp. "Here's a present for the hotel. Compliments of Bummer Dan, who won't be needing it anymore."

"Why, thank you, Captain. We can always use another lamp around here!"

Jack walked into the dining room filled with men. One small table was open for him. He would be eating alone, which was just fine with him. He wanted to collect his thoughts from the day. Lou and her staff were busy waiting on customers and had no time to chat. Stonewall ran off to the kitchen for his repast. One of Lou's helpers brought Jack a plate of tonight's dinner—ham, peas, and mashed potatoes, all delicious and washed down with a bottomless pot of coffee.

When he was done, the helper punched his ticket, and he got up to leave. Stonewall had not returned from the kitchen, but this was nothing unusual. Sometimes he spent the night there with the help, and why not? It was nice and warm and he was always able to get a snack if he begged just enough.

Jack climbed the stairs to the common sleeping room he shared with other men. He found his trunk in the dim lamplight and removed a set of clean clothing. He returned down the steps to the hotel's washroom, where the attendant provided him with a pitcher of hot water and a large washbowl. He stood in front of the only mirror and trimmed his beard and shaved off facial and neck hair that grew in the wrong places. He then removed his clothes and washed up the best he could. Come Saturday, it would be time for his weekly bath. He felt refreshed after completing all his toiletries and putting on fresh clothes for the evening's festivities.

It had been quite awhile since he had last attended a play. He had seen *The Streets of New York* years ago. It was one of those classic standbys most people could see again and again. Jack gave the washroom attendant a tip and handed him his dirty clothes to be washed and cleaned at the nearby Chinese laundry. Actually, there were no other laundries in town other than Chinese.

He walked by the Grand Central's barroom, but saw no one he knew. Jack looked at the regulator clock over the front desk as it started to chime. It was 10 o'clock, still plenty of time before the play was to begin. He left the building and walked down Main Street past the Deadwood Theater to the Senate Saloon. A crowd of people were lining up to enter the theater and others were in the saloon, having one last drink to get themselves in the proper mood before heading into the theater. Jack entered the Senate to see what, if anything might be going on, and to have one brief drink before entering the theater. He approached the bar. The same bartender who he had talked to earlier in the day came over to him.

"You need more information or are you drinking this time?" the barkeep asked.

"Drinking," Jack responded.

"What'll it be?"

"Got any Old Crow?"

"You bet," the barkeep answered as he found a bottle on the backbar. He poured Jack a shot and said, "That will be twenty cents."

Jack found a quarter and said, "Keep the change."

"Thank you, sir," the barkeep said. Jack took a sip of the whiskey and turned. Leaning his back on the bar, he surveyed the dimly lit room. Sitting by himself toward the back was Texas Jack. *This might be a good time to ask him a few questions*, Jack thought.

"Barkeep, another shot of Old Crow," Jack called to the bartender. After receiving and paying for the second shot, Jack carried both drinks over to the table where Texas Jack sat with his Bowie knife out, whittling a stick.

"You look like you could stand a shot of good whiskey," Jack said.

"I sure could," Texas Jack said. "I don't think I've had the pleasure to meet you, sir."

"My name's Jones, Jack Jones," he said as he stuck out his hand. Texas Jack shook Jack's hand without standing up from his stool. Jack handed him the drink as he pulled up a stool.

"Mind if I join you for a minute?" Jack asked.

"Well, it looks like you already did. What can I do for you?"

"I have several questions I'd like to ask. But first, I should tell you I'm a reporter for the *Chicago Inter-Ocean* newspaper."

Texas Jack's demeanor changed. He sat up from a slouching position and became more animated.

"You say you report for a newspaper?"

"That's right."

"And you want to write about me, maybe make me famous?"

"Well, I can't guarantee I can make you famous, but I would like to get some information from you that could add to the story of the murder of Preacher Smith."

"Sure thing, Mr. Jones."

"Jack, just call me Jack."

"Sure thing, Jack."

"The first thing I'd like to ask has nothing to do with the story, but it's information you might have that can help me out. Do you know California Joe and do you know where I might be able to find him?"

"To the best of my knowledge, California Joe is still out prowling the hills around Deadwood lookin' for Injuns to keep the town safe." Texas Jack downed the whiskey in one gulp. "What else do you want to know?"

"Do you know where Laughing Sam is?"

"No sir, ain't seen him since yesterday."

"You were at the incident last night where Harry Young was almost hanged. You were one of the two men who placed the noose around Harry's neck."

"So what if I was? Young had it coming. He shouldn't have gunned down poor old Bummer Dan."

"I imagine we'll find out tomorrow what his fate will be after he stands trial."

"I suppose so," Texas Jack said. "All this talking is making me thirsty. You want to buy me more whiskey?"

Jack looked at his pocket watch. It was twenty after ten. It probably wouldn't hurt if he was a little late for the show, and after all, he knew the plot. As long as he was there before the end, Lil probably wouldn't mind.

"Yes," Jack said.

"Hey, Jim!" Texas Jack shouted to the bartender. "Send over two more shots of that whiskey this feller bought. He's buying two more!"

"Sure thing," the barkeep responded. He walked over with the Old Crow bottle and poured them both another shot. Jack handed the barkeep a half dollar and said, "Keep the change." Turning back to Texas Jack, Jack said, "You were one of those who first found Preacher Smith's body. Is that correct?"

"That's so," Texas Jack responded.

"Can you tell me what happened?"

"Sure," Texas Jack said. "We was out huntin' in the hills around Crook City and we was on our way back to Deadwood."

"Just out of curiosity, what were you hunting? Deer?"

Texas Jack's face broke into a nasty grin. "We was huntin' Injuns. That's what we was huntin'. Didn't find none though, not until later."

"Go on," Jack said. *This is going to take longer than I was thinking*, Jack thought.

"Me and the boys, we was on the trail headed back to Deadwood when we came upon this body. One of the boys reckoned it was that preacher feller. We looked around, took out our pistols and carbines and were ready in case the Injuns were still lurking about."

"How did you know Indians had killed Preacher Smith?"

"Well, hell! Who else would have done such a thing? No white man would go an' kill a man of God! They'd roast in hell," Texas Jack said, with indignation dripping from his lips.

"What signs did the Indians leave behind? I hear he wasn't scalped or otherwise mutilated."

"That's right. Those Injuns didn't harm a hair on his head. He looked so peaceful with his eyes closed, lying there on his back, his hands clasping his Bible to his chest. There was even a slight smile on his lips. He looked angelic. He looked as if he was only asleep—except for the bullet hole through his heart."

"None of this proves Indians killed him. I heard that his offering was taken—dust, coins, chips, and markers. You didn't find any of those on him?"

"What do you take me, Texas Jack, for? A criminal that would go through the pockets of a dead parson? For shame!"

"You still haven't told me why you think Indians did it."

"Think about it, Mr. Know-It-All Reporter," Texas Jack spat and poked his finger in Jack's chest. "It was the same day those heathen devils attacked the Montana herd out on Centennial Prairie and drove off hundreds of horses and killed two good men—the same day!"

"Still, that doesn't prove those Indians killed the preacher."

"What about this then?" Texas Jack spoke with the voice of authority. "As we was gettin' ready to bring back the preacher's body, a crafty Injun slowly and deliberately walks his horse toward us, makin' the sign of peace. I can tell you, that crafty devil was just trying to deceive us so he could get close enough to murder us all, just like he did to the poor old preacher. I shot at the Injun and wounded him and Lou Mason shot and killed his horse. The Injun ran into the brush. We fired at him and he fired back for a time, but then all was quiet. Lou says, 'He's got to be dead. I'm goin' in after him.' The rest of us boys told him to be careful, but he was all-fired certain that Injun was dead. Well, he wasn't. Lou got close to that Injun and he gut shot old Lou then and there. We poured in the lead into that Injun's hidin' place until a gopher couldn't survive in there. Then cautious, we went in and found the Injun dead. I took out my skinnin' knife and cut off his head. While the others took care of Lou's and that preacher feller's bodies, I raced my horse back to town to show the folks we had taken revenge for the preacher and the others. It was a fine time. I took that head around to all the saloons. All the boys bought me drinks and when I was done showin' off my trophy, the good businessmen of Deadwood paid me fifty dollars in gold dust for the head. They took it and buried it out behind the Cricket Saloon. Not sure why. It was fun to look at and carry around."

"So you believe Indians killed Preacher Smith because one of them approached you near where Preacher Smith was killed and made the sign of peace to you."

"That's correct, Mr. Reporter," Texas Jack said, slamming his empty glass on the table. "Don't you think I deserve another drink for that?"

Jack looked at him and was about to say no, that Texas Jack didn't know that the Indian had killed the preacher, but then thought better of it. *Why cast pearls before swine?* He thought. "Sure, Texas Jack. One more drink for you, but I must go. I have a show to catch."

Jack called the bartender over and paid for one more drink for Texas Jack. Jack tipped his hat to the headhunter and walked away.

He looked at his pocket watch. Time had flown. It was well past eleven o'clock. He hurried out the door and walked next door to the Deadwood Theater. He approached the doorman.

"I'd like to buy a ticket, if you please," Jack said.

"I'm sorry, sir, it's too late. I can't let you in," the doorman responded.

"I've seen the play before. Can't I just sneak in the back? I'll be quiet."

"Sorry, sir. It's the theater's policy."

"Oh, policy be damned!" Jack said.

"Oh, really, sir?" the man said as he unbuttoned his coat to reveal a holstered pistol hanging from a waist belt.

"Humph!" Jack said, turning away fuming. He marched down the street, with no particular place to go, his thoughts dark and brooding. The nightlife in town was loud and raucous. Some buildings had music spilling out into the street. Most of it was either from banjos or fiddles. *When is someone going to ship a damn piano to this hellhole?* Jack ranted to himself. After walking as far as the Cricket Saloon, he had cooled down considerably. *Now what?* He thought. "I suppose I'll head back to the Deadwood Theater, wait until it's over, find Lil, and apologize." Jack said aloud to himself. He turned around and headed back up the street.

When he reached the theater, the show was over and a happy throng emerged from the front entrance. He waited until most had come out, and then he slipped in while the front doorman was busy talking to one of his cronies. Inside, Jack made his way to the front, where a few people were still there conversing. John Langrishe was on stage talking with a few actors about the evening's performance. Jack spied an actress who was rearranging a few props.

"Excuse me, miss," Jack said.

"Yes?" she said.

"Can you tell me where I might find Miss Rochelle?"

"I believe she is in the back," the actress said, "removing makeup and changing clothes from tonight's performance. Third room on the right."

"Thank you," Jack said. He walked back behind the stage where there were several small dressing rooms. He found the room he was looking for and knocked on the door.

"Who is it?" Lil's voice asked.

"It's Jack."

"Go away. I don't care to talk to you right now."

"Lil, I apologize. I was going to come to your performance tonight, but my interview with Texas Jack took longer than I thought. I am very sorry."

There was a long period of silence. Finally, the door slowly swung open. Lil stood before him. She had been crying.

"Jack, I have strong feelings for you, but it seems that you are so reserved, that you don't want to get close."

"No, that's not it, Lil."

"Then what is it, Jack?" said one of the actors who was standing close by. Jack glared at the man, who smirked and left.

"Lil, can we go for a walk?" Jack asked.

"I suppose," she said. "Let me get my shawl."

Jack borrowed a lantern from the theater. They walked out and headed uptown, with Lil holding on to his arm. As they slowly picked their way between stumps, rocks, and the ruts, they talked.

"I was so disappointed when I did not see you in the audience," Lil said.

"I understand," Jack said.

"You could have at least come in for the end of the show."

"I tried, but your guard wouldn't let me by."

"He takes his job too serious. Some people like it when they get a little power."

"Again, I do apologize."

"Jack, sometimes I feel—well, I feel that you are standoffish. I try to get close, but you seem distant."

"I don't mean to be."

"Then why are you?"

"I feel very close to you. I want to be with you all the time. You make me happy. When I think of you I always smile."

"But still, I sense there is something dark there. Something you won't share with me."

"It's not that I don't want to share it. I just don't know how. I'm afraid of it. I'm afraid that if I share it with you, you will think less of me. I try not to think of it myself, but it always resurfaces."

Lil stopped dead in the street and removed her hand from his arm. Facing him, she said, "Jack, you can tell me. I will not think any less of you whatever you tell me. That is my promise."

Jack stood for the longest time, staring at her. Finally, he said, "All right." He stood silent, trying to formulate his words.

"I was married and I have a daughter," Jack blurted. Lil was silent for a moment, then said, "'married.' You use the word 'married.' Does that mean you are no longer married?"

"That is correct. I was married. My wife, her name was Mary."

"I see," Lil said.

Neither said a word for a long time.

"She is dead," Jack said.

"Oh, Jack, I am so sorry to hear that."

"Thank you. It's hard. I think of her every day."

"You said you have a daughter. What about her?"

"Mary died in childbirth. A little girl was born to us. My sister took her in and named her Sarah. She has raised her as her own child."

"Have you helped raise her? Does she know who you are?"

"I have seen her on occasion as she grows up. I send money to help my sister's family. My job as a reporter keeps me traveling, just the way I like it. Keep active—try not to think too much. Sarah knows me only as Uncle Jack."

"Do you think you will tell her someday?"

"I don't know. I feel so ashamed about it all."

"In what way? Why?"

"You see, Lil, I was away when the birth and death occurred. I was in the army during the war. I found out about Mary's death just before the fight at Chancellorsville. Our regiment's time was up. We were to go home, but the fight was on and we fought anyway. I was numb. I didn't care if I lived or died. I should have been by Mary's side. I fought with no thought of my own preservation. All I could think of was Mary dead." He paused for a long time. "I returned home to Pennsylvania, but there was no joy. I was ashamed and heartsick that I had not been there with Mary. My sister was happy to raise Sarah as her own. I sold my farm and began traveling. I eventually found a job as a reporter. I just keep moving and try not to make any close human attachments."

"I see," Lil said, looking away from Jack. There was a long moment of silence.

"Until now," he said.

"Oh, Jack!" she said, looking back at him. "Don't think you are the only one who hurts. I too have loved and lost. Only my story is pitifully plain and not as heartbreaking as yours."

"Tell me, if it is not too painful," he said.

"A year after I had joined my uncle and aunt in the theater troupe, a handsome actor joined us. He was pleasant and enthusiastic. He helped me learn my lines for the plays and taught me all the latest melodies. He was always happy and interested in my accomplishments and me. We went for long walks, horseback rides, and picnics. I was in love with him and he professed his love for me. Since we were in Colorado and my father and mother were so far away, Uncle and Auntie stood in their stead as my guardians. He asked Uncle for my hand in marriage, which Uncle agreed to. He then asked me and I jumped at the chance. We were so happy together until about a month before the wedding, when Uncle happened upon him and one of the actresses in a dressing room, completely undressed and ... Oh I can't go on." Lil paused for a long time. "Let's just say Uncle let them go then and there. That was the end of the engagement, and that was the end of my happiness." Again, a long pause. Lil looked up at Jack. "Until now," she whispered. They touched and they kissed—long and deep.

"Oh Jack, I love you."

Jack looked up into the night sky at the waxing moon. He felt at peace.

"Lil…" A long pause, then a sob. "I love you, too."

CHAPTER SEVEN

ℰᴑᏰᏉ

Thursday Morning, August 24, 1876—Jack sipped his coffee as he reviewed his notes from the day before. Male patrons filled the Grand Central's dining room. Lou and her assistants were busy in the kitchen cooking, bringing out breakfast foods, and clearing plates from those finished with their meals.

Pounding hoof beats sounded outside the building. Shots rang out in the street. No one looked up from what he or she was doing. Pistol shots in the street were a normal occurrence in Deadwood.

Probably some exuberant young buck excited over some eureka moment. Jack thought. He smiled. *Exuberant, that's me. I have not felt this whole, this complete since...since Mary. I do love Lil.*

Jack went back to reviewing his notes and making corrections. He heard rapidly approaching leather boots striking wood flooring and coming down the hallway, a jingling of spurs and raucous laughs and curses as a mob of men shoved their way into the dining room. All conversations and movement ceased. Jack looked up from his notebook.

Poncho stood in front of the mob, grinning from ear to ear. Carlos stood slightly behind Poncho, with his hand on Poncho's shoulder. He, too, grinned.

"*Amigos!*" Poncho shouted. "Gaze upon the face of my new Indian friend!" Holding a sack in his left hand, Poncho reached in with his right hand and pulled out a human head. He held the grizzly remains aloft by its long black hair. The diners looked in horror at the sightless, glazed eyes. The men behind Poncho started to laugh, started to make their crude comments. One diner gagged, then retched.

A deep, guttural scream, followed by a crash of dishes hitting the wood floor, startled all to speechlessness. Lou stood in the doorway of the kitchen. A large knife lay with other utensils on a table near the door. Lou picked up the knife and rushed the mob, shouting, "Get out of here! Get that man's head out of here. Get out, you animals! Now!"

The mob turned tail, rushing out of the room, out into the hallway and back into the street, followed by Lou, wielding her knife. The diners heard Lou shouting, "I don't want to ever see any of you ever again in my dining room. Do you hear! Don't ever return!"

The men in the dining room sat silent. No one moved. Lou appeared in the doorway, knife hanging limp in her hand. She faced the diners and said, "Gentlemen, I apologize for the intrusion of those reprobates. Please try to enjoy the rest of your meal." And to her staff she said, "Scrub the floor where those men stood, make sure it's clean, and please clean up my mess by the kitchen. I need to see about the food on the cook stove." Someone began to clap, and all the men and the help joined in. They stood and gave Lou three cheers. She nodded acknowledgement and disappeared into the kitchen.

Jack sat stunned by what he had seen. He had witnessed plenty of carnage during the war, every conceivable aspect of man butchering man, but he had never been in a relatively civilized, relatively peaceful setting eating a quiet breakfast and had a severed human head thrust unexpectedly into that setting. Lou had acted heroically, charging those men and throwing them out. He made note of it in his book, finished his meal, and left the dining room.

The regulator clock showed that the time was approaching ten a.m. He was getting a late start today, and there was much to do: check on his horse, see about renting mules, track down Laughing Sam and California Joe, check in with Star and Bullock on his supplies, observe the setup of the court and jury selection, and above all, make sure to attend the play tonight. With Stonewall by his side, Jack stepped out of the hotel onto the front porch. He looked up at a partly overcast sky. He looked across the street to see if there were any goings on at the Deadwood Theater, but none of the theater people were to be seen.

"Good morning, Jack!" Pete said, standing up. He had been sitting on the edge of the front porch, whittling a stick.

"Good morning to you, Pete!"

"I was waiting for you. You said you wanted me to report on the doings up at Lead."

"That's right! Sorry I forgot. Things got a little busy yesterday. Let's just sit right here and you can tell me your information."

"Sure thing," Pete said as they sat side by side. Stonewall saw another dog and chased after him. Men going about their business walked past. Workers were unloading freight from a bull train down the street.

Jack pulled out his notebook and pencil and said, "I'm ready."

"There's lots going on up at Lead," Pete began. "They say that's the source of all the placer gold being found in the streams here. Men are digging adits all over the hillsides there and a few true hard rock mines have started up. Some think these mines are going to be big bonanza moneymakers."

"I can't remember, who did you work for up there?"

"Why, none other than Mister Smokey Jones himself at his Golden Star Mine. He sure is a nice fellow. He treated us kindly as we loaded the ore into the wagons, paid us well, and when we were done, gave us each a half-cup of whiskey and treated us to his wolf howl," Pete said and laughed. "That man sure can howl! Anyways, they have over ten thousand pounds of ore they are hauling back to Omaha to be smelted."

"What about the Manuel Brothers, Fred and Mose? I hear they have a mine that shows a lot of promise, The Home Stake."

"They have mined over fifty tons of rock, but they have no way to reduce it until a stamp mill is built. People say it could yield up to $500 in gold per ton. They left their claim to look for better prospects until stamp mills are built."

"Interesting," Jack said, writing down everything Pete said.

"Anything else?" Jack asked.

"No, I think that covers it."

"What are your plans today?"

"It's getting rather late in the day to find a job now. I might try to get a job as a pitman for the day at one of the sawpits."

"That's a dirty, strenuous job, sawing upwards through logs all day."

"That's for sure. If I don't find a job today, I think I might sit in on the Harry Young trial. That should be quite interesting."

"Maybe I'll see you there then, as that's where I'll be, reporting on the trial for the paper. By the way, I don't suppose you found time to put those greenbacks in the bank. You can't be too careful around this town."

"Thank you, Jack, I may do that. As I said, I have an aversion to banks, but I did buy a little protection with yesterday's earnings." Pete unbuttoned his coat, revealing an old army waist-belt and holster. Out of the holster, he pulled an old cap-and-ball Navy Colt.

"I was able to pick this up from Star and Bullock for a few dollars," Pete said. "This will provide me protection better than any old bank."

"Suit yourself," Jack said.

"Have you found any more information on Bummer Dan or Laughing Sam?" Pete asked.

"I haven't been able to locate Laughing Sam yet. Hopefully he'll be at the Young trial. I found out Laughing Sam and Bummer Dan were partners. They were not the most likable men in town. Bummer Dan's haversack is still missing and someone ransacked his shanty, most likely looking for valuables."

"The oddest thing about your story is why did Bummer Dan wear Laughing Sam's clothes into Saloon Number 10?"

"Especially if those two were in cahoots," Jack said. "Bummer Dan should not have worn Laughing Sam's clothing into Saloon Number 10, a place where he had to know that Harry Young might shoot Laughing Sam on sight. Why would anyone in their right mind want to walk into a situation such as that, knowing it could amount to suicide?"

"There had to be some angle to it," Pete mused. "An angle that would be to their advantage so much so that Bummer Dan was willing to risk his life."

"That's a good point. I hadn't considered that."

The sounds of the street changed. Pete and Jack looked up. Jack recognized a familiar sight from yesterday.

The two Cantonese men were again carrying the Asian beauty. But now he knew her name, Di Lee. Both Pete and Jack stood as one and swept the hats off their heads. Di Lee was dressed in a blue robe, girded by a white sash. She lowered the fan as she smiled and spoke in perfect English, "Good morning, Captain

Jones. Good morning, young sir." She gave a light chuckle, brought the fan back up to her lower face, and spoke a command to the men to proceed on. Pete and Jack put their hats back on their heads and watched as the two men and woman disappeared into the crowd.

"Who was that?" Pete asked.

"Her name is Di Lee. I don't know much more than that except I hear she is single and rich," Jack said. "How does she know my name?" he asked himself more than Pete.

"Di Lee," Pete spoke the name slowly. "She is so beautiful. She could be a doll." He paused and then said softly, "A china doll."

"Humph, maybe so," Jack said. "In any event, I need to get moving. I have a few errands I need to finish today, and I need to make sure I don't miss the play tonight."

"Sure thing, Jack, maybe I'll see you later at the trial," Pete said.

"And thank you again for the information concerning the hard rock mining in Lead. I need to ask Colorado Charlie if he's seen a fellow called California Joe."

Jack stood up and walked to the corner of Main and Gold. Colorado Charlie was not in the street. Jack poked his head in the Lee & Brown Store but did not see him there. He turned left onto Gold Street. Stonewall caught up with him by the time he reached the Montana Feed, Livery, and Stable. Paco nickered a welcome as he entered the building. Jack walked over to Paco and rubbed his forehead and scratch behind his ears.

"*Bonjour*, Monsieur Jack!" Old Frenchy said.

"Good morning, Old Frenchy. How are you this fine morning?"

"Good, Monsieur! And you?"

"I haven't felt this good in years, Old Frenchy," Jack said. "Years!"

"Ah, very good, Monsieur!"

"Any news on my horse?"

"Ah Monsieur Jack, I am afraid I will make you less happy. One of the herders arrived this morning with a count and listing of the horses. Your horse unfortunately is counted among the missing, but we are still looking for him."

"Thanks, Old Frenchy. He is a good, solid horse. I bought him in Fort Pierre for the journey here. He and I became close on the trail. I'm still hopeful he will be found so I can ride him when I leave to find General Crook."

"The herders are still searching for any horses that may have scattered that were not run off by the Indians."

"I leave in several days, whether my horse is found or not. If he is not found I'll need to rent a horse from you, and I'll also need to rent two mules and packs for carrying supplies."

"That can be arranged, Monsieur Jack."

"I don't suppose you have heard anything about Laughing Sam Hartman?"

"No, *mon ami.*"

"Or that you have seen California Joe?"

"I have not seen him, but I hear he is in town."

"Thank you, Old Frenchy! That's good news. I must be on my way. I'll stop back tomorrow to see if there's anything new on my horse."

"*Bonjour, mon ami.*"

Jack strode out of the livery stable. Now at least he had a good chance of tracking down California Joe. He walked over to the *Black Hills Pioneer* building.

Maybe Merrick has some new information, he thought. Jack tried the door handle but it was locked. Then he saw the sign, "Closed. Be Back Soon."

"Humph," Jack grunted. *Merrick must have left early for the jury selection.*

He walked back to Main Street, turned left and headed north, scanning the crowd for Laughing Sam or anyone who might look like California Joe.

Jack did not see either of them, but he did see a familiar figure—Fat Jack. He was standing in front of a building, a party to one of the many outdoor faro games. Jack walked up and joined the small crowd of onlookers. The dealer drew a card. Fat Jack looked at the checks he had laid on the wrong card. "B-Busted!" he cried.

"Ha! Ha!" the dealer laughed. "Care to wager again?"

"I said I'm b-busted. I'm b-broke!"

"Then get yer carcass out of the way," one of the onlookers said. "So someone who's flush can win this bloke's pile."

Fat Jack stood and moved away, dejection written across his face.

"Fat Jack!" Jack said. "A moment of your time?"

"S-Sure, Captain."

"Any sightings of Laughing Sam or California Joe?"

"N-Nothing on Laughing Sam, but I do know where C-California Joe is."

"Where?"

Fat Jack grinned, fishing a pair of cotton socks out of his pocket. "You n-need socks, don't you?"

Jack could not help but smile. "Yes I do, Fat Jack. Yes I do," He handed Fat Jack fifteen cents and took the proffered socks.

"I saw C-California Joe not more than a h-half hour ago at the S-Senate Saloon. He should s-still be there. If you see a m-mule tied to the hitching rail, you'll know he's s-still inside. He was working on a t-tankard of beer when I s-saw him last."

"Thanks, Fat Jack!"

"H-Happy to be of service to you, Captain," Fat Jack said sweeping off his top hat and bowing. He quickly straightened and, placing his hat on top of his head, muscled his way through the crowd back to the faro layout shouting, "M-Make way, boys, for a man with m-money!"

Jack smiled, shoved the socks in his coat pocket, and walked back up the street to the Senate Saloon. A saddled mule stood at the hitching rail outside the building. The same sign still hung on the outside wall, "No Dogs Allowed." Fortunately, Stonewall had run off to join a pack of mongrels roaming the street for whatever dog mischief they could get into.

Jack walked through the door into the cool, dark barroom. A different bartender was serving the already larger than normal crowd for this time of day. They were getting primed for the big show, the trial proceedings set to soon begin.

As his eyes adjusted to the dim light, Jack spied a mountain of a man who appeared to fit Colorado Charlie's description of California Joe. A long-haired, red-bearded, blue-eyed, buckskin-clad man wearing a wide sombrero was regaling an enraptured crowd with his hair-raising narrow escape from certain death at the hands of Indians during Custer's attack on the Cheyenne village at the Washita.

"Oh Emma! Those Injuns came boilin' out of their teepees upriver and downriver," the man mountain exclaimed. "If we hadn't skedaddled when we did, we all would have been butchered and our topknots would be adornin' those Cheyenne and Arapaho braves' lances, just like what happened to Major Elliot and his men, who Custer left behind. Old Hard-Ass Custer must have tried his same tricks at the Little Big Horn that he did at Washita back in '68. He must have been thinkin' his luck would hold out again and that he could get away with it. But Custer's Luck didn't work for him this time!"

The man mountain took a break from his harangue, puffed on his pipe, and hoisted a tankard of beer. He took several large gulps, slammed the tankard on the table, and shouted, "More beer!" as he swiped a greasy sleeve across his lips. The bartender walked over to the table and picked up the empty tankard. Jack motioned to the bartender and said, "Is that fellow doing all the talking over there California Joe Milner?"

"He's the one and only California Joe," the bartender answered.

"Thanks. I'll pay for his beer and bring one for me, too. And I'll take it over to him for you."

"Thank you," the bartender said. "He's been a handful!" He returned with two frothing tankards and Jack paid him.

California Joe continued to expound on the state of the countryside. "Most of the Injuns are tryin' to make it back to the agencies without the troops catchin' them. The Grey Fox probably won't catch any of them."

"Grey Fox?" one listener asked.

"The Grey Fox, that's what the Apaches named Crook. He was relentless. They finally gave up and made peace with him, after he hired Apaches to hunt down Apaches and used mules to haul his supplies instead of using wagons. But here the Grey Fox ain't got no Lakota or Cheyenne huntin' their own people. They'll stay out of his way until they get back to the agencies and claim they were nowhere near the Little Big Horn." California Joe's thirst got the better of him.

"Hey! Where's my beer!" he shouted.

"Right here," Jack answered. "And I've already taken care of its payment."

California Joe looked up and squinted at Jack as he set the tankard on the table in front of him.

"Well, that's right neighborly of ya, Mister! Mister? Can't say as we've met before."

"We haven't. My name is Jack Jones."

"Jack Jones. Say, is you the feller some people call Captain?"

"That's correct. I was a captain in a Pennsylvania regiment during the war."

California Joe stretched out a begrimed hand. "Glad to meet ya, Captain. Pull up a stool. One of ya loafers who ain't bought me a beer, give your seat to the Captain here."

California Joe glared at the man sitting next to him, and the man stood up and left. Jack took his stool and after taking a drink, set his beer on the table. His boot struck something firm but at the same time soft. Whatever it was, it moved. He looked under the table and came eye to eye with a large hound.

"What's this?" he said.

"Why, that's my hound dog, Lester," California Joe said.

"But the sign outside reads "No Dogs Allowed," Jack said.

California Joe took another drink, puffed on his pipe, and then thoughtfully said, "That's a silly sign. Everyone knows dogs can't read."

Everyone around the table roared with laughter as Jack smiled and shook his head.

"So, Captain, why are ya bein' so neighborly to old California Joe?"

"I'd like to talk with you about a little business when you have some free time."

"I have free time right now! The rest of ya loafers clear out of here. The good Captain and I are goin' to conduct a little business."

Jack and California Joe each took a gulp of their beer as the others cleared away from the table.

"I need to find Crook," Jack said. "And I hear you're the man who can take me to him."

"I'm the only man who can take you to him and keep your topknot intact," California Joe said, then took another long drink. "Why do you need to find Crook?"

"I'm a reporter for the *Chicago Inter-Ocean*. My editor wants me to find out what Crook and his men have been doing and report back."

"Hell, you can stay right here, because I'll tell you what Crook's doin'. He's runnin' in circles, using up his supplies, and not findin' any Injuns."

"Thanks. I believe you, but my editor requires I physically find him. I'll pay you ten dollars a day and a bonus of twenty-five dollars if you find him for me within ten days."

California Joe picked up his tankard and drained it.

"Buy me another beer, would ya?"

"Right," Jack said and shouted to the bartender, "Another beer for California Joe, if you please."

The bartender walked over to the table and took the empty tankard. California Joe stared at the ceiling. "If I did this, I'd want thirty-five dollars bonus. I'm currently employed by the good folks of Deadwood to patrol the perimeter to ensure Injuns don't attack the town. I could stretch my patrol further to the north, takin' ya with me. But once we find Crook's troops, I leave ya there and return to Deadwood, as I must make sure Deadwood is protected. Also, ya would pick up all the provisions."

The bartender returned with California Joe's beer and Jack paid him for it.

"Agreed," Jack said and held out his right hand. "Agreed!" California Joe said, shaking Jack hand.

"I'm having Star and Bullock prepare a list of provisions for us. I plan to stop there later today to check the list. If you get the opportunity, you should do likewise and add to it if you see something I left off."

"I can do that later today."

"I also plan to rent two mules to haul our supplies."

"Good move. I love mules. I ride one myself. When do we leave?"

"My hope is to leave as early as Sunday. I want to stay around town for Harry Young's trial."

"That's a travesty right there, if ya ask me," California Joe said.

"In what way?"

"Somethin's awry there. I heard that weasel Bummer Dan walked into Saloon Number 10 wearin' Laughing Sam's clothes. And you know what I hear tell, that Laughing Sam was seen sneakin' into Saloon Number 10 just as Bummer Dan walked in wearin' his clothes."

"What!" Jack said, about to take a drink of his beer.

"That's right, friend. I hear Laughing Sam was in the saloon when Bummer Dan was shot by Harry Young."

"If true, what does that mean?"

"It means it was a setup, a setup that went wrong," California Joe said. "I think Laughing Sam was goin' to kill Harry Young. Here's how I sees it. Bummer Dan is the distraction. Harry was to see Bummer Dan and focus on him, meanwhile Laughing Sam was goin' to sneak up on Harry when he wasn't lookin' and shoot him. The problem was, Harry got nervous and shot Bummer Dan thinkin' he was Laughing Sam come to kill him. Laughing Sam seein' Bummer Dan shot and killed, runs out into the dark and leaves town before anyone puts two and two together."

"You put two and two together."

"Right, and do you see Laughing Sam anywhere in town?"

"No."

"I rest my case. I bet ya won't see him at jury selection or at the trial, even though his good friend and partner was murdered."

"I won't bet against that."

"I'll tell ya what, if they hadn't assassinated my good friend, Wild Bill, none of this bullshit would be happenin'."

"What do you mean by 'they'? Jack McCall shot and killed Wild Bill."

"I mean 'they' put McCall up to it. He was the instrument of the murder, he pulled the trigger, but they paid him to do it to get Wild Bill out of the way."

"Who are they? And why did they want Wild Bill out of the way?"

"Why? Hell, everybody knows there's a criminal ring in this town controllin' things. Some of the good folks in town wanted to hire Wild Bill as a lawman to control the criminals. The criminals got wind of it, paid McCall to do their dirty work for them, then set it up that he could make his getaway."

"How so?" Jack asked.

"First of all, they had a horse tied to a rail outside Saloon Number 10. If McCall could have gotten on that horse, he would have been able to ride out of town before anyone could mount a good pursuit. The stupid bastard forgot to tighten the cinch before walkin' into the saloon and assassinatin' Wild Bill. When he went to mount up, the saddle, not bein' cinched up, slid with him as he tried to get up. It wound up under the horse's belly." California Joe took a gulp of beer and let out a loud, long belch. "So the ring of criminals had to come up with another plan to save their boy from the noose, as he was about to be hung. And they sure as hell didn't want him to rat on them. They cried for law and order so the mob relented. The ring then made sure they had enough people on the jury to make sure McCall got off and that's exactly what happened. I hear from Colorado Charlie Utter that the weasel is down in Cheyenne, braggin' about killin' Wild Bill. If he ever runs into me, I'll be the last thing that son of a bitch sees."

"Do you have any proof?"

"Proof! Hell! I ain't got no proof! What do you expect them to do? Write it down on paper? Publish it in the *Black Hills Pioneer*? It's all hearsay. People whisper and say Johnny Varnes is the head of it too!"

"What!" Jack said.

"You heard me," California Joe said.

"Prove it," growled a voice behind them.

They turned and there stood Texas Jack.

"You heard me," Texas Jack said. "Prove it, you greasy windbag."

"I don't need to prove nothin' to you, ya bastard polecat!" California Joe shouted, whipping out an Arkansas Toothpick. But as he stood with knife in hand, Texas Jack leveled two Army Colts at his gut.

"I repeat," Texas Jack said, his face contorting in a snarl, "prove it."

"I can't," California Joe said.

"Then shut up! You can't go around badmouthin' good honest citizens without any proof of wrongdoin'. The next time I hear you spoutin' off your nonsense, I'll end it with a bullet in your fevered brain." Texas Jack holstered his pistols and swaggered out the door. California Joe picked up his tankard and drained it.

"I'll need another," he said to Jack.

"Me too," Jack said. "Barkeep, another round if you please."

The bartender returned and took the tankards. *That was ugly*, Jack thought.

"Texas Jack, he's one bad *hombre*," California Joe muttered. "I ain't shuttin' up because of the likes of him." He motioned with his hand for Jack to lean in closer. It was hard for Jack to do because of California Joe's stench, but he did. California Joe continued in a low voice, almost a whisper, "You know, Texas Jack and Mason were the first to find Preacher Smith's body. Who's to say, they didn't kill the good preacher themselves and then pilfer the collection. And who's to say Texas Jack didn't get greedy and gut shoot Mason just to keep all the loot for himself. Then how convenient that poor Injun comes ridin' along, makin' the sign of peace. Texas Jack kills him too, slices off his head, rides into town, claims the Injun done it, and takes credit for revengin' the poor old preacher. He wins every which way."

"That's an interesting theory," Jack said.

"Theory!" California Joe shouted, then realized he had shouted. "Theory!" he said in almost a whisper again. "Why, it ain't no theory. Where's the money? Huh? If the Injun killed the good padre, Texas Jack should have recovered the money, and he didn't. Or so he says."

"So you think Texas Jack killed Preacher Smith for his collection, then killed Mason to keep it all for himself."

"Ha! For a reporter feller, you're catchin' on quick."

"It is a plausible story, but wouldn't hold up in court."

"Court? There ain't no court! Not that so-called play that will take place later today. Mark my word, nothin' will come of that trial. The only judge, jury, and justice out here in Dakota Territory is a man who can back up his word with his gun. Remember that, pilgrim."

"Thanks for the advice."

Jack finished his beer. *I need to get out of here before he wants me to buy him another round*, Jack thought, and then said, "I need to get down to Star and Bullock's and see about that supplies list. I'll tell them you'll stop by and add to the list anything you think useful."

"I'll do that as soon as I finish here. Most of the foodstuffs should be food that we can eat without cookin'. Most of our camps will be cold camps. We don't want to attract no Injuns with our camp smoke. After I stop by Star and Bullock's, then I'll have to head back out on my patrols through the Hills."

"As I said, I want to leave Sunday. How about we meet at the livery stable at sunrise on Sunday?"

"That sounds good. I'll be there then." They shook hands, Jack pushed back from the table, and left California Joe and his beer.

Back out on the street, Stonewall joined Jack as he slowly walked toward the emporium. His mind was racing. *What if everything California Joe says is right? A ring of criminals running the town behind the scenes? If so, who is involved? They assassinated Wild Bill Hickok to protect their illicit business, which is what? Robbery? They murder Preacher Smith for his gold. Was Bummer Dan killed for his gold? But that was probably a case of mistaken identity. How many unsolved killings in town and disappearances are due to this ring? If indeed a ring exists. Maybe I can spend a little time with Bullock and Star and see what they think.*

When Jack reached Star and Bullock's, he realized he would not be able to spend any time alone with them. Men filled the store, examining the latest goods that had arrived by bull train. Jack did not see Bullock. Star had his hands full collecting gold dust from his customers. Jack worked his way to the makeshift counter behind which Star stood. Star looked up from weighing gold dust on a small set of scales.

"Why, good morning, Jack," Star said. "How are you this fine morning?"

"Good, Sol. And you?"

"Very good, and very busy, as you can see."

"Where's your partner?"

"He has gone to watch the trial proceedings. He was so excited about it, I told him to go, I could handle the store, but *oy vey iz mir*, I had no idea I would have a mob of shoppers descend upon me. I have your list of supplies right here, if you wish to take a look at it?" Star said, opening a lidded box, removing a sheet of paper, and handing it to Jack. "Look it over and add anything you think we missed," Star said returning to help the next customer.

Jack sat on an empty crate and slowly went over the items on the list, making a few additions and corrections as he thought about what he and California Joe would need for their trip.

The buzz of male voices subsided. Jack looked up from the list to see why. Twirling a parasol on her shoulder, Dirty Em strolled into the store, wearing a dark blue ankle-length dress and a short-brimmed matching hat. Most likely the latest fashion shipped by rail straight from New York to Cheyenne, then by wagon to Deadwood.

"Good morning, Ma'am," Star said.

"*Guten Morgen*, Herr Star. Good morning, boys." Dirty Em greeted the crowded room and smiled. "Go on about your business. I'm just perusing the new bolts of cloth Monsieurs Star and Bullock received."

Jack went back to reviewing his list. Dirty Em moved among the various goods and worked her way close to Jack who looked up and smiled.

"Good morning, Em."

"Good morning, Captain Jones," she said, flashing him a smile. "I can tell from your breath, you've been imbibing ale already this morning."

"Only to entertain our friend California Joe Milner and get him to agree to help me find Crook," he said, standing up.

"A disgusting fellow! He needs to soak in a hot tub for a good hour and then be scrubbed until his skin glows red."

She examined the bolts of cloth laid out on a table next to Jack. Her floral scent was faint, but noticeable. She held up a bolt of purple cloth saying, "Captain Jones, does this appear to be too rich a fabric for your tastes?"

"I have to admit, I haven't paid much attention to high fashion."

"Oh, you men are all alike!" she said in a voice louder than it needed to be. Moving closer and in a low whisper meant for only him, she said, "I'm going to pass some information to you, but I'm afraid if others find out, I may be hurt or worse, so play along with me when I need you to."

Jack nodded.

"If you go to the trial today, watch Swearengen," she whispered. "I overheard him and Johnny Burns talking. Swearengen plans to rig the trial."

"What?" he said in surprise, loud enough for several men to turn in their direction. She glided close to him and whispered, "Place your arm around my waist." He complied.

"I said it's twenty dollars and no less!" Dirty Em stated loudly. The men chuckled and turned back to their examination of the store's goods.

"How does he think to rig the trial?" Jack whispered.

"He plans to have jurors selected who will vote the way he and his friends want the verdict to go," she whispered drawing nearer. He sensed the closeness of her well-formed body. His pulse raced.

"Which way, which way do they want the verdict to go?" Jones said, losing himself in her dark brown eyes.

"I wasn't able to hear that part," she whispered, her breath sweet, her lips inches from his.

"Have you heard about a criminal ring in town?" he said, his eyes now drawn to her glistening lips.

"Yes, I've heard rumors of such," she softly spoke. "If it's true, I wouldn't put it past Al and Johnny to be a part of it. Other than that, I really don't know much."

"Thanks." He was perspiring.

"You're welcome," she murmured, pressing her body firmly to his. Her essence was overwhelming. He felt he was losing control.

She laughed and drew away. "Oh, it's no use, Captain," she proclaimed loudly. "I'll not go lower than twenty dollars. But if you're interested in a little game of chance, stop by my faro game at the Cricket Saloon this evening."

"I'll do that," Jack croaked. Dirty Em moved away to examine other items. Jack composed himself, then finished reviewing and making minor changes to the list before returning it to Star.

"If California Joe wants to add to the list, that's fine with me," Jack said.

"Sure thing, Jack," Star said, gazing past him. Jack turned to see what Star was looking at and saw Dirty Em walking out the door.

"Dirty Em sure does have a well-turned ankle, does she not?" Star said.

"She certainly does," Jack agreed.

"Well, back to the business at hand. When do you want the supplies ready by?" Star asked.

"I'd like them by Saturday. If you could have the items delivered to the Montana Livery, I'll also pay for the delivery. I plan to hire two pack mules, and so I'll need to spend the time sorting and distributing the loads for the mules' packs."

"That won't be a problem," Star said.

"Thanks, Sol," Jack said and left the store.

The temperature was increasing and so was the cloud cover. He turned left on Main Street and began walking toward the Deadwood Theater. He had lots to consider. There might be a ring of criminals who had Wild Bill Hickok assassinated, killed Preacher Smith for his money, and killed who knows how many other unknown victims for their gold. Then Harry Young kills Bummer Dan in a case of mistaken identity. Al Swearengen wants to rig the jury for a verdict, but I don't know in which direction or why.

Stonewall ran off to join California Joe's hound. They were having a great time roughhousing. California Joe's mule was gone from the hitching rail, indicating that California Joe must be on the move. *A good thing*, Jack thought.

"Well, lookee thar!" An inebriated loafer shouted to his bummer friends. The drunk stood in the middle of the street looking up at the sandstone cliffs to the west. "Look at that big buzzard!" Jack looked in the direction the drunk was pointing. A large golden eagle soared out from the cliffs and over the street.

"Two bits says ya can't hit him, Jeb!" one of the loafer's friends shouted. Jeb, the loafer, shouted back, "I'll take that bet!" Men were quickly making side bets around Jeb as he pulled out a pistol, took an unsteady aim, and started blazing away at the eagle. Untouched, the bird banked and soared back the way he had come. Jeb continued blasting holes in the sky until his gun was empty. The friend who had made the bet pounded Jeb on the back saying, "That was mighty fine shootin', Jeb. You sure did show that buzzard a thing or two," as Jeb handed him a coin.

Bullock is right. There needs to be some law and order in this town, Jack thought.

The drunks stumbled and continued to weave their way down the street, clogged with humanity and bull wagons. Two familiar figures trotted their horses toward Jack. It was Poncho and Carlos, minus the head. Carlos laughed as he held up his Lakota possible bag.

"*Gracias,* Deadwood!" Poncho shouted.

"*Gracias* for this fifty dollars of gold dust!" Carlos shouted, lifting the possible bag high over his head. Grinning, Carlos lowered the bag, then pointed the pistol in his left hand over his head and shot straight up into the air.

"We celebrate your good fortune and our good fortune, *amigos!*" Poncho shouted. "One less Indian for you to worry about, and fifty more dollars for us to worry about!"

They laughed and shot their pistols again into the sky as they trotted north past Jack, down Main Street.

Deadwood Dead Men

CHAPTER EIGHT

၏ℭ

Thursday Afternoon, August 24, 1876—Stopping in front of the Deadwood Theater, Jack looked at his pocket watch. The time was half-past noon. He had a dilemma, either find something to eat and possibly miss some of the court proceedings, or eat later. He decided to eat later and joined the throng pushing to get inside.

Men were rapidly filling up the benches. Langrishe had ingeniously built a large seating capacity by driving rows of wooden posts into the ground then nailing wooden planks across the tops of the posts to create benches for theatergoers to sit upon. Instead of boards, the floor was made of graded placer mine tailings covered with sawdust. The stage at the far end of the building was built of wood and raised off the floor to create a better view for the audience. Curtains were suspended at the front of the stage for scene changes and back curtains hid props and dressing rooms. The theater's walls were frame, but the roof was canvas which had been partially rolled back to let in more light for the court proceedings. Jack looked for an empty place to sit.

"Ah, Captain Jones," a voice behind him said. Jack turned and there stood John Langrishe.

"Welcome to our humble theater, Captain," Langrishe said.

"Thank you, sir," Jack responded. "This is quite the theater you have here."

"Thank you. We have tried to create at least one establishment where folks can enjoy good clean wholesome entertainment in Deadwood Gulch."

"That is quite admirable, sir."

"I now have enough funds to construct a proper roof for the building before cold weather sets in. I'm just waiting for a builder to roof it over for me. There are several building projects ahead of mine it seems. After the roof, I'll have a floor and then it will be just like any theater in Cheyenne or St. Louis. Once people enter and the show begins, they can transport themselves anywhere we create the illusion to take them."

"Very good, sir, but if I might ask, how is Miss Lil today?"

"She is well. Lil and the other actors have left for the afternoon to practice elsewhere for tonight's performance so the business at hand can be attended to. She is excited you will be here tonight to witness her acting. If you are unaware, she is playing the part of Lucy in *The Streets of New York*, a modern adaptation of the classic *The Poor of New York*. Have you seen the play, Captain Jones?"

"Yes I have, but it was a long time ago. It does have a good moral to it."

"Yes, even though for a time greed appears to triumph over virtue, good will always trump evil!"

"I wish it was that way in real life,"

"Oh it is, Captain, it is. It may not come about for years or even in this lifetime, but good always trumps evil!" Langrishe said and then changed subjects. "I spy Mr. Merrick sitting in the crowd. He is now standing and beckoning you to join him at his bench, and I have to go on stage and start this real-life performance."

"Thank you, sir. Give Lil my best and tell her I look forward to seeing her performance tonight."

"I will, Captain, I will," Langrishe said and began making his way through the crowd toward the stage.

Jack walked down the aisle several rows until he reached the one where Merrick sat. Merrick had saved a space for Jack between himself and Bullock.

"Glad you finally decided to join us. I was just about ready to give up the place I was saving for you here, but Mr. Bullock was certain you would not miss the festivities," Merrick said as Bullock grinned.

"I thank you both," Jack said as he opened his notebook and found his pencil. He scanned the crowd to see if Laughing Sam Hartman was in the audience, but if he was there, Jack did not spot him. Jack opened his penknife and sharpened the point of his pencil.

Langrishe stood in the middle of the stage. Behind him, Keithley sat at a small table that must have been a stage prop. At stage left, two men sat on stools at another small table, and at stage right sat three men on stools behind a third table.

"Ladies and gentlemen!" Langrishe shouted. The buzz of voices in the theater subsided only slightly. "Ladies and gentlemen!" Langrishe shouted stronger, and the buzz died down.

"Where are the ladies?" a man shouted from the crowd. "I don't see no ladies!"

"From a back row a woman roared, "Come up here and say that, ya bastard!"

Jack turned and saw Calamity Jane standing, hands on hips, glaring at the speaker. On each side of her sat Tid Bit and Kitty Arnold.

"Sorry, Calamity Jane!" the man apologized.

"Well, all right then," she said and sat back down to the laughter and increased buzzing in the theater.

"Ladies and gentlemen!" Langrishe shouted. "Let us proceed with this trial! I have a show to perform tonight, so much as I would like to have this merriment continue, we must begin. And by the way, I suggest you return this evening for a stellar performance of *The Streets of New York*. I promise you will not be disappointed. And now, I think the best way to proceed in our nation's most democratic manner—and since we do not have an established form of government—is to vote. Yes, vote for our temporary representatives to carry out justice on behalf of we, the people. Since this is my establishment, I propose we vote for the officers of the court. Do I hear a motion to that effect from the floor?"

"I make that motion, that we the citizens of Deadwood elect the officers of the court," a voice shouted.

"And for the record, who, sir, makes this motion?" Langrishe asked.

"It is I, Johnny Varnes who makes this motion."

Jack saw that Varnes was sitting several rows from the front at an aisle position.

"Very good, sir!" Langrishe said. "And do I have a second?"

"Second!" shouted a voice from near the front.

"And again for the record, sir, who are you?"

"Swearengen, Al Swearengen."

Jack saw that Swearengen sat at an aisle position directly across from Varnes.

"Very good, sir!" Langrishe said. "Now for the vote! All in favor signify by saying aye."

The crowded theater erupted with shouted ayes.

"And those opposed signify by saying nay."

"Nay!" shouted one lone voice.

"What's wrong with you?" shouted the man's partner, who was sitting next to him.

"Aw, I just didn't want it to be unanimous!" the naysayer explained. The crowd roared in laughter.

"Order! Order!" Langrishe shouted. The crowd noise subsided and Langrishe continued. "Tuesday evening, the evening of the loss of life, W. R. Keithley agreed to act as judge. But to confirm that and give these proceedings legality, we the people need to elect a judge. Is there a motion to nominate W. R. Keithley as judge?"

"I make that motion!" a voice shouted.

"And for the record, sir, your name?"

"Charlie Walker!"

"Very good. And is there a second in the house?" Langrishe asked.

"Seconded by Tom Short!"

"We have a nomination by Mr. Walker and a second by Mr. Short to elect W. R. Keithley as judge. Are there any more nominations in the house?"

Silence.

"Hearing no further nominations, I rule the nominations be closed. All in favor of electing W. R. Keithley judge signify by saying aye!"

"Aye!" roared the crowd.

"Opposed signify by saying nay."

"Nay!" shouted the same man who had shouted nay earlier. His partner hit him with his hat. "What's wrong with you?"

"I still don't mean nothin' by it. Just don't want nothin' being unanimous!"

The crowd roared in laughter. "Order! Order in the court!" Langrishe shouted. He produced a Bible. Keithley rose and stood to the right of Langrishe. Langrishe held out the Bible, Keithley placed his left hand on it, and held up his right. Langrishe did likewise saying, "In the name of the people of this community, the Territory of Dakota, these United States of America, and under the direction of the Lord Almighty, do you, W. R. Keithley, solemnly swear to uphold the laws of the Territory of Dakota and the United States?"

"I do with the help of God."

The crowd roared its approval again as the two men shook hands.

"I turn the rest of these proceeding over to Judge W. R. Keithley!" Langrishe shouted. The crowd clapped and hooted its approval.

"Looks like Old Necessity is judge," Merrick muttered to himself shaking his head.

Jack glanced at him and said, "What are you talking about?"

"I'm talking about Keithley. That's his nickname, Old Necessity. For a lawyer, he is so ignorant of the law. Remember the old saying 'Necessity knows no law?' That's Keithley. He's not well-learned in the technicalities of the law."

"Humph," Jack grunted and turned back to the stage.

"Thank you, John," Keithley said to Langrishe, and then to the crowd he said, "I humbly accept your vote of confidence in me to uphold the rule of law. I will hold court until the case has been tried and then like Cincinnatus, I will withdraw and retire from this judgeship. I have a copy of the laws of Dakota Territory which we will use to guide us through these proceedings."

The crowd murmured its approval. Merrick and Jack began to scribble furiously in their notebooks.

"Mr. Whitehead and Mr. Simington have volunteered to represent the people in the prosecution of this case against Mr. Harry Young. Unless I hear any dissension, in the name of the people, I will accept them as the people's prosecutors."

Jack looked over at the man who had dissented before and found that his friends were restraining him. One had his hand over the man's mouth. Jack smiled, nudged Merrick to look, and continued to write.

"Hearing no dissent, I recognize Mr. Whitehead and Mr. Simington as representing the people. And as for the defense, Mr.

Young has asked for Mr. McCutchen, Mr. Miller, and Colonel May to represent him. And I do so accept their representation."

There was a buzzing murmur of approval through the crowd.

"Now we will begin to impound the jury and begin our selection of its members. Please bring in the defendant."

From stage right Harry Young, hands bound behind him, walked onto the stage. Two heavily armed men guarded him. One of them, carrying a double-barreled shotgun tucked under one arm, was Old George, whom Jack had met yesterday. Old George's eyes scanned the stage, obviously looking for a place to spit excess tobacco juice. He finally saw the sawdust on the floor beyond the stage, and he shot out a stream in its direction, although most of it hit the stage and some stayed in his beard.

"Gentlemen, please unbind the prisoner," Keithley said.

"What?" Old George shouted.

"I said release the prisoner!" Keithley shouted. The other guard had already started untying the rope binding.

"Why didn't you say so!" Old George shouted as the crowd roared in laughter.

"Silence!" Keithley shouted as he reached for a hammer and pounded on a block of wood he had placed on the table. The hall quieted down.

"The defendant may take his seat," Keithley said. Young sat on a stool set aside for him at the defense table.

"The prosecution may present its first potential juror," Keithley said.

"We don't have anyone preselected," Simington said. "We call for volunteers from the spectators."

"So be it," Keithley said. "Do we have anyone who wishes to do their civil duty and volunteer for the jury?" A mass of hands went up from the crowd. Simington and Whitehead scanned the audience. Finally settling on an individual who appeared clean and well dressed, they pointed to him.

"You sir, please come up on the stage. The man walked up on the stage and sat on a waiting stool.

"State your name, sir," Whitehead said.

"It's Tim. Tim Anderson, but my friends just call me Big Tim." Jack wrote in his notebook, Big Tim is rather short.

"Big Tim," Whitehead said. "What do you do in town, sir?"

"I've just arrived in town a few days ago. I sell a variety of medicines that will cure your ills. I've not opened my shop as yet, but I am staying at the Grand Central Hotel, if any of you in the audience are in need. My tonic will cure gout, rheumatism..."

"That will be enough, Mr. Anderson," Whitehead said. "Let me ask this, do you know the defendant sitting to your left?"

"I do not."

"Did you know the deceased? Myer Baum, also known as Bummer Dan?"

"I did not."

"Were you present the night of Mr. Baum's demise?"

"I was not."

"Do you think if the evidence showed Mr. Young did wantonly kill Mr. Baum that you could vote to have him pay the full penalty of the law and have him executed?"

Anderson looked over at Young, who stared back at him. Anderson gulped and said, "Yes."

"I have no further questions," Whitehead said. "We accept Mr. Anderson as a juror."

"Representatives for Mr. Young, what say you?" Keithley asked.

Jack happened to notice Varnes glance over at Swearengen, who looked back at Varnes. Varnes gave a slight negative shake to his head and looked away. Swearengen's eyes quickly returned to the stage. Miller looked toward Swearengen, who gave a slight negative shake to his head. The exchange took only seconds, but Jack had caught it. It appeared no one else in the room had seen it.

"Your Honor," Miller said. "If I might question Mr. Anderson?"

"Proceed, Mr. Miller."

"Mr. Anderson, you say you just now arrived in Deadwood?"

"That's correct, just a few days ago."

"Mr. Anderson, you say you sell medicines that can cure just about any ills known to mankind?"

"I don't claim that they will cure everything, but they will cure a good deal of what ails you."

"I see," Miller said as he stood up and paced back and forth across the stage. "Are you, sir, the same Big Tim Anderson who sold so-called medicine in Sidney, Nebraska, where several people became quite ill?"

"I am not, sir!" Anderson said. "I have never been to Sidney, Nebraska. I came to Deadwood by the Fort Pierre trail."

"Why sir, I've heard of you before and I've heard that your medicine is more akin to poison than to health elixir!" shouted Swearengen from the audience.

"Enough!" Keithley shouted, banging the hammer on the wood block. "There will be no more outbursts from the audience. If so, I will have anyone who does forcefully removed."

Swearengen appeared cowed, saying, "Sorry, your Honor, it won't happen again."

"I ask that Mr. Anderson be dismissed from further questioning and step down," Miller said.

"So be it," Judge Keithley said. "Mr. Miller, it is your turn to present a potential juror."

"We ask for Henry Varnes," Miller said.

"Is Mr. Henry Varnes here?" Keithley asked. "If so, will Mr. Varnes come to the stage?"

Henry Varnes moved through the crowd, walked up onto the stage, and sat on the waiting stool. Jack was startled. He stopped writing. The man was Henry Varnes, the brother of Johnny Varnes, the same Henry Varnes who had almost hanged Harry Young.

"Please state your name for the court," Miller said.

"Henry Varnes."

"And what do you do, Mr. Varnes?"

"You might say I work in the entertainment business, providing amusement and the lure of profit for the hardworking miners and merchants of Deadwood Gulch."

"I see," Miller said. "Do you know the defendant, Mr. Young?"

"I certainly do. Most people who visit Deadwood's watering holes know who Harry Young is."

"Do you believe you could give a fair and impartial verdict on Mr. Young's situation, after listening to all the facts?"

"Yes I could."

"No further questions. We ask your Honor that Mr. Henry Varnes be impaneled as a juror."

"Does the prosecution have any questions it would like to ask?" Keithley said.

"Yes, your Honor," Whitehead said then to Varnes, "Mr. Varnes, if it can be shown by evidence that Mr. Young did indeed kill Mr. Baum, are you prepared to pronounce a guilty verdict of death on this individual?"

Varnes stared at Young and said, "Yes, I can do that."

"No further questions, your Honor. We accept Mr. Varnes as a juror."

"Very well," Judge Keithley said. "Mr. Varnes, do not wander anywhere as we will be needing your services shortly. And now, Mr. Whitehead, please present your next candidate."

Jack was frantically writing and at the same time trying to determine what this latest development implied. *I think the selection of Varnes means the ring is in fact real and that Varnes and friends plan to have Harry executed, no matter what.*

Whitehead had summoned the next potential juror on stage and was questioning him. Jack had not heard his name. He needed to talk to someone, someone he could trust about the criminal ring theory. Merrick was engrossed in the jury selection proceedings. He was mumbling under his breath as he wrote, and Jack heard the word "tedious." That left Bullock. Bullock seemed to be a man of honor, what little Jack knew of him. Had he not been a law officer in Montana? Jack felt the need to see if he could talk to him.

"Seth, I'm stepping outside to stretch my legs," Jack whispered. "I need to talk with you at some point."

"I feel the urge myself and will head out with you," Bullock whispered. "Merrick can fill us in on any details we might miss."

"A. W., Seth and I are stepping out to use the privy. Let us know what happens while we're gone," Jack whispered to Merrick.

"Oh, don't worry," he whispered back. "I'll enlighten you with the latest and newest way to reject a juror."

Jack and Bullock stood and maneuvered through the crowd that was intent on the latest drama unfolding on stage. They passed through the doorway into the bright light of a still partly cloudy day. Stonewall was waiting in the shade for Jack. The men turned the corner of the building and walked to the rear, where the Deadwood Theater's privy stood. Jack used it and then Bullock. They walked toward Whitewood Creek and stopped at an abandoned pit where prospectors had dug through the gravel to the bedrock, removing any gold encountered. No one was nearby.

"Can I speak to you in confidence?" Jack asked.

"You can trust that I won't divulge what you might say, not even to my partner, Sol Star," Bullock said.

"I really don't know you, but I feel I can trust you."

"On my honor, which is the one thing I hold dearest, I will not discuss what you might tell me with anyone."

"I will tell you, but again if word gets out, I am afraid some people may be hurt, even killed."

Bullock stopped walking and turned to Jack, saying, "I'm listening."

"This sounds farfetched as I turn it over in my brain, but I've been trying to figure out these recent killings. Today two people independent of each other warned me about a criminal ring here in Deadwood that has been responsible for several murders and is now in the process of fixing the jury for the Harry Young case." Jack paused.

"Go on," Bullock said. "I'd like to hear more about the facts that brought you to this conclusion."

"Let's start with the murder of Hickok. Both of his friends Colorado Charlie Utter and California Joe Milner believe Jack McCall was a hired assassin, whose mission was to kill Hickok. Some of the town's more respectable element was thinking of hiring Hickok to act as a lawman and clean out the rougher element in town. The criminal ring got wind of it and hired McCall to carry out the assassination. They had a horse ready for him to make his getaway, but he failed to tighten the cinch on the horse's saddle before he shot Wild Bill. When he stepped into the stirrup, the saddle turned on him and he tried to escape on foot, but they caught him. At the trial, the criminal ring arranged for the jury to be bribed or otherwise compromised so that they arrived at a verdict of 'not guilty' when McCall said that Wild Bill had shot his brother, which some people believe never happened."

Jack stopped for a moment, picked up a stick, and tossed it for Stonewall to chase.

"There's the matter of Preacher Smith, which we discussed yesterday. It has a suspicious odor to it," Jack continued. "It just doesn't sound like the work of Indians. Then there is the killing of Bummer Dan. On the surface, it appears to be a case of mistaken identity. Harry Young shoots Bummer Dan by mistake because, of all things, Bummer Dan is wearing Laughing Sam's clothes. Laughing Sam just happens to be in the midst of a feud with Harry Young, both of whom have made statements about killing each other. Why does Bummer Dan have Laughing Sam's clothes on? Is it possible that he was to be a distraction to Harry Young? California Joe told me a rumor that Laughing Sam was seen in

Saloon Number 10 at the same time Bummer Dan walked in wearing Laughing Sam's clothes. Was Laughing Sam going to shoot and kill Harry while he was distracted by Bummer Dan? If so, things went awry when Harry shot first, killing Bummer Dan. Laughing Sam takes off because he does not want to be blamed for this accidental shooting. And by the way, Laughing Sam is still missing. No one has seen him since the shooting."

"That's all very interesting information, but it doesn't prove there is a criminal ring in Deadwood," Bullock said.

"Right, but there are a few more pieces."

"Go on, you've got my interest."

"Bummer Dan had a large nugget that he showed me a couple of hours before he was killed. That nugget is missing. I visited his shanty to find that the shanty had been ransacked and there I found what appeared to be his poke sack. It had been emptied of any gold that it had held except for several fine particles we found after turning the sack inside out."

"You just said 'we.' Who's 'we'?"

"A Cantonese acquaintance who lives near Bummer Dan. Fee Lee Wong is his name."

"Hum," was all Bullock said.

"Finally, I was given a tip by a working girl in town, in fact right in your very store this morning, that certain individuals are setting to fix the jury so the verdict will go in the direction the ring wants it to head. And from what I could see, it appears to me that the ring wants the jury rigged so Harry Young is sentenced to death."

"Now for the question that is just itching to be asked," Bullock said. "Who do you believe are members of this criminal ring?"

"Two names I think are part of this ring are Johnny Varnes and Al Swearengen. I've heard Varnes's name associated with the assassination of Wild Bill and the working girl had overheard Swearengen mention that they needed to fix the jury verdict today by selecting the right jurors. I saw Varnes and Swearengen in action as Big Tim was eliminated from the jury. Varnes signaled Swearengen with a slight negative shake of his head. Swearengen then did the same to Miller, who was watching him. Once Miller knew what the others wanted, he made damn sure Big Tim was excluded."

Stonewall returned with the stick. Jack grabbed it from him and tossed it again.

"Finally," Jack said. "Don't you think it's odd that Henry Varnes, the brother of Johnny Varnes, is selected for the jury?"

"There's nothing suspect in that," Bullock said.

"Only that Henry Varnes was one of the two men who had the noose around Harry Young's neck and was leading him to a tree to be hanged."

"I see," Bullock said, stroking his long mustache in thought.

"That's why I believe if there is a ring, it is setting the stage to have the jury declare Harry Young guilty and then have him executed."

"That's very interesting, but you haven't been able to figure out a motive for why the so-called ring would want to eliminate Harry Young."

"Correct."

"Let's keep our eyes open during the trial and maybe we can discover more to this theory of yours," Bullock said. "I have to say, it does have merit, but I am not one-hundred percent sold on it."

"I have to admit I'm not either," Jack said. "But I am a writer!" They both laughed. Bullock slapped Jack on the back and said, "We best be returning to the theater. By now, hopefully, they have selected the rest of the jury."

They walked back along the side of the theater to Main Street. An enterprising peddler was selling cold beef to the trial spectators who had stepped out of the building for a break and another vender had a cask out of which he was selling beer. Jack and Bullock bought themselves slabs of beef and each downed a beer before returning inside to their seats. Jack leaned over to Merrick and whispered, "What have we missed?"

"You were gone?" Merrick sarcastically answered. "Hardly any progress. They have selected two additional jurors. The defense repeatedly finds reasons for excluding volunteers from the pool. You had better settle in for a long session. I only hope we're done before the Lord's Second Coming!"

Merrick was right. The process was taking too long. Time seemed to slow down. Jack saw that the signals between Varnes, Swearengen, and Miller continued. He nudged Bullock, who took notice. He scanned the crowd again but saw no sign that Laughing Sam had entered. After hours of questioning, the audience was becoming bored. Many had left. Merrick, with elbow propped on one knee and head held in hand, wrote in large capital letters TEDIOUS! Jack smiled at that. By this time, they had selected ten of the twelve jurors. Langrishe appeared on stage.

"Your Honor," he said to Keithley. "Can you please conclude this soon? I need to prepare for this evening's performance."

"Thank you, Mr. Langrishe," Keithley said, and to the lawyers he said, "Gentlemen, you heard Mr. Langrishe here. We need to move this along. I want the jury selected today at the very least and then tomorrow we will hold the actual trial."

"Yes, your Honor," Whitehead said.

"We agree, your Honor, but we are only looking out for the best interest of our client, whose life is at stake here," Miller responded.

"Very well, gentlemen, proceed."

Jack looked at his Elgin pocket watch. The time was five o'clock.

"Do we have another volunteer in the audience?" Whitehead asked the crowd.

"I volunteer," a voice sounding familiar to Jack shouted. The volunteer stood and approached the stage, and Jack saw that it was none other than Texas Jack.

The rowels of Texas Jack's spurs jangled and the jinglebobs chimed as he slowly mounted the steps, crossed the stage, and took his seat.

"Please state your name, sir," Whitehead said.

"Texas Jack."

"Your full name, sir," Judge Keithley interjected.

Texas Jack scowled and said, "Percy Hollingberry."

"Hollingberry?" Whitehead said.

"Hollingberry!" Texas Jack snarled.

"I can see why you go by Texas Jack, Mr. Percy Hollingberry," Simington said. The audience roared in laughter. Texas Jack rested his hands on his pistols. *If eyes could bore holes through bodies*, Jack thought, *Simington would be a dead man.*

"Order in the court," Keithley shouted, pounding his hammer. "There will be no more snide remarks in this courtroom. Is that clear?"

"Yes, your Honor," Simington said to Keithley, and to Texas Jack he said, "I apologize, sir."

Texas Jack did not respond.

"Let us continue," Whitehead said. "Where do you hail from sir?

"West Texas," Texas Jack said.

"Can you be more specific, sir?"

"Eagle Pass, Texas."

"Thank you," Whitehead said. "Do you know the defendant?"

"Yes."

"Did you know the deceased?"

"Yes."

"If called upon after hearing all the evidence and if that evidence clearly shows that Mr. Young did murder Mr. Baum, would you have any reservations rendering a guilty verdict?"

Texas Jack's face broke into a large grin. "No, I would have no reservations. I would be proud to do my civic duty."

Jack leaned over to Bullock and whispered, "Texas Jack was the other person who helped put the noose around Young's neck. I have no doubt he would vote for the death penalty."

"Hum," Bullock grunted.

"I have no further questions, your Honor," Whitehead said. "We approve of Texas Jack to be a member of the jury."

"Mr. Miller, please proceed," Keithley said.

Without looking to Swearengen, Miller said, "We have no objection to this man being seated as a juror."

That clinches it, Jack thought. *They are out to ensure the jury will find Young guilty.*

"You may step down, Mr. Hollingberry," Keithley said. "But do not stray too far, as we will require your services tomorrow." And to Whitehead he said, "Please find another candidate, sir."

"Do we have another volunteer?" Whitehead asked the audience in a loud voice. He scanned the crowd for any hand that might be raised, but there were none. "Well, I suppose I might just pick a volunteer myself," he muttered, more to himself than to the audience. He pointed to the front row. "You, sir! Please come forward! Yes, you."

Jack saw a man stand, and as he stood Jack realized it was Pete.

Pete climbed the steps to the stage and sat on the empty stool.

"State your name, young fellow," Whitehead said.

"Pete. Pete Adams, sir."

"Well, Mr. Adams, do you know the defendant?"

"No, sir."

"Do you know the deceased? Myer Baum, alias Bummer Dan?"

"No, sir."

"How long have you been in Deadwood, son?"

"Since Tuesday evening, sir. I was a bullwhacker on a bull train from Fort Pierre."

"I see, and where are you from, Mr. Adams?"

"A small farm in Iowa."

"Um-hum, all right, Mr. Adams, if it came down to it, and Mr. Young was found guilty of murdering Mr. Baum, could you vote for the death penalty?"

Pete glanced at Young, who stared steely-eyed back at him. "Yes I can, sir," Pete said, as he locked in and matched Young's stare.

"We qualify this man for seating on the jury," Whitehead said.

"Very well, Mr. Whitehead," Keithley said. "Mr. Miller, do you have questions for Mr. Adams?"

Jack was watching Varnes and Swearengen. Varnes gave a brief negative shake of his head, Swearengen gave a similar brief shake of his head, and Miller saw the signal to reject Pete Adams.

"I do have questions for Mr. Adams."

"Proceed, Mr. Miller."

"Mr. Adams, how old are you?"

"I'm twenty-one, sir."

"Thank you. So you are old enough to sit on the jury," Miller said in more of a statement than a question.

"Yes, sir."

"Pete, if I may call you Pete..."

"Yes, sir."

"Pete, you know this man's life is in the balance. Do you think you could make a decision that may end this man's life and then live with that decision? A decision that may affect you for the rest of your life?"

"Yes sir, I am prepared."

Miller slowly shook his head negatively from side to side. "Pete. Pete, I wish you would reconsider. I wish you would voluntarily step down for your own good."

"Sir, I am ready to do my duty."

"Judge Keithley, I request that you dismiss Pete Adams. Even though he is of age, I believe he is not wise in the ways of the world and would not make an informed decision."

Keithley looked at his pocket watch and frowned. "Mr. Miller, you have asked for the dismissal of many well-qualified candidates this afternoon, and the court has graciously complied with all your requests. It is late in the day, and the theater must be prepared for this evening's performance. I see absolutely nothing wrong with this young man. Therefore, I overrule your request. Mr. Pete Adams will be seated as the twelfth juror."

"But, your Honor..." Miller began.

"It is over, Mr. Miller," Keithley said.

"Hallelujah," Merrick muttered.

"Jurors, attorneys, and people," Keithley announced. "This court will reconvene tomorrow morning, nine a.m. sharp. Do not be late. Court is adjourned!" And with that, he brought the hammer down hard on the slab of wood, cracking it. The theater erupted into a cacophony of conversations.

"I need to return to my shop!" Merrick said as he stood to leave. "I've wasted too much of my time here today. Good day, messieurs!"

Jack turned to Bullock. "Well, what do you think?" he asked.

"You may be on to something here," Bullock said. "There were clearly signals between Varnes, Swearengen, and Miller."

"I fear, whether right or wrong, they have unduly stacked the jury so that the verdict will be against Young and he will pay the ultimate penalty for it."

"We will have to wait and see how this plays out," Bullock said.

"Should we go to Keithley and let him know of our concerns?" Jack asked.

Bullock thought for a moment. "I don't know him. Do you?"

"No, I don't."

"What's our proof? That we thought we saw signals between two men in the audience and one of the attorneys for the defendant. That we think at least one of the attorneys for the defendant wants to see Young lose and then swing for it. Does that sound logical or a little farfetched?"

"I agree it sounds farfetched, but I think it's worth a try."

"All right, let's see if we can talk to him alone for a few moments."

"Good."

Bullock and Jack made their way against the flow of the crowd and then climbed the steps onto the stage. Keithley and Langrishe were finishing discussing the setup for the next day's court proceedings. They shook hands and Langrishe walked away.

"Judge Keithley," Bullock spoke, "may we have a moment of your time, please?"

Keithley looked at the two men and said, "Yes, briefly. We need to clear out of the theater."

"Judge, my name is Seth Bullock of Star and Bullock and late of Montana, where I was a lawman," Bullock said, shaking Keithley's hand.

"And I am Jack Jones, reporter for the *Chicago Inter-Ocean*," Jack said.

"Nice to meet both you gentlemen," Keithley said.

Bullock looked around to ensure no one was close enough to overhear. "Sir, to cut to the heart of the situation," Bullock began. "Mr. Jones and I have reason to suspect there may be collusion to rig the jury so that there is a verdict of guilty, with the death sentence then being pronounced for Mr. Young."

"So you think the prosecutors have somehow weighted the jury in their favor, even though the defense were the ones who kept throwing out the potential jurors?"

"Not the prosecution," Jack said. "The defense."

"The defense? That's absurd, gentlemen."

"Hear us out, sir," Bullock said.

"All right, but you must make it quick."

"Mr. Jones and I saw Johnny Varnes and Al Swearengen passing signals to Mr. Miller to reject certain potential jurors. Also, we think it is very strange that two jurors, Henry Varnes and Texas Jack, were the very men who placed the hangman's noose around Young's neck. The defense had no opposition whatsoever to those two men. We think the signals to Miller and the placement of Henry Varnes and Texas Jack indicate that the defense is going to allow Young to be convicted of murder and hanged."

Keithley stared at the stage floorboards, stroking his salt and pepper beard. "That may be, gentlemen, but we are too far along in the process to do anything about it. I will be on my guard to watch for any indication the defense, or for that matter, the prosecution may be doing something to rig the court proceedings or the jury's verdict. I thank you, gentlemen. Now we must be gone. I see Mr. Langrishe approaching, and I know he is going to shoo us out of here. Again, I thank you for your vigilance and concern."

With that, Keithley left the stage, followed by Bullock and Jack. As they reached the rear of the building, Jack noticed Texas Jack sitting on a bench in the shadows. How much, if anything, had he heard of their conversation? Texas Jack was using his Bowie knife to whittle away at the back of the bench in front of him. He smirked and tipped his hat to Jack and Bullock as they passed. When they reached the street, they stopped at a position where there were few people.

"What do you think?" Jack asked.

"I think the judge probably believes something is unusual but he wants the case to proceed. Think about it, the evidence is fairly flimsy. He would have to use our testimony that we saw collusion and he would also have to throw out two jurors who the defense had already accepted. I don't think he will do anything, but I believe he will keep a close eye on things."

"You're probably right," Jack said. "I suppose we'll have to wait and see how it turns out tomorrow."

Two horseback riders trotted down Main Street—Poncho and Carlos again. They reined in their horses in the middle of the street, pulled their pistols from their holsters, and each shot once straight up into the sky. "Citizens of Deadwood!" Poncho shouted. "Carlos and me, we thank you again for your generosity in giving us fifty more dollars in gold dust for another poor Indian who lost his head! Ha! Ha!" Carlos held up their possible bag and shook it. The two Mexicans spurred their horses, continuing north at a fast trot, firing their pistols into the sky and laughing. Bullock was shaking his head. "It's a damn shame the merchants are paying for these killings, it only leads to more problems," he said. "I must get back to the store and help out old Sol. He's probably run ragged by now."

"And I need to visit Fee Lee Wong. He has invited me for tea this afternoon."

They shook hands and parted, Bullock heading north on Main Street and Jack south.

CHAPTER NINE
ɛɔɔ

Thursday Late Afternoon, August 24, 1876—Jack continued to dwell on what had taken place that afternoon. Stonewall trotted behind him as he crossed over the Lee Street Bridge and into the camps. Jack paid little attention to his surroundings, as he was deep in thought. He was startled out of his musings when someone set off several strings of firecrackers, sounding like the massed, rapid-fire musketry he had experienced during the war. Jack arrived at Fee Lee Wong's simple but neat dwelling and shouted "Halloo, anyone home?"

"Yes!" Wong's voice rang out from within. "Is that you, Jack?"

"It is, Fee Lee."

Wong emerged from the house and bowed to Jack, which Jack attempted to copy. Wong laughed and held out his hand to shake.

"Please enter my humble abode," Wong said. Jack, followed by Stonewall, entered the home.

"Have a seat." Wong pointed to where Jack had sat yesterday. Wong went through the same ritual of pouring tea for both of them and then sat down to join Jack.

"Have you learned anything new about the murder of Bummer Dan?" Wong asked.

"No, not much more than yesterday," Jack said. "Have you seen Laughing Sam Hartman?"

"No one in camp has seen him. It looks like he has not returned to his home."

They both sipped and enjoyed the tea in silence.

"Fee Lee, have you ever heard of a ring in Deadwood?"

"A ring? I am not sure what you mean by ring?"

"A group of organized criminals who may do some legitimate business but may also be involved in criminal activities."

"Oh, that would be similar to our tongs. Chinese formed these organizations when they came to America. Tongs help the individual Chinese become more familiar with America and help him stay in touch with his family back home. The tongs will ensure that if the man dies, his body is returned to China for burial, but some tongs are involved in the opium trade, attempting to enslave the minds and souls of our people. Some tongs control prostitution and practice extortion and murder. So yes, I am familiar with criminal rings."

"I believe there may be a criminal ring in Deadwood," Jack said.

"Why do you believe this?" Wong asked.

"There have been a series of murders that may be connected. I learned from two different sources who believe that Jack McCall was paid to kill Wild Bill Hickok. Indians may not have killed Preacher Smith, but white men may have killed him for his gold and made it look like Indians did it. Then there is the murder of Bummer Dan. I'm not sure his murder is tied to the ring, but maybe the removal of the gold from his shanty might somehow be connected to it. Finally, I sat in on the jury selection for the trial of Harry Young, and it appeared that some of the men who might be in this criminal ring were trying to rig the jury selection so Young is convicted of murder and then hanged."

"Who are these men?" Wong asked.

"Al Swearengen, owner of the Cricket Saloon, and Johnny Varnes, a professional gambler."

"I see," Wong said, then thoughtfully sipped his tea. "I do not know these men, but I will ask friends and see if they know anything about them."

"Thanks, Fee Lee," Jack said. "Let's change subjects. Tell me about your family. Are you married?"

"Ah, not yet, but here is my plan. I am betrothed to a beautiful girl back in Guangdong. When I have made enough money to begin an emporium, I will marry her and bring her back here."

"That is commendable. I wish you luck, my friend."

"And what of you, Jack?"

"I was married to the love of my life. She died in childbirth. I have a daughter, who my sister is raising as her own. My daughter knows me only as her uncle."

"I see. Will you tell her someday who you are?"

"I don't know," Jack said as he stared at his teacup. "But there is now new joy in my life. I have met someone who has rekindled love in my heart."

"Ah, tell me about her."

"Her name is Lillian Rochelle. She is an actress at the Deadwood Theater. We have expressed our love for each other. I'll have to see where this leads."

"I am very happy for you, my friend."

"I hate to leave you, but I must return to Main Street to prepare to attend the show at the theater tonight. I missed it last night and disappointed Lil by not showing up."

"Let me not detain you. If you have time tomorrow, stop by again. We can further discuss rings and tongs."

"I'll do that, Fee Lee. Thank you for your hospitality."

They bowed to each other and Jack, followed by Stonewall, retraced his steps through the camps. The sky was cloudy, casting a gloom over the landscape. A single rifle shot rang out from the slopes of Hebrew Hill. No other shots followed. *Someone must have been shooting at a critter for tonight's supper or maybe shooting at a varmint*, Jack thought.

Jack crossed the bridge over Whitewood Creek and entered the Grand Central Hotel. No one was present behind the counter. The regulator clock showed the time to be seven p.m. Jack walked into the dining room, and the fragrance of this evening's meal made him realize just how hungry he was.

"There you are, Captain Jones!" Lou scolded. "You have been keeping irregular hours," she said, leading him to an empty table and bringing out his writing paraphernalia.

"Come along, Stonewall," she said. "Let me see what I can find for you in the kitchen."

Lou returned with a plate of steaming ham, potatoes, and cornbread. Jack wolfed down the food. Lou saw how quickly he had eaten and brought him a second helping. One of Lou's helpers cleared his empty plate and Jack began writing as he sipped his coffee. Most of the diners had finished their meals and were leaving as he finished his notes for the day. Jack saw Lou emerge from the kitchen.

"Aunt Lou, do you have a few spare minutes to talk?" Jack asked.

"Not really, but I'll make an exception," she said and sat down.

"This has been a long day. It started out eventful for you, didn't it, with those crazy Mexicans."

"I have never in my life, ever had something remotely akin to that happen to me and in a regular folks' dining room! Those boys must have had some bad liquor to make them behave as savages."

"You were certainly brave to chase them out of here the way you did."

"That wasn't bravery—that was pure excitability. After I chased them out, I started to shake like a leaf."

Jack looked around to see if anyone was sitting close enough to overhear their conversation and saw that there was no one. He lowered his voice as he said, "Can I ask you a few questions that might be considered dangerous?"

"Go ahead, Captain, I'm not afraid to discuss whatever it is you are about to say."

"Very well, I have a theory that there is a criminal ring here in Deadwood that had Wild Bill assassinated, killed Preacher Smith for his collection, and possibly had Bummer Dan murdered, or if not murdered, made sure they stole his gold."

"Why do you say that?"

"Two people told me they think Wild Bill was assassinated. Preacher Smith was shot but not mutilated, and Bummer Dan had gold on his person and in his shanty that is now missing."

"That all may be true, but how do you know there is actually a criminal ring behind all this?"

"I had one person tell me it was so, and today I saw two people who I think may be members of this ring in action at the jury selection. I believe they have rigged the jury so Harry Young will be convicted of murder and hang."

"But again, it might be all the actions of individuals and not an organization of criminals."

"That's true. So I take it you have never heard of a criminal ring in town?"

Lou leaned forward and whispered, "I didn't say there was no such thing in town. I'm only saying it would be hard for you to prove it. Even if you did prove it, what good would it do you? It would only get you crosswise with the bad element in town and who knows what they would try to do to you and any of your friends? After all, there is no one in town to protect you from them. There are no police."

"Well, right you are again," Jack said. "I'll be more discreet."

"I better get back to work," Lou said and stood. "Please be careful."

"Thank you, Aunt Lou, I'll try."

Jack stood and walked out of the dining room. He washed up and then changed into clean clothes. *I had better not be late this time,* he mused.

Walking past the hotel's regulator clock, Jack noted that the time was 8:45 pm. He checked his Elgin pocket watch, which indicated the same time. Lou had agreed to take care of Stonewall for the evening, which was just fine with the hound.

As Jack stepped out into Main Street he decided he had time to check with Dirty Em and see if she had learned anything new since the afternoon. The night was darker than normal, and the stars were not visible. A cool breeze blew down from higher elevations. Men crowded the street, picking their way around the stumps and rocks. Lights flared in front of saloons, enticing men as moths to flames.

Jack reached the Cricket Saloon and walked into its well-lit interior. A banjo plucker was playing a rousing rendition of "Kingdom Coming." Shouts and raucous laughter came from groups of liquored-up men. A few sporting girls laughed with them.

Jack spied Madame Mustache running a faro spread near the front of the building. A sizable crowd gathered round her table, laying down bets. She was busy, and Jack thought not to disturb her, so he began to walk by. But Madame Mustache saw him and shouted above the loud-talking punters and the side-bet takers, "Captain Jones! Captain Jones! If you are looking for Dirty Em, she is running her faro game at the back of the saloon!"

"Thank you, Madame Mustache!" Jack said, tipping his hat. He slowly made his way through the crowded saloon. He had to squeeze through and excuse himself several times until he found Dirty Em at her faro layout. She had left several buttons of her burgundy-colored bodice unbuttoned at the top. She appeared radiant as she controlled a crowd of mesmerized men.

Excited punters were making their bets, and men behind them were making their side bets. Jack saw it was coming down to the end of the hand. The case keeper sitting opposite Dirty Em held the abacus-like case showing that Dirty Em had played most of the cards in the deck. Looking up, Dirty Em spied Jack.

"Care to buck the tiger, Captain Jones?" Dirty Em said, raising an eyebrow and flashing a smile.

"Yes, Ma'am."

"One dollar for a check," Dirty Em responded. Jack handed her a ten-dollar gold piece and she handed him ten ivory checks.

"Place your bets, gentlemen," she announced. Jack looked at the complete suite of Spades pasted and lacquered on the layout table. He placed five of his checks on the Jack of Spades as the other punters let their checks ride on the layout cards or changed to new ones.

"Anyone care to copper the bet?" Dirty Em said as she held up an Indian-head penny.

"I will," said one of the punters. "I'll bet to lose!" She handed him the penny and he placed it on top of his ivory checks.

"Betting is now over, gentlemen!" Dirty Em announced.

She pressed the dealing box and out sprang the top card, the dealer's card. It was a Ten of Hearts. Any player who had a check on the dealer's card in the layout would lose. She pressed the box again and out sprang the player's card. It was a Three of Diamonds. Any player who had a check on the player's card in the layout would win. One of the punters had two checks on the Ten and Dirty Em swept them to her. No one had a check on the Three.

"Place your bets, gentlemen," Dirty Em announced again. Jack decided to let his ride on the Jack of Spades. The other punters made their bets.

"Betting is over, gentlemen," Dirty Em announced as again she pressed the box. The dealer's card was an Ace of Hearts, and the player's card was the Jack of Diamonds. She swept the checks from the Ace and doubled Jack's pile. "Captain Lucky-Jack Jones!" she said.

"Dirty Em, we are down to the last three cards," the case keeper announced, showing the case to the punters. "The cards are Queen of Diamonds, Five of Clubs, and Nine of Hearts."

"Thank you, sir," she said. "Gentlemen, as you know, with the last three cards I can call the turn, which I do so now. Place your bets, and if you call the turn correctly by calling the correct sequence of the cards, you can win four to one." Several punters called the turn and placed their bets, including Jack who said

"Queen, Five, Nine." Dirty Em hit the box and out came in sequence Nine, Five, Queen. No one had the correct sequence, and she raked in the checks from the layout.

"Thank you, boys!" she said. "I need to take a little break. We'll reconvene this faro game in fifteen minutes."

The men on stools pushed back from the table and stood. Some headed to the bar to refill their cups and glasses. The banjo plucker began playing "The Girl I Left Behind Me," and a prospector brought out his bones to keep time.

"Captain Jones," Dirty Em said, "Will you escort a lady outback to the privy?"

"I would be honored, Ma'am," Jack said. He held out his arm and she took it. He had to part the sea of men as she followed behind in his wake. At times, he felt her body press up against his. They reached the saloon's backdoor and stepped out in the cool of the night. The privy was several paces beyond the rear of the building.

"How chivalrous of you, Captain, to escort me to the necessary house," Dirty Em said loudly, then in a low voice that was almost a whisper, she continued, "I'll tell you quickly, Al returned to the Cricket after the jury selection. I overheard him telling Johnny Burns that he and Johnny Varnes were pleased with the jury selection. They were happy that brother Henry and Texas Jack were on the jury and that they could count on most of the other jurors voting their way. The only juror they are worried about was some kid new to town. They have no idea which way he will vote. That's all I know. I couldn't overhear anymore."

"Thank you, Em," Jack whispered.

"And now, Captain," she said in a loud voice. "If you would be so kind as to wait for me, I will be only a few minutes."

She took a small lantern hanging by the privy and entered, closing the door behind her.

A few other men joined Jack as they waited in line for Dirty Em to emerge from the privy. He had time to think.

Jack saw that Swearengen and Varnes were happy that Henry and Texas Jack are on the jury. They seemed satisfied with all the other members of the jury except for the new kid, which had to be Pete. They were looking to convicting Harry Young for murder, but why? *Why would they need to have him found guilty?*

The privy door opened and Dirty Em handed the lantern to the first man in line. She took Jack's arm.

"Captain Jones, may I speak to you in private for a moment?"

"Certainly, Em."

They walked away from the men and the lantern light. Dirty Em swiveled, facing Jack. She circled her arms around his shoulders. She leaned into him softly pressing her body against his. Her eyelids half closed as she seemed to study his mouth. Her perfume mixing with her perspiration created a scent, a desire, overwhelming Jack's senses. His arms circled her slim waist, drawing her even closer. He felt her body yield to his. "Captain Jones, thank you," she whispered. Her body pressed hard against his. Her breath was sweet as her lips brushed his. She then pressed them gently to his. He responded harder. She opened her mouth. He was losing control. He wanted her.

"I'm yours tonight," she murmured.

He stopped himself. He backed away and gently held her at arms' length.

"Thank you, Em. Thank you. But I'm in love for the first time in a very long time, I'm in love and I'm going to be true to her. But I sincerely thank you."

"You are an honorable man, Captain Jones. She's a fortunate woman," Dirty Em said, then smiled.

He escorted her back into the Cricket Saloon. The constant roar of men's voices filled the barroom. The banjo plucker had moved on to the next piece, "Lost Indian," the bones adding to the tune.

They reached the faro table. Dirty Em turned and kissed Jack on the cheek.

"Thank you, Captain." she said, flashing him her smile.

"Good evening, Em, and thank you—for everything." Jack smiled and tipped his hat.

The banjo plucker finished "Lost Indian." Over the roar of the crowd, someone shouted to the banjo plucker "Why don't you play a piece for the old Confederacy! Most of what you've been playin' tonight have been Yankee tunes."

"Play Dixie!" another man shouted. The banjo plucker thought a moment and shouted, "Here's a little song for all you Southern boys!" This announcement generated rebel yells and applause. The banjo plucker started with a fast little picking introduction and then broke into the Union anthem of "Marching Through Georgia." Some of the Unionists in the crowd who could sing—and many who could not—joined in shouting the words as the banjo plucker shouted out:

Ring the good ol' bugle, boys, we'll sing another song,
Sing it with the spirit that will start the world along,
Sing it as we used to sing it 50,000 strong
While we were marching through Georgia.
Hurrah, hurrah, we bring the jubilee!
Hurrah, hurrah, the flag that makes you free!
So we sang the chorus from Atlanta to the sea
While we were marching through Georgia!

The banjo plucker didn't make it to the next verse. A Southerner punched him in the mouth as another grabbed his banjo and smashed it on the stage. A Unionist grabbed the banjo-smasher and threw him to the floor. Fists started flying right and left. Some of the bystanders jumped into the fight and started swinging, not knowing if they were hitting friend or foe. Some entered the fight not caring who they hit. They just wanted to hit someone.

Jack hung back. It seemed to him a stupid reason for fighting. He looked for Swearengen but did not see him in the crowd. However, his henchman, Johnny Burns, weighed into the melee, knocking heads together and shouting "Enough! Stop this! Drinks half price if you stop this now!" After five minutes of punching and wrestling, the men participating in the fight wore themselves down to the point where they wanted to get back to drinking and gambling. The fight fizzled out and the men drifted back to what they had been doing before, all, that is, except for the banjo plucker, who stood at the bar consoling himself over the loss of his banjo with a large glass of whiskey.

Jack walked out of the Cricket and into Main Street. The wind was coming up and felt cooler. He crossed over to Saloon Number 10 and entered.

Anson Tipple was one of the two bartenders working the bar. Tipple saw Jack and reached under the counter for Jack's bottle, which he handed him along with a glass.

"Anything of interest happen since I last visited?' Jack asked as he poured himself a drink.

"Nothing newsworthy," Tipple replied. Jack scanned the room but did not see Johnny Varnes.

"Where's Johnny Varnes?"

"Haven't seen him since you talked with him this morning."

"Humph, that's unusual."

Tipple shrugged his shoulders and moved on to the next customer. Jack checked his Elgin pocket watch and found the time to be 10:30 pm. He downed the Old Crow and handed the bottle back to Tipple.

Jack left the saloon and walked quickly up Main Street. He saw there was no longer a line in front of the Deadwood Theater. The same old curmudgeon stood at the door.

"You again!" the ticket taker said. "Jones, right?"

"Yes," Jack said. The roar of laughter from inside interrupted them.

"You need to be more punctual, sir," the man growled. "But Mr. Langrishe gave me strict instructions I was to let you in no matter how late you arrived. Enjoy the show, but don't disturb those guests who know how to get here on time!"

With that admonition, the man stepped out of the way and let Jack enter. He heard the muffled voice of a speaker on stage and again the crowd roared in laugher. As he entered the main hall, he saw it was a packed house. John Langrishe stood on stage entertaining the audience. Jack spied an empty place on a bench in the last row and had to cross in front of several people to reach it. As Jack sat between two men he did not know, Langrishe continued with his comedy act.

He was wearing a long frock coat and a tall stovepipe hat that accentuated his length. His nose looked longer than it should be, and then Jack realized that Langrishe wore a false, elongated nose. Langrishe's facial expressions were so exaggerated and comical that Jack could see them clearly, even from the back of the hall. Jack settled in and listened to Langrishe's performance.

"I told my wife, let's be happy, and live within our means," Langrishe said. "Even if we have to borrow the money to do it." The crowd howled with laughter. He waited until the volume died down then said, "Ladies and gentlemen, let me introduce you to my beautiful wife, Mrs. John Langrishe!" Mrs. Langrishe walked on stage. She was a stunning redhead and was dressed in a green, sleeveless, low-cut dress, most likely one of the latest New York fashions. The audience erupted in applause as she curtseyed to them.

Ladies? Jack thought. He looked around the theater and there in one of the middle rows sat Calamity Jane, Kitty Arnold, and Tid Bit. A few rows back sat Mr. and Mrs. Al Swearengen. Jack looked in the other direction and saw no women, but he did see Johnny and Henry Varnes sitting side by side. He concluded that that was why he had not seen either Swearengen or Varnes. They had decided to experience some wholesome entertainment for a change.

When the applause died down Langrishe asked his Mrs. a question. "My dear, why is a dog like a tree?"

"I don't know, sir," she answered. "Why is a dog like a tree?"

"Because they both lose their bark once they're dead!" he responded. The audience groaned.

"What kind of customers do pawnbrokers prefer?" Langrishe asked.

"I don't know. What kind of customers do pawnbrokers prefer?"

"Pawnbrokers prefer customers without any redeeming qualities." The audience laughed and groaned.

"You loved me before we were married!" Mrs. Langrishe said.

"Well, now it's your turn!" Langrishe replied. The crowd roared.

"I'm a millionaire," Langrishe said. "Haven't I got money enough for both of us?"

"Yes," Mrs. Langrishe responded. "If you are moderate in your tastes." The audience again laughed.

"Give Mrs. Langrishe a hand again, ladies and gentlemen!" Langrishe shouted over their applause, as she curtsied and left the stage.

"And now, ladies and gentlemen, while we prepare for tonight's performance of that classic drama, *The Streets of New York*, enjoy Banjo Dick Brown and his fellow musicians in their rendition of 'New York Girls!'" Banjo Dick, followed by his fellow banjo player, and the fiddler Lil called Professor, walked on stage with their instruments and sat on stools that were waiting for them. The Professor ran his bow over the fiddle's catgut strings and the banjos joined in as both the banjo players sang:

As I walked down the Broadway
One evening in July
I met a maid who asked me trade

And a sailor John says I.
And away, you Santee
My Dear Annie
Oh, you New York girls
Can't you dance the polka?

As they continued on to sing of the sailor who is drugged and waylaid by the maid and her mother and left with not even a stitch of clothing, Jack's thoughts were of Lil and how happy he had been with her the last twenty-four hours. Just to be in her presence made him feel complete, made him feel happy. He could not wait to see her on stage and then spend time with her after the show. The performers were on the last verse when Jack broke away from his thoughts.

I joined a Yankee blood-boat
And sailed away next morn
Don't ever fool around with gals
You're safer off Cape Horn
And away, you Santee
My Dear Annie
Oh, you New York girls
Can't you dance the polka?

The crowd applauded. The musicians stood, bowed, and filed off stage. The crowd grew quiet. A strong gust of wind shook the canvas roof. The booms of distant thunder foretold the possibility of rain. The theater's canvas roof was notorious for its leaks during rainstorms.

An actor Jack did not know walked on stage. "Good evening, ladies and gentlemen, tonight Langrishe's Theater Troupe brings you *The Streets of New York* a remake of Dion Boucicault's classic *The Poor of New York* a drama in five acts. Act 1 takes place during the Panic of 1837, and then Act 2 and the rest of the acts take place during the Panic of 1857. Scene 1 begins in the private office of Gideon Bloodgood's banking house in New York. And now let us transport you to *The Streets of New York!*" The actor walked off the stage to the applause of the audience.

The curtain opened. Another actor Jack did not know was playing Gideon Bloodgood. He sat behind a roughly cobbled-together desk, reading some papers. Edwards, a bank officer, entered with a sheet of paper.

"The stock list, sir," Edwards said.

"Let me see it," Bloodgood said. "Tell the cashier to close the bank on the stroke of three, and dismiss the clerks." Edwards left the stage as Bloodgood read the sheet of paper.

"So—as I expected," Bloodgood soliloquized. "Every stock is down further still, and my last effort to retrieve my fortune has plunged me into utter ruin!" He crushed the paper and threw it on the floor. "Tomorrow, my drafts to the amount of eighty thousand dollars will be protested. Tomorrow yonder street, now so still, will be filled with a howling multitude, for the house of Bloodgood the Banker will fall, and in its fall will crush hundreds, thousands, who have their fortunes laid up here."

Jack had seen the play before and knew the story well. Fairweather, an old sea captain, arrives to deposit his lifesavings, one-hundred thousand dollars. This saves the day for Bloodgood. Fairweather learns within minutes of giving Bloodgood his money that Bloodgood is insolvent and is about to flee the country. Fairweather tries to recover his money from Bloodgood, but Bloodgood will not give it back. Fairweather has a heart attack and dies. Bloodgood, with the help of Badger, played by Langrishe, keeps Fairweather's money for his own. He tells Badger to destroy Fairweather's receipt, but Badger saves it in case he might need it in the future. Then Badger leaves New York.

Twenty years later, it is the Panic of 1857. Fairweather's wife and daughter are destitute, while Bloodgood and his family live the life of luxury. Mrs. Langrishe was playing the part of the widow Mrs. Fairweather and Lil was playing the part of Lucy, Mrs. Fairweather's daughter. Mrs. Langrishe made her first appearance in Act II, Scene 1. Jack had to wait for quite awhile until Lil would be on stage.

The wind whipped the canvas and the thunder sounded closer. Finally, Lil appeared on stage in Act II, Scene 3. Mrs. Fairweather was arranging dinner on a table in a poor, but neat, rented apartment. Lil as Lucy entered. Jack felt his heart race when he saw her. He hoped she would look in his direction and see him, but she was intent on the acting.

"My dear mother," Lucy said.

"My darling Lucy," Mrs. Fairweather said. "Ah, your eye is bright again. The thought of seeing Mark Livingstone has revived your smile."

A crash of thunder and the flash of lightning illumined the canvas roof for a brief second. The slow splat of raindrops on canvas began.

"I have seen him," Lucy said. "He and Paul called at Madame Victorine's."

"Is your work over, Lucy, already?"

The raindrops were hitting the canvas harder.

"What we expected has arrived, mother. This dress is the last I shall receive from Madame Victorine—she is discharging her hands."

The downpour hit the canvas and streams of water hit members of the audience. The actors had to shout above the torrent.

"More misfortunes—and Paul has not been able to obtain employment," Mrs. Fairweather shouted.

The deluge did not last long and settled down into a slow steady rain. Most of the cast and audience were wet, but they did not care. The show must go on.

The situation was bad for the Fairweathers, as Bloodgood made life even more miserable for them. Lil never did look in Jack's direction. *It is almost as if Lil does not want to look at me,* Jack thought.

The story deteriorates for the Fairweathers. They are destitute, with no income and nothing to eat. Mrs. Fairweather and Lucy decide to commit suicide from asphyxiation by gas fumes in their apartment, but at the last minute Mark Livingstone and Lucy's brother, Paul, break into the apartment and begin to save them from their fate.

"Too late!" Paul said. "Too late! They have committed suicide!"

"They live still!" Mark Livingstone said. "Quick, bear them outside into the air."

They pick up the two women to carry them out.

A loud hock and splat of spewing tobacco juice broke the silence of the audience.

"Oh hell!" Calamity Jane shouted. "That's a put-up job!"

The audience was stunned, and then a few people started to laugh. It was contagious, and soon the whole theater was laughing, even the actors. The actors regained their composure, the audience settled down, and the play proceeded.

The rain had died down, but the edges of the canvas still dripped onto the muddy ground and onto the backs of the patrons. It was toward the end of the play. Badger had returned from his self-imposed exile from New York. He presented the receipt showing that Bloodgood had indeed absconded with Captain Fairweather's money. The fortune was then restored to the Fairweather family. Lucy and her lover, Mark Livingstone, were reunited, and Bloodgood was led away to jail. In the final scene, the entire cast was on stage. Lil looked radiant.

"And now Lucy, I claim your hand," Livingstone said. "All is ready for the ceremony."

Two gunshots rang out outside the theater. The shots sounded like they had come from behind the theater. *Must be someone celebrating*, Jack thought. The audience must have thought the same as Jack. No one left to investigate.

"You have seen the dark side of life," Badger said. "You can appreciate your fortune, for you have learned the value of wealth."

"No," Mrs. Fairweather said. "We have learned the value of poverty. It opens the heart."

Paul Fairweather, the son, turned to the audience and said "Is this true? Have the sufferings we have depicted in this mimic scene touched your hearts, and caused a tear of sympathy to fill your eyes? If so, extend us your hands."

"No, not to us," Mrs. Fairweather said. "But when you leave this place, as you return to your homes, should you see some poor creatures, extend your hands to them, and the blessings that will follow you on your way will be the most grateful tribute you can pay to the Poor of New York—or in our case, the Poor of Deadwood!"

The crowd stood and applauded while the actors bowed and curtsied. Jack waved to get Lil's attention, but she did not look in his direction. He made his way toward the stage against the flood of humanity leaving the theater. As Jack came near the stage, he saw Lil turn her back, heading for the dressing rooms. "Lil!" he shouted as he mounted the stage. "Lil!" She had to have heard him, but she continued to walk away from him. As Jack started to pursue her, John Langrishe stepped in front of him.

"Captain Jones," Langrishe said. "May I have a word with you, sir?"

"Yes," Jack said, looking beyond Langrishe as Lil disappeared into a dressing room. Langrishe grabbed Jack's arm and led him to the side of the stage.

"Captain Jones, I must tell you that my niece is very distraught with you."

"What!" Jack said in surprise. "I don't understand."

"It seems that word has gotten back to my niece about your liaisons today at Star and Bullocks and in the Cricket Saloon with the harlot, Dirty Em. Lil is very upset. And can you blame her? Here the man she loves is propositioning a courtesan and is seen cavorting with her, even up to right before our show this evening."

Jack was stunned and felt that a mule had kicked him in the gut. "I-I don't know what to say!"

"I think you need to contemplate your actions and what consequences they have led to. I don't believe Lil wishes to see you again, and I can't say that I desire to spend any more time with you. Good night, sir."

"Wait!" Jack said, grasping Langrishe's elbow. "Hear me out, sir, please!"

Langrishe stopped and turned, saying, "Very well, what have you to say for yourself?"

"Has Lil told you at all about my theories as to the murders of Wild Bill, Preacher Smith, and now Bummer Dan?"

"No, I don't see what this has to do with your dealings with Dirty Em."

"It has all the world to do with them."

"I don't understand, but go ahead. I'm listening."

Jack looked around to see if there was anyone close by who could overhear what he had to say. Seeing no one close, Jack said, "I believe there is a criminal ring in town that has murdered several individuals to steal their money and gold. In order to gather more information I have been working with Dirty Em, who has been giving me vital information on my theory. These people have killed before and there is no reason why they would not kill again. In order to protect Dirty Em, we pretended in Star and Bullock's that I had propositioned her, so she could pass information to me. At the Cricket Saloon, I escorted her to the privy so she could safely pass on more information to me. That is all that was going on."

Langrishe had a thoughtful look on his face, then blew out some air from his mouth, and said, "Hell is empty and all the devils are here."

"What?" Jack said.

"Oh, that's Shakespeare from *The Tempest*, Act 1, Scene 2."

"Will you pass my explanation on to Lil for me, please? Let her know there was nothing to my communications with Dirty Em. I was only getting information from her and trying to protect her at the same time. I love your niece, sir, and would do anything for her. I would never do anything to dishonor her."

"Captain Jones, I believe you." Langrishe reached out and took Jack's hand. "I will tell Lil what you have told me and I hope she will understand and forgive you."

"Thank you, sir," Jack said. "I greatly appreciate this."

"See me tomorrow and I will let you know her reaction."

They shook hands and Jack left the stage. The audience had cleared out of the theater except for several small groups still discussing the night's performance.

Jack walked to the back of the theater and out the door onto Main Street. The air was cool and invigorating from the recent storm, but instead of enjoying it, he was miserable and dejected. How could he have been so stupid as to give observers the impression he was attempting to buy the favors of Dirty Em? He realized that he loved Lil so much that to lose her would crush any remaining joy he had.

"Hey! Over here!" a man shouted. "Help!" The voice seemed to be coming from back behind the Deadwood Theater. Jack and several other men ran in the direction of the voice. They saw a man holding a lantern back by the privy, near the exploration pit. "Hey! Here!" the man shouted. "They need help!"

"Who?" shouted one of the men running towards the man holding the lantern.

"Why, these two fellas lying over here!" shouted the man with the lantern. As Jack and the others ran up to him, the man raised his lantern and pointed. Lying on the ground faces up were two men. They were not moving. The small group of men crowded around the two prone men. Jack bent over the closest one. The lantern illuminated his face. It was Poncho. A bullet hole oozed blood from his chest. The man with the lantern shone it over the other person, revealing that it was Carlos. Both were dead. The crowd grew as the news raced through the street that two men had been shot and killed. More men arrived with lanterns to illuminate the bodies.

"Look!" said a smooth-shaven man. "They both hold pistols in their hands!"

"I bet Poncho and Carlos shot each other over their bounty money that they received today for that Injun head," an old-timer said.

"Makes sense," another man said. Jack saw that they both did have their pistols in their hands. *Wait a minute*, Jack thought. *There is a lot that does not seem right.*

"Yes!" someone else said. "They must have quarreled over the money and shot each other dead! Why else would they have their pistols drawn?"

Jack examined Carlos's body. He searched for but did not find Carlos's beaded possible bag. Jack thought that was strange. Carlos would have kept that possible bag with him so no one could steal it. He squatted down by Poncho's body. The possible bag was not on his body. He looked up at the man with the lantern. *Could he have taken it?* Jack thought. The man wore only a shirt, pants, and hat. Hardly anything that could conceal the possible bag.

"Do you mind if I borrow your lantern for a few minutes?" Jack said to the man.

"Go right ahead," the man answered. As Jack took the lantern, he examined the man closer just to see if he might have overlooked the possible bag stashed under the man's shirt or down his pants. But Jack could not detect that it was hidden anywhere on the man's person. Jack then walked around the bodies, shining the lantern on the ground to see if the possible bag might have been flung from the grasp of one of the men. *I cannot believe Carlos and Poncho would have drawn their pistols and shot each other*, Jack thought. *They seemed too good of friends.*

By the time he handed the lantern back to its owner, the crowd had come to its own conclusion, that Carlos and Poncho had fought a duel over their payment for the Indian chieftain's head and had simultaneously killed each other.

There was still something wrong with this that Jack could not figure out. He looked closely at the bodies again. As he studied

Carlos for the third time, he saw it. Carlos's pistol was in his right hand. Nothing out of the ordinary with that. Then Jack remembered his conversation with the bewhiskered miner during yesterday's horserace. The miner had said that Carlos shot with his left hand. Then it dawned on Jack. Carlos and Poncho had not killed each other in a duel. Someone had shot them for their money, then placed the guns in their hands to make it look like they had killed each other. The killer did not know that Carlos did not use his right hand to shoot his pistol. The killer had placed the gun in the wrong hand, the right hand. Carlos shot with his left hand.

CHAPTER TEN

℘℧

Friday Morning, August 25, 1876—Jack was in a foul mood. He dabbled at eating his pancakes and bacon. The coffee mug was poised halfway to his lips.

How dumb I am, he told himself. His only hope was if Langrishe would convince Lil of his sincerity that his conversations with Dirty Em were only a ruse to protect Dirty Em from members of Deadwood's criminal ring.

"Captain Jones!" Lou spoke standing beside him. "Captain Jones, you have hardly touched your food. Are you sick?"

Jack looked up at her. "In a way, I suppose I am."

Lou looked around to see if any customers needed help that her waitresses were not handling. Seeing no one was in need at that moment, she sat down across from Jack.

"Captain, do you want to tell me what is going on?"

Jack stared at his coffee mug for a moment then said, "I did some stupid things that hurt Lil. She is upset and refuses to see me."

"Hum," was all Lou said.

"As you know," Jack said in a low voice. "I have been investigating the possibility of a criminal ring in Deadwood. I am now convinced there is one. Dirty Em passed sensitive information to me at Star and Bullock's and to provide cover for her, we pretended I was negotiating her services."

"Um hum," Lou said.

167

"That evening at the Cricket Saloon, I escorted Dirty Em to the privy as she divulged more information to me. The telling of those two meetings made their way to Lil. She believes my dalliances with Dirty Em were real, and now she will not even look at me."

"I see," Lou said.

"So you asked, and that's why I'm despondent."

Lou stared at Jack for a moment, then said, "Captain Jones, I know you are an honorable man. When I see Miss Lil again, I'll let her know your story. I know she will believe you. I can see the way she looks at you. She loves you. This little incident will pass, and you'll get back together. You'll see. Now buck up! Eat your food. You've got work to do. You have a trial to cover today." She smiled, stood, and patted him on the shoulder.

"Come on, Mr. Stonewall Jackson, let's find you a nice bone out in the kitchen," Lou said to the hound, and he followed her out. Jack finished his breakfast. Stonewall did not come back from the kitchen. Jack knew he was in good hands.

As Jack walked into the lobby, Charlie Wagner greeted him, "Good morning, Captain Jones."

"Good morning, Charlie," Jack said as he pulled out his Elgin pocket watch. He checked it against the regulator clock, which indicated the time was ten minutes before eight o'clock. "I need to make sure I'm on time for meals."

Wagner chuckled and along with a shake of his head he changed the topic. "That's a sorry business what happened to those two Mexican fellas last night. They appeared to be such good friends. It's hard to believe they would go and shoot each other over their poke."

"It is hard to believe," Jack said. "You haven't heard any mention of Laughing Sam, by chance, have you?"

"Nary a word on him."

"Thanks. If anyone is looking for me, I think I'll check in at the Montana Livery on my missing horse, and then stop by the *Black Hills Pioneer* before I head over to the Deadwood Theater for the trial."

"I'll be sure to let them know," Wagner said.

Jack had a little time to kill before the trial started again at nine a.m. As he stepped out onto the front porch, the sun peeked over the top of Hebrew Hill, blinding him for an instant. The town was bustling with the same sights, sounds, and smells of yesterday, with one exception. Looking left down Main Street to the north, Jack saw a horseback rider trotting up the street, leading two other saddled horses. The rider was Texas Jack. His jinglebobs chimed in rhythm with the steps of his horse, which was wearing the silver inlaid bridle Poncho had won from Texas Jack at the end of the race two days before. Jack recognized the two saddled horses as those belonging to Poncho and Carlos.

"Whoa!" Texas Jack said, reining his horse to a stop in front of Jack and stopping the two other horses. The smirk seemed permanently plastered on his face.

"Good morning to you, Mister Reporter," Texas Jack said. "Just for the record, since I know you keep a record, I figure these here horses, the saddles and tack, and my bridle that Poncho won only because my horse slipped, they all belong to me now!"

Jack could not help but glare at him.

"You see, Poncho and Carlos have no next of kin here in Deadwood to claim their animals and gear," Texas Jack continued. "So I figure I'm the closest thing they got for family. I paid for their carcasses to be buried at the cemetery and so in payment for my good deed, I'm claiming their critters and gear. You got a problem with that?" he said, resting his right hand on the butt of one of his pistols and breaking into a wide grin.

"Does that go for their possible bag too?" Jack asked.

"I don't know nothin' about that," Texas Jack snarled. "There weren't no possible bag with their gear. They must have spent all their take on their spree."

"Humph," was all Jack responded.

Texas Jack clicked his tongue to the horses and continued riding to the south. "See you at the trial!" he said as he clicked again and spurred his horse into a trot. Jack followed him with his eyes until he disappeared.

Jack figured that Texas Jack had something to do with Poncho's and Carlos's murders and had their possible bag. But he didn't know how to prove it, or if he did, would anyone in town care?

Jack walked down Main Street and stopped in at the Lee & Brown Store, where Colorado Charlie Utter had his office. Charlie was not there, but the clerk behind the counter told Jack that Charlie had sent off his dispatch rider to Cheyenne. The clock was now ticking for Jack. He would have to leave town by Sunday to chase after Crook.

Jack walked to the Montana Livery. Old Frenchy was working on the books. Pacho was not in his stall.

"Good morning, Old Frenchy," Jack said.

"Ah Monsieur Jack, *bonjour!*" Old Frenchy responded.

"I see Pacho is not in his stall."

"Yes, he was rented this morning for the day and earns his keep."

"Any news on my horse?"

"I am afraid he is still listed among the missing," Old Frenchy said, with a negative shake of his head.

"I saw Texas Jack this morning leading Carlos's and Poncho's saddled horses."

"*Oui,* he came in here this morning demanding their horses, saddles, and tack. He said they belonged to him now because he paid for their burial. I said I would have to wait until the livery owners told me I could release them. He struck me with his quirt and shouted, 'Don't talk back to me. Get those horses now and saddle them pronto!' Then he pulled a pistol on me, so I saddled them for him. He is a very bad man."

Jack could feel his blood boiling. "I agree he is a very bad man. Speaking of bad men, have you heard anything about Laughing Sam?"

"It is as if he has dropped off the face of the earth."

"Thank you, Old Frenchy. I must be off."

"Ah, I must also tell you that two mules will be here tomorrow for your use. You may want to stop by and examine them to see if they are suitable. And we will have two packs for you to start packing when you are ready."

"Thank you."

"You are most welcome, Monsieur Jack."

Jack walked the short distance to the *Black Hills Pioneer* building. Merrick was closing and locking the front door.

"Good morning, Jones!" Merrick shouted. "Beautiful day, is it not?"

"That it is, A.W."

"I deduce that you are coming to visit me, but I, like you, need to be walking toward the theater, where we will witness a real show, an extravaganza of life and death. Come join me on my walk."

"That I will, A.W., but I thought this was not that big of a show for you. I thought you were more interested in the development of this town."

"Right you are, Jones. This trial is important because it shows we are not savages here in Deadwood. It shows when right-minded men gather together justice prevails and that is progress. That is civilization!"

"Humph," Jack grunted.

"Look at Tom Short and all the wonderful goods that Omahoss has brought with him from Omaha. Even a rocking chair! Now, that item smacks of civilization! I wish I could get my hands on it, but he won't let anyone even sit in it!"

"A. W.," Jack said.

"Huh?" Merrick appeared lost in thought. "What?"

"What do you think about the double murder of Carlos and Poncho last night?"

"What's to think about? Those two yahoos shot and killed each other."

"Maybe not."

"How so?"

"What if someone murdered them for their poke and made it look like they killed each other over it."

"Prove it," Merrick said, stopping in the middle of Gold Street.

"What if I told you their poke was not on them?"

"So? Maybe they spent it before they killed each other. Maybe some bummer lifted it from their bleeding carcasses. Just because their poke is missing doesn't mean someone killed them."

"What if I told you Carlos used his left hand to shoot his pistol, and when I saw his body, the pistol was in his right hand?"

"Interesting," Merrick said, stroking his chin, pondering. "But it is still not proof. Even if what you say is correct, that someone shot both men, making it look like they shot each other and then stealing their poke, you don't know who the murderer is. No one saw it happen."

"I think I know who did it," Jack said.

"Who?"

"Texas Jack."

"Why would he do that? What's his motive?"

"To begin with, there appeared to be some competition between Texas Jack and the two Mexicans in the killing of Indians. Then Poncho wins Texas Jack's bridle in the horse race.

Texas Jack was furious about that. Earlier this morning, Texas Jack took possession of Carlos's and Poncho's horses, saddles, and tack, saying they belonged to him since he had paid for their burial."

"Texas Jack sounds like a Good Samaritan."

"I believe Texas Jack killed Carlos and Poncho."

"I'm sure you do and you build a plausible case, but it's all circumstantial. Until you find a witness, I don't believe you have a case. Even if you did, could you convince the mob in this town to hold another trial? I think not."

They resumed their walk in silence to Main Street and turned right toward the Deadwood Theater.

"I'll need to find more evidence," Jack said. "If I find that possible bag on Texas Jack, that could clinch the deal."

"That just might do it," Merrick said. "Look, here we are at the theater."

They joined the line of men slowly moving through the door. Merrick and Jack took the same seats they had had yesterday. Jack scanned the inside of the building, hoping for a glimpse of Lil. His heart sank even further as he thought of the hurt he had caused her and realized she may never wish to speak to him again.

The members of the jury were straggling in with the crowd. They were directed to sit in two rows on the right, closest to the stage. Pete stood facing the crowd. When he spied Jack, he broke into a big grin and waved to Jack, who waved back.

"I take it you know that young fellow?" Merrick said.

"Yes, Pete Adams from Iowa. He's a good kid who just arrived in town. Still a little wet behind the ears and honest as the day is long."

Judge Keithley and the prosecution and defense lawyers assembled on stage. Keithley sat down and gaveled the hammer onto the already split board on top of the table.

"Take your seats, gentlemen! Silence! Silence in the court!" Keithley pronounced. Langrishe walked out with several spittoons, placing them at strategic positions to help save his stage floor from expectorants.

Jack scanned the crowd to spot Laughing Sam Hartman, but there still was no sign of him. With Laughing Sam not being there that confirmed to Jack that there was something amiss with Hartman's involvement with the murder of Bummer Dan.

Keithley looked at the jury. His lips moved as he silently counted the jury's members and then stated, "We seem to have a problem here. We are short one juror."

Jack looked at the jurors and saw that the missing juror was Texas Jack. He saw Varnes was strategically sitting behind the jury, but there was no sign of Swearengen. Varnes turned around, scanning the audience, probably looking for Texas Jack. It was plain on his face he was visibly upset.

"Who is missing from the jury?" Keithley asked.

"It appears it's that Texas Jack feller," one of the jurors responded.

"Does anyone know the whereabouts of Mr. Percy Hollingberry?" Keithley asked.

"I'm here!" Texas Jack shouted from the back of the building as he strode down the aisle. "I just had a little matter to attend to with some horseflesh."

"Very well, Mr. Hollingberry but in the future, please be on time, as you are holding up these proceedings."

"Yes, your Honor," a sneering Texas Jack replied. Varnes glared at Texas Jack as he found a seat at the end of the row.

"Bring in the prisoner," Keithley said. Old George and the other guard from yesterday escorted a bound Harry Young onto the stage.

"Release the prisoner," Keithley said.

"What?" Old George shouted.

"Release the prisoner!" Keithley shouted.

"Humph," Old George grunted, then spat a stream of tobacco juice toward a spittoon, hitting it this time. The guards untied Young and left.

"The prisoner may be seated," Keithley said. "Mr. Whitehead, what are the charges brought forth by the people?"

"Judge Keithley," Whitehead said as he stood. "The people present the case that the prisoner, Harry Young, also known as Samuel Young, employed as a bartender by Messieurs Mann and Lewis at Saloon Number 10, did on the evening of August twenty-second in the year of our Lord 1876, shoot and murder Myer Baum, also known as Bummer Dan, and we on behalf of the people ask that if found guilty, Harry Young be executed by hanging."

"Thank you, Mr. Whitehead," Keithley said. "And what say you, Mr. Miller?"

Miller stood and placed his hand on Young's shoulder. "Your Honor," Miller began. "We do not deny that the defendant Harry Young did fire a pistol and kill Myer Baum, also known as Bummer Dan, but we will show that he shot in an act of self-defense, and we would ask that he be declared not guilty, as he did not kill the man he intended to shoot."

The crowd broke out in a loud murmur. Keithley gaveled the hammer onto the wood. "Order! Order in the court!" The crowd settled down. "Very good, Mr. Miller, please be seated."

"Mr. Whitehead, call your first witness."

"Thank you, your Honor," Whitehead said. "The people call E. B. Farnam as their first witness."

Farnam rose from the audience and mounted the stairs to the stage. He stood facing Keithley.

"Raise your right hand, Mr. Farnam," Keithley said and Farnam complied. "Do you solemnly swear to tell the truth, the whole truth, and nothing but the truth? So help you God?"

"I do," Farnam said.

"Mr. Farnam, please be seated," Keithley said.

Farnam sat on the witness stool beside the judge's table.

"Mr. Whitehead, please proceed with your witness," Keithley said.

Whitehead left his stool and stood before Farnam.

"Please state your name for the record," Whitehead said.

"E. B. Farnam."

"Mr. Farnam, how long have you resided in Deadwood?"

"Several months."

"And what is your occupation?"

"I own a store on Main Street, next door to Saloon Number 10."

"Tell us what you know of the events of Tuesday night, August 22, 1876, if you would please, sir."

"Certainly," Farnam said. "About ten o'clock, Tuesday, I was closing my store for the night when I heard two shots in succession. I ran out the door and heard a man say, 'I am murdered.' I then found Mr. Baum dying in the street. Along with Mr. Short and others, I entered Saloon Number 10, where we pursued the prisoner sitting over there. On confronting him with the fact that Mr. Baum had been shot, the prisoner said, 'If I am the man you are looking for, I deliver myself up.' The prisoner also said he had done the shooting and all he wanted was a fair trial."

"Very good, Mr. Farnam," Whitehead said. "Do you have anything else to add?"

"No sir."

"Your Honor, I have no further questions."

"Mr. Miller," Keithley said. "Do you have any questions for Mr. Farnam?"

"Yes I do, your Honor," Miller answered and rose from his stool. "Mr. Farnam, when you confronted Mr. Young about the shooting of Mr. Baum, did he say why he shot Mr. Baum?"

"The prisoner said nothing about shooting Mr. Baum."

"In fact, is it not true that Mr. Young was surprised and shocked to learn that the dead man was Mr. Baum?"

Farnum looked toward the canvas ceiling and then slowly answered, "Yes, that is true. The prisoner showed surprise and shock that he had shot Mr. Baum."

"Did Mr. Young tell you who he thought he had shot?"

"The prisoner said he thought he had shot Laughing Sam Hartman."

"Thank you, Mr. Farnum. No further questions, your Honor."

"The witness may step down," Keithley said.

Farnum stood and began to leave the stage as Keithley said, "Mr. Whitehead, your next witness, please."

"The people call Tom Short as our next witness," Whitehead said. Short arrived on stage, took the oath, and sat down. Through the questioning, Short had no new information to provide, and so it was for the next few witnesses.

Jack's pencil had stopped moving. The lead point rested on the notebook's paper. Jack looked at Merrick, whose eyes were closed. Soft snoring came from his mouth. Jack's mind wandered from the trial proceedings. Lil was all he thought about. Jack wondered how he could be so stupid? How could he convince Lil he was not with Dirty Em, that it was only to further his investigation into the murder? How could he restore Lil's confidence in him and their happiness? Merrick snorted, waking himself and bringing Jack back to the business at hand.

"Judge Keithley, that concludes the witnesses for the prosecution," Whitehead said.

"Very good, Mr. Whitehead," Keithley said. "Mr. Miller, you may now call your witnesses."

"Thank you, Judge Keithley," Miller said as he stood. "We call Carl Mann as our first witness."

Carl Mann arose from the audience, made his way to the stage, and Keithley swore him in as he had the others.

"Mr. Mann, please take the stool," Keithley said.

"Thank you, W.R., I mean, your Honor," Mann said as he sat down.

Miller approached Mann and started his questioning, "Mr. Mann, how long have you been in Deadwood?"

"Well, I've been here several months."

"And what is your occupation?"

"I own Saloon Number 10 on Main Street, with my partner Jerry Lewis."

"Do you know the defendant, Harry Young?"

"Yes, I employ Harry as bartender in the saloon."

"What do you know of the events that led up to the shooting of Myer Baum?"

"As I understand it, Laughing Sam Hartman had for several days before the shooting been making threats against Harry Young."

"What type of threats?"

"Hartman made threats that he was going to kill Harry."

"Who did he make these threats to?"

"Several different people, including me."

"Please explain further, Mr. Mann."

"Three days before the shooting, Laughing Sam approached me and wanted to borrow a gun. I refused."

"Why did Hartman want to borrow a gun from you?"

"He said he had no quarrel with me, but he was out to get Harry. He said, 'That Harry Young, the son of a bitch, I will kill him.'"

"What happened the evening of the shooting?"

"Tuesday evening, things heated up between Harry and Hartman. Hartman baited Harry in the saloon and Harry threw him out, stating he would kill Hartman if he came back in Saloon Number 10. Matters had assumed a threatening aspect. I told Harry to continue to work in a dimly lit part of the bar, in case Hartman should return to do him harm. I then tracked down Hartman who had returned to that dancehall, the Senate Saloon. There I told Hartman 'If you kill Harry, you will go up in a second.'"

"You mean hang?"

"Yes."

"Please continue, Mr. Mann."

"As I said, I told Hartman he would hang if he killed Harry. Hartman replied to me, 'Young won't speak to me. I have only a little while to live, and I will kill that Young and that whore. If they hang me tonight, so be it.' I left the dancehall and ate a late supper. It was later that I learned about the shooting of Bummer Dan. That's all I know."

"Is there any reason that you know why Harry Young would have shot Bummer Dan?"

"No, Bummer Dan was Laughing Sam Hartman's partner, but he was relatively harmless. Don't forget what everyone knows, that Bummer Dan was wearing Laughing Sam's hat and coat when he walked into Saloon Number 10, and I had sent Harry to a dim part of the saloon. It being dark and what with Bummer Dan wearing Laughing Sam's clothes, I could see why Harry would think it was Laughing Sam come to do him harm and shoots him."

"Your Honor!" Whitehead said, standing up. "I object! The witness's statement is pure speculation, and I wish it stricken from the record."

"Your objection is accepted, Mr. Whitehead. Jury, you are to disregard the last statement by Carl, I mean Mr. Mann. Proceed, Mr. Miller."

"I have no further questions for the witness, your Honor."

"Very well, thank you, Mr. Miller. Mr. Whitehead, you may cross-examine the witness," Keithley said.

Whitehead, with hands clasped behind his back and staring at the floorboards, walked up to Mann. "Mr. Mann, how long have you known the prisoner, Harry Young?"

"I have known Harry for several months, ever since he arrived from Custer City."

"You stated that the prisoner threatened to kill Laughing Sam. Is that not so?"

"Yes."

"And is it not true that Bummer Dan was the partner of Laughing Sam, and that Harry Young knew they were partners?"

"Yes."

"So, since Young was feuding with Hartman, and knowing that Hartman and Baum were partners, Young sees Baum and shoots him because he knew Baum could be out to kill him, as well as Hartman."

"No. I don't know that to be the case."

"Mr. Mann, Young was angry that night, and he was ready to kill anyone who he thought would be against him. Isn't that right?"

"No. No," Mann responded.

"I object to this badgering of the witness, your Honor!" Miller interjected.

"Objection overruled," Keithley said. "I see no badgering going on here. Mr. Whitehead is only trying to get to the truth."

"Thank you, your Honor," Whitehead said. "Mr. Mann, you mentioned Laughing Sam said he was going to kill Young and 'that whore.' Why did he make that statement, and who is the whore he is talking about?"

"I have no idea. That is all he said."

"Hum," Whitehead said and paused for what seemed an eternity. "That is all the questions I have, your Honor."

"Carl, I mean Mr. Mann, you may step down," Keithley said. "Who is your next witness, Mr. Miller?"

"I call Anson Tipple to the witness stand," Miller said. The Saloon Number 10 bartender walked to the stage, took the oath, and sat on the stool. He looked over at Young, nodded, and smiled.

"Mr. Tipple," Miller said. "Do you work at Saloon Number 10?"

"I do, sir," Tipple answered.

"Do you know the defendant?"

"I do, he's Harry Young, who works with me in the saloon as a bartender."

"How long have you known Mr. Young?"

"Oh, about three months."

"Tell us about what went on Tuesday night at Saloon Number 10."

"Well, to save time, I agree with everything Carl Mann said."

"That's the most sensible thing anyone has said so far!" Calamity Jane's voice shouted from the back of the hall. Jack turned around and saw her standing in the back with her hands on her hips. The crowd roared with laughter as Keithley pounded the hammer on the board, shouting, "Order! Order in the court!" The crowd noise subsided as Keithley continued, "And you, young lady, any more outbursts from you and I'll have you bound and gagged!"

Calamity Jane sat down without a word.

"Continue, Mr. Miller," Keithley said.

"Mr. Tipple, tell us what happened in the saloon."

"Well, sir, as Mr. Mann said, he sent Harry to the back of the building, behind the bar, where there is poor lighting, because he was afraid Harry would be an easy target for Laughing Sam, who had vowed to kill him."

"And where were you?"

"I took over the bar in the front, where it is better lighted."

"I see. Then what happened?"

"Well, sir, through the door I see what at first I think is Laughing Sam, but when I look closer, it's Bummer Dan, wearing Laughing Sam's slouch hat and checkered coat."

"Why was he wearing Laughing Sam's clothes?"

"I have no idea."

"What happened next?"

"The next thing I know, Laughing Sam walks into the saloon and comes up to the bar. He's bare-headed, wearing only a shirt and vest. He asks me where he can find the boss, Carl Mann."

Jack jerked up straight. This confirmed Laughing Sam was in the saloon! Jack's mind was racing. Why was he there?

"You say Laughing Sam was also in Saloon Number 10?" Miller asked.

"That's right," Tipple said. "I have no idea what his game was because about that time, Bummer Dan had walked to the dimly lit part of the saloon and was shot by Harry."

"What happened to Laughing Sam?"

"As soon as Bummer Dan was shot, Laughing Sam skedaddled out the front door."

"I see. So is it fair to say Harry Young feared for his life, since his enemy and his enemy's friend were in the saloon and were approaching him? If so, Harry Young fearing for his life, shot in self-defense."

"Yes," Tipple said. "I believe that is correct. Harry shot in self-defense."

Whitehead jumped to his feet. "Your Honor!" he shouted. "The defense attorney and the witness are drawing legal conclusions on the ultimate issue of self-defense. That is a subject for the jury to decide."

"Duly noted, Mr. Whitehead," Keithley said, and then turning to the jury, he continued, "The jury will disregard the last exchange between Mr. Miller and Mr. Tipple." Finally, turning to Miller, he said, "Proceed, Mr. Miller."

"Mr. Tipple, what was the feud about between Young and Hartman?"

"Well, I believe it was all about a woman. It was about the trick Laughing Sam Hartman played on the working girl, Tid Bit."

"That son of a bitch, Hartman!" Calamity Jane shouted. Keithley rose and pointed his hammer at her shouting, "I told you, young lady, the next outburst from you, I would have you bound and gagged. Officers of the court, proceed against that trollop!"

Before anyone could act, Calamity Jane disappeared from the building.

"Mr. Miller proceed with your witness," Keithley said, straightening his coat and returning to his stool.

"Mr. Tipple, please tell the story succinctly."

"Well, several weeks ago, Laughing Sam spent the night with Tid Bit and instead of paying her in gold, he tricked her with copper filings. Harry became close friends with Tid Bit, in fact, if you ask me, I think he's sweet on her. Anyway, Harry confronted Laughing Sam about cheating Tid Bit and their feud blew up from that."

"So Laughing Sam Hartman was out to get Harry Young because Harry stood up for a woman who had been wronged by Hartman."

"That is correct."

"Thank you, Mister Tipple," Miller said, then turned to Keithley, saying, "That concludes my questioning, your Honor."

"Very good, Mr. Miller. Mr. Whitehead, you may cross-examine the witness," Keithley said. Whitehead arose from his stool and approached Tipple.

"Mr. Tipple," Whitehead said. "Are you not good friends with the prisoner?"

"Yes."

"You would do anything for the prisoner, wouldn't you?"

"Yes."

"Even lie?"

"I don't know what you mean!"

"You don't know what I mean? Ah, sir, but I think you do know what I mean. After humiliating Mr. Hartman Tuesday night, the prisoner and you knew Mr. Hartman would come back into Saloon Number 10. You both knew he would come back to restore his honor, and you both lay in wait for him to come back so you could murder him. That's why the prisoner stayed out of the light in the shadows, waiting to assassinate Mr. Hartman. Is that not true?"

"No!" Tipple shouted. Beads of sweat broke out on his forehead.

"Then, when out of kindness, Mr. Hartman gives poor Bummer Dan his hat and coat and Bummer Dan enters the saloon and is only passing through to leave through the back door, you give the signal to the prisoner that the man you perceive is Hartman is passing by. The prisoner lurks in the shadows and ambushes a defenseless Bummer Dan, thinking it is a defenseless Laughing Sam Hartman. Pure and simple premeditated murder! Is that not right, Mr. Tipple? You and the prisoner conspired to murder a defenseless Laughing Sam Hartman. Only your nefarious scheme went awry when the two of you murdered the wrong person. Even though you both killed the wrong person, it is still murder, the unlawful taking of a life."

"No! No! No!" Tipple shouted as sweat streamed down his face.

"The witness will control himself," Keithley said to Tipple.

"I have no further questions for this witness, your Honor," Whitehead said.

"Mr. Tipple, you may step down," Keithley said to a visibly shaken Tipple, who quickly left the stage.

Jack and Merrick were frantically writing. Whitehead's line of questioning stunned the crowd.

Time seemed to slow down as the defense marched through a string of witnesses, all who testified to the same set of circumstances laid out by the first few witnesses for the prosecution and the defense. A bored Merrick doodled pictures of animals and caricatures of the principal members on stage, while Jack's mind drifted to Lil, and how he could return things to the way they had been. After the defense's last witness was grilled by the prosecution, Keithley asked, "Are there any other witnesses?"

"No, your Honor," Miller said.

"I agree with Mr. Miller," Whitehead said. "There are no further witnesses."

"There is a key witness missing, gentlemen," Keithley said. "And the obvious question is why have you not produced the key witness? Where is Laughing Sam Hartman?" Whitehead and Miller looked at each other.

"Your Honor," Whitehead said, "Both the prosecution and the defense have looked for Laughing Sam Hartman, but he has disappeared from Deadwood."

"This is true, Mr. Miller?" Keithley asked.

"Yes, your Honor," Miller responded. "We planned to place the defendant on the witness stand next."

"Very well, gentlemen," Keithley said, looking at his pocket watch. "The time is now fifteen minutes past noon. The court will adjourn for lunch and reconvene at two o'clock." With that, Keithley brought the hammer down onto the wood with a resounding crack, and the theater erupted into loud conversation.

Merrick stood and let out an explosive sigh.

"Come on, Jones, let's grab a bite to eat and we can piece together what we have heard so far."

"Sounds fine to me," Jack said, as he rose tucking away his notebook and pencil.

"What say we try Eggerts's California Chop House? They have first-rate pies."

"Let's go, then," Jack said. He scanned the theater one last time, hoping he might spot Lil. But nary a glimpse of her.

The sun was high overhead and not a cloud in the sky. The bright light made the two men squint as they left the theater, turning to their right and heading north on Main Street. Three doors to their right they came to a building with a sign reading California Chop House & Bakery, Eggerts & Co. They entered and found an empty table near the front. The owner, Eggerts, approached their table and said, "Good afternoon, gentlemen. Welcome to the California Chop House. Mr. Merrick, you did an outstanding job advertising our establishment in your fine paper. It has brought in increased business."

"Why, thank you, Eggerts. I do believe you have one of the best cooks from the Pacific coast, and that's how I wrote it. What do you have simmering in the kitchen for us today?"

"We have a nice venison stew with potatoes, carrots, and onions."

"What do you say, Jones? Venison stew and coffee?"

"Sounds good to me," Jack responded.

"Very well, gentlemen," Eggerts said. "I'll be right back with your food and drink."

"So Jones, what do you think of this morning's proceedings?"

"I knew most of the facts already, but the number one thing that took me by surprise was the confirmation of a rumor that Laughing Sam Hartman was in Saloon Number 10 at the time of the shooting."

"Yes, that is a valuable piece of information."

"Right, and now Laughing Sam is nowhere to be found."

"Why do you suppose that poltroon has fled the town?" Merrick asked. Eggerts returned and placed before them two large bowls of steaming venison stew, a fresh loaf of bread, and two mugs of coffee.

"Enjoy, gentlemen," he said.

"Smells delectable," Merrick said. They both dug into the stew and bread. After they had devoured all the food in silence, Jack said, "I never answered your question." He took a sip of coffee.

"Go on," Merrick said.

"After listening to all the testimony, here's what I think happened and why Laughing Sam is gone. I think after Harry Young threw Laughing Sam out of the saloon, Laughing Sam was so angry he was going to kill Harry. Remember, Laughing Sam and Bummer Dan were partners. Laughing Sam devises a plan to sneak up on Harry to kill him. What Laughing Sam does is he gets his good friend Bummer Dan to wear his hat and coat into Saloon Number 10, in full view of everyone. Laughing Sam also enters the saloon but dressed differently, hoping no one notices him. His plan is to have Harry distracted by Bummer Dan, sneak up on Harry, and shoot him before he knows what's happening. Only the plan goes wrong. Bummer Dan's disguise is too good, and Harry shoots him before Laughing Sam can act. Laughing Sam tries to leave quickly, but not before Anson Tipple and a few others recognize him. He decides the best thing to do is leave town. Too many questions will be asked. Bummer Dan must have given him his haversack with the gold nugget in it that..."

"Stop!" Merrick said. "What gold nugget?"

"Sorry, the night Bummer Dan was murdered, he showed me a large gold nugget he had in his haversack. He also told me he had more gold hidden somewhere."

"I see," Merrick said.

"After the murder, Bummer Dan's haversack was missing and when I visited his shanty, I found that it had been ransacked, but left behind was a discarded poke bag, with several gold flakes remaining inside. So my theory is Laughing Sam goes to Bummer Dan's shanty, digs up Bummer Dan's poke and flees town. That's what I think."

"A convincing tale, Jones. It sounds plausible."

"But what baffles me is, could Bummer Dan and Laughing Sam have been a part of the criminal ring in town? And if so how does that fit into all this."

"Will you drop your ring theory," Merrick said. "You have no solid evidence the criminal element in town has banded together. The way you portray it, every evil deed committed in Deadwood has a sinister connection to your mythical band. Next thing you know, you'll be telling me Jesse and Frank James have been spotted here in town!"

Jack grinned. "I haven't seen them yet."

"Your whole ring theory is based on hearsay from individuals of the lowest class or those who have no reputable standing in town—prostitutes, faro dealers, drunkards, servants, and heathen Chinese."

Jack felt himself becoming agitated, but regaining control he said, "Look, A.W., I consider these folks my friends, and I believe them."

"I'm just saying their testimony would not stand up in any court of law, even Old Necessity Keithley's court."

Eggerts returned to their table. "Can I interest you gentlemen in a slice of freshly baked apple pie? It's still warm out of the oven."

"Yes, indeed!" Merrick said. "Jones?"

"Yes."

Eggerts returned with two slices of apple pie, which Jack and Merrick had no problem consuming. Eggerts returned after they were finished.

"What did you think of the pie?" Eggerts asked.

"Delicious!" Merrick said.

"Yes, it was," Jack agreed.

"And now for the bill, Eggerts, if you please," Merrick said.

"No bill," Eggerts replied. "It's on the house for the excellent advertising."

"Thank you, sir!" Merrick said.

"Yes, thanks!" Jack said. Jack and Merrick left the chophouse and looked at their pocket watches.

"We have a little time before the trial reconvenes," Jack said.

"I need to head back to the office to see if I have any messages or work," Merrick said.

"I'll meet you back at the theater," Jack said as they parted. He walked north to Star and Bullock's and entered the building. The room was full of customers. Star waved to Jack and went back to adding up a customer's purchases. Bullock left a customer and walked over to Jack.

"I can only talk for a moment," Bullock said. "As you can see we are very busy. How goes the trial?"

"They have questioned all the witnesses, and at two o'clock the court will reconvene, with Harry Young on the stand."

"I'll try to break away if I can, I'd like to hear what he has to say."

"I think another interesting development is that it was confirmed Laughing Sam Hartman was in Saloon Number 10 when Bummer Dan was killed."

"That is interesting, and I'm assuming Laughing Sam is still missing."

"That's correct. When you have time, I would also like to discuss with you the shooting of Poncho and Carlos. I don't believe they killed each other."

Bullock looked at Jack with no expression on his face as he said, "That's one I'd like to hear."

"Seth!" Star called. "I need your help over here!" The line of customers wanting assistance was increasing.

"Thank you, Jack, got to get back to work. We'll talk later. Oh—by the way, we have all your supplies and gear ready for you and will have them at the livery this evening so you can begin packing tomorrow."

"Thanks, Seth, I hope to see you later at the trial."

Bullock returned to helping customers as Jack walked out the door and back up the street towards the theater.

Oh Lord, Jack prayed. *I know I don't talk to you as much as I should, but help me figure out a way to get back into Lil's good graces. I do love her so.*

CHAPTER ELEVEN
๕ว๊อ

Friday Afternoon, August 25, 1876—Jack walked into the Deadwood Theater hoping to see Lil, but again she was absent. He was late. The proceedings had already started. He took his seat by Merrick, pulled out his notebook and pencil, and noticed the pencil needed sharpening. He found his penknife and began shaving the point as he picked up on the proceedings. Young was already on the witness stool, and Miller was addressing the next question to him.

"Is it true, Harry, that you and Laughing Sam Hartman were feuding?" Miller asked.

"Yes."

"Tell us the nature of the feud."

"It's just as the others said earlier and what they said was true. That low-down skunk, Laughing Sam Hartman, had cheated Tid Bit. She's a poor working girl just trying to make ends meet and he takes advantage of her, and I let him know he was a no good, egg-sucking dog!"

"Tell us about Bummer Dan and your relations with him. Did you have a grudge against him, or make any threats against him?"

"No. I had no grudge against old Bummer Dan, and I made no threats against him. Even though he was Hartman's partner, I had no cause to feud with him."

"Tell the court in your own words what happened Tuesday night in Saloon Number 10."

"As Carl Mann said, after I told Hartman to leave the saloon, Carl sent me to work in the dimly lit part of the bar. He was afraid Hartman was going to return and try to murder me. Carl's reasoning was if Hartman could not see me at first, they would have time to stop him before he attempted to shoot me.

"As I was working in the back, I saw rapidly approaching me a figure who I thought was Hartman. I recognized his hat and his colorful checkered coat. The man was coming so fast I thought for sure he was coming after me, so I pulled out one of the pistols we keep behind the bar and shot first, thinking he was coming right at me to kill me. So I shot first in self-defense. He continued to approach me after the first shot, so I fired again. He then turned and ran out of the saloon."

"I see, then what happened?"

"I was scared. I was shaking. I wasn't sure if I had hit him, or if he was going to come back again after me. The whole saloon cleared out. It seemed as if it was forever until a mob led by Mr. Farnum and Mr. Short entered the saloon and told me I had not shot Hartman, but I had shot and killed Bummer Dan. Believe me, I am sorry. I did not mean to harm Bummer Dan."

"So if I may restate for the court, you are saying you thought you were shooting Laughing Sam Hartman. The same Laughing Sam who earlier threatened to kill you. You shot in fear of losing your life. You shot in self-defense. Is that correct?"

"Yes, that is correct. I shot in self-defense."

"Shot in self-defense," Miller slowly, emphatically repeated. "No further questions, your Honor."

"Mr. Whitehead," Keithley said. "You may question the defendant."

"Thank you, your Honor," Whitehead said. "Mr. Young, may I call you Harry?"

"Yes, sir."

"Harry, I won't go over again any of the questions that were previously asked of you by Mr. Miller, but I do want to clarify a few things," Whitehead said. "First of all, did you or did you not threaten to kill Laughing Sam Tuesday night in Saloon Number 10?"

Young stared at the floorboards for the longest time, then looked up at Whitehead and said, "Yes, I did, but I was angry and

I didn't mean it, I didn't mean I would actually kill him. But he did some horrible things and never even apologized for them. I said I would kill him, but it was all talk."

"Harry, you went to a dimly lit portion of the bar, correct?"

"Yes."

"You waited there because you were afraid that in the stronger lamplight you could easily be seen by Laughing Sam, correct?"

"Yes."

"You and your good friend, Anson Tipple, were in cahoots to waylay Laughing Sam when he walked through the saloon. When you saw Laughing Sam's hat and coat you naturally thought it was Laughing Sam and shot twice to kill him because you had a rage against him."

"No! No!"

"Yes! You shot first, hoping to get Laughing Sam out of the way. Only you did not check out your target, and you shot and killed the wrong man, Bummer Dan. It was not self-defense. It was a cold, calculated maneuver to assassinate your rival. Murder is murder!"

"No! No! It wasn't like that at all!"

"Your Honor, that concludes my line of questioning of this cold-blooded killer."

"Thank you, Mr. Whitehead, but must I remind you that the term 'cold-blooded killer' crosses the line in our judicial system," Keithley said. "The jury will disregard Mr. Whitehead's final remark. We will now move to closing arguments. Mr. Whitehead, please go ahead and make the people's case."

"Thank you, your Honor," Whitehead said, as he approached the jury sitting below him in the first two rows. "Gentlemen of the jury, you have heard lots of testimony here today concerning the murder of poor old Myer Baum also known as Bummer Dan. Bummer Dan may not have been one of Deadwood's stellar citizens, but he never hurt anyone and he certainly did not deserve death. We think much of the mayhem that occurred Tuesday night in Saloon Number 10 can be laid at the feet of Laughing Sam Hartman. Unfortunately, he is nowhere to be found. However, the indisputable facts are that Harry Young threatened to kill Laughing Sam if Laughing Sam stepped back into Saloon Number 10. Young went to the darkened part of the bar of Saloon Number 10 and waited there for Hartman. When he saw Hartman's hat and coat, he fired his pistol. Not once to scare him off or wound him, but twice. Twice, to make sure he killed him. Unfortunately, it was Bummer Dan and not Laughing Sam, but murder is murder. It was premeditated. The facts cannot be denied. The people ask that you find Harry Young guilty of murder, and we ask that Harry Young be hanged by the neck until dead. Thank you."

Whitehead returned to his stool. Keithley looked up from his papers and books spread out on the table in front of him, saying, "Mr. Miller, you may now address the jury."

Miller arose from his stool and walked to stand in front of the jury. "Gentlemen of the jury," he began. "I won't repeat or refute most of what my esteemed colleague just went over. We admit that on Tuesday night, Harry Young did shoot and kill Bummer Dan. But know this, Laughing Sam had made numerous threats to many people that he was going to kill Harry Young. Harry was afraid for his life. Carl Mann was afraid for Harry's life, and that's why Carl told Harry to work in the dimmer part of the saloon—so he would not be an easy target for Laughing Sam."

"Now comes Bummer Dan," Miller continued. "Bummer Dan is wearing Laughing Sam's distinctive clothing. And why is this?" Miller paused for a moment for the jury to hang on his next words. "Because Bummer Dan was a decoy, a distraction for Harry to look at while Laughing Sam was sneaking up on him to murder him. The plan backfired. Harry instinctively shot Bummer Dan to preserve his own life. It...was...self-defense! Harry Young shot and killed Bummer Dan thinking it was Laughing Sam come to murder him. That is the only reason he shot, to preserve his own life. And where is Laughing Sam? Why isn't he here to testify for his dead friend, his partner? Why isn't he here demanding justice? I'll tell you why, because Laughing Sam and his partner Bummer Dan were out to kill Harry Young, pure and simple."

"Yes, Harry Young killed Bummer Dan," Miller continued, "But he did not kill the man he intended to kill. I ask that you declare Harry Young not guilty, as he shot in self-defense. Thank you." Miller strode back to his chair and sat down.

Jack and Merrick had both stopped writing. They had furiously written until the lead in their pencils blunted down to the wood, and they were now quickly using their pocketknives, shaving the wood and lead to new points.

"Thank you, Mr. Miller, and thank you, Mr. Whitehead," Keithley said. "And now, jury, all eyes turn to you. You must decide who is telling the correct story. Both are similar, but different on this one point—did the prisoner, Harry Young, decide to murder his rival, Laughing Sam, only to kill the wrong person, Bummer Dan? Was it a premeditated act, or did Harry Young shoot in self-defense to protect his own life?"

Keithley paused and flipped through one of his law books to find the territorial law he was looking for.

"The Territory of Dakota has not yet codified all its law, but I have found the Dakota Territory Penal Code in one of my books. Let me read a portion of Chapter 17 to you. Section 242 states:

> Homicide is murder in the following cases: (1) When perpetrated without authority of law, and within a premeditated design to effect the death of the person killed, or of any other human being. (2) When perpetrated by any act immediately dangerous to others, and evincing a depraved mind, regardless of human life, although without any premeditated design to offset the death of any particular individual. (3) When perpetrated without any design to effect death, by a person engaged in the commission of any felony.

Keithley flipped a few pages further into the book and said, "I need now to read to you what is Excusable Homicide, also found in Chapter 17 of the penal code. This will be excerpts from Sections 262 and 264:

> Homicide is excusable in the following cases: (2) When committed by accident and misfortune, in the heat of passion, upon any sudden and sufficient provocation, or upon sudden combat: providing that no undue advantage is taken, nor any dangerous weapon used, and that the killing is not done in a cruel or unusual manner. Homicide is also justifiable when committed by any person in either the following cases: (1) When resisting any attempt to murder such person, or to commit a felony upon him or her, or upon or in

any dwelling-house in which such person is; or (2) when committed in the lawful defense of such person...when there is reasonable ground to apprehend a design to commit a felony, or to do some great personal injury, and imminent danger of such design being accomplished...

Keithley closed the book and looked down at the jury. "Gentlemen of the jury," he said, "your charge is to determine the guilt or innocence of the prisoner, Harry Young, in the death of Myer Baum, alias Bummer Dan. If you find Harry Young guilty, and your verdict must be unanimous, we will promptly execute him by hanging until dead. You will hold your deliberations right here in this theater. The officers of the court and the public will leave the premises. You are not to further discuss this case with anyone outside your fellow jury members. Elect a foreman who will guide your deliberations. Good luck and Godspeed, gentlemen. Either I or one of the officers of the court will be located outside the front door for you to notify us when you are through and ready to announce your verdict. With that..."

Merrick jumped to his feet and said in a loud voice, "Your Honor! Please excuse this outburst, but how will we, the public, know when the jury is ready to give its verdict, so we can be here to hear it?"

"That is a very good question, Mr. Merrick," Keithley said and then sat silent, pondering.

"If I may interject, your Honor?" Whitehead said.

"Go head, Mr. Whitehead."

"What if after we learn the jury is ready to deliver its verdict, we have Old George stand in the middle of Main Street and fire off his double-barreled shotgun into the air? He could fire one shot, wait ten seconds then fire the second shot."

"That is a wonderful idea, Mr. Whitehead. That is what we shall do. I will explain this plan to Old George later. As for now, the court is adjourned until the jury is ready to give its verdict." Keithley brought the hammer down on the block of wood, further splitting it. The audience erupted into animated conversations as the men began to leave. Jack and Merrick left the theater and stood on the street.

"I need to return to the office, Jones," Merrick said. "See you when we return for the verdict!"

Jack searched the immediate area for any theater troupe member he might ask after Lil, but no one was in sight. Bullock had failed to make the courtroom, so Jack concluded he and Star must still be overwhelmed with customers. He had time to kill and decided to return to the camps to visit Bummer Dan's and Laughing Sam's shanties for any additional clues and to visit Wong. He looked at his Elgin pocket watch. The time was fifteen minutes past three o'clock.

Jack crossed the Lee Street Bridge into the camps. The same activities were going on as in previous days. As he picked his way through the shanties and shebangs, he noticed something different about Bummer Dan's shanty. Bummer Dan's sign was gone. Jack walked up to the tent flap and was about to announce his presence in case anyone was about, when a man rushed through the tent flap with his right fist raised and pulled back.

"What are ya snoopin' about here for? Come to rob me, have ya?" the man shouted.

"No! No!" Jack said, with hands up, palms forward. "I'm a reporter investigating the murder of Bummer Dan. I had no idea his living quarters were now occupied."

"Well, as ya can see, they are now occupied—by me! That fellow is dead, and I claim this shanty as me own since he has no kin here and I bein' the first to claim it. Now bugger off!"

Jack could feel the heat in his blood rise, but realized it would do him no good to argue with the man. So he said, "So be it, good day to you, sir." As he turned away from the man, he looked in the direction of Laughing Sam's shanty and saw a stranger smoking a pipe sitting in front of it.

Jack strode away from the squatter toward Fee Lee Wong's dwelling.

"Halloo!" he said. Wong's grinning face poked out of the flaps of the tent's entrance.

"Jack! Greetings!" Wong said. "Come in! Come in!"

Jack entered and Wong insisted he stay for tea. After they had settled in at the table, each with a cup of tea, Jack asked, "When did the squatters move in?"

"Those fellas are hard characters," Wong said, his brow furrowing. "They moved in without asking any of the neighbors if they could. They have been insulting to me and anyone else who is not like them."

"I am sorry to hear that, Fee Lee."

"It is nothing new. I have run into people disliking me in other towns because I do not look exactly as they do. But here in Deadwood, most people are friendly toward each other because we all have to live so close together, and we all are here to make money," he said and smiled.

"I take it you have heard nothing new about Laughing Sam?"

"You are correct, there is nothing new."

"I just came from Harry Young's trial. The jury is now deliberating his guilt or innocence."

"I see," Wong said.

"Did you hear about the two Mexicans shooting each other last night?"

"Yes," Wong said, his face wooden and expressionless.

"Is there something wrong? Jack asked.

Wong stared at his teacup for what seemed a long time.

"I am not sure I should tell you this. I do not want to see you hurt," Wong said.

"Please go ahead, I'm always careful."

Wong let out a sigh, then said, "I will tell you, but promise me you will not do anything rash?"

"I promise."

"We Cantonese are everywhere in town, doing many jobs for many people, day and night. Many Cantonese understand English, but do not speak it very well, so they don't. It is part of our pride. We will not speak unless the word is spoken correct."

"I understand, your English is perfect, and I am sure you know I know no Cantonese and would butcher the words if I tried."

Fee Lee smiled, then said, "Last night a Cantonese man was cleaning the Deadwood Theater's privy, knowing it would receive heavy use once the performance was over. He was inside cleaning when he heard the two Mexicans and a white man arguing. The white man demanded the Mexicans give him their money. They told him no. One of them said, 'Texas Jack, you are a pig.' Two shots were fired. The man inside the privy peeked out the door and could barely see a man moving two bodies in a line across from each other and then placing guns in their hands. He took a bag from them and walked toward the privy. Of course, the man inside the privy was frightened and quietly closed the door, hoping the murderer would not enter. Fortunately for my friend, the murderer passed by. He said the man's footsteps made music such as from tiny bells."

Jack was silent, his mind racing. *It was Texas Jack! Here is irrefutable evidence Texas Jack killed Poncho and Carlos!*

"Fee Lee, would this man be willing to tell his story?"

"Tell it to whom?"

"Well..."

"There is no law in town. Who would really care? I know you care and a few others care, but you are powerless. Would you shoot and kill Texas Jack? I think not. If I bet on it, I would have to bet he would shoot and kill you. That is why I made you promise. You promised you would not do anything rash and I hold you to your promise."

"Humph, all right, but I don't like it."

"Very good," Wong said and smiled.

"So here is the irony..." Jack said.

"Irony? What is irony?" Wong interrupted.

"Irony is hard to explain. It is expressing humorously something that is the exact opposite of what is real. For instance, if I said something tasted good, but actually it tasted bad."

Wong looked puzzled. Jack held up his teacup and said, "If I drop your teacup and instead of saying 'That is a bad thing,' you say 'Oh good,' that is irony."

"Oh," Wong said not sounding convinced.

"So here is the irony. Texas Jack kills two men. He commits murder, and now he sits as part of a jury trying another man, Harry Young, for murder. This is irony!"

"Oh now I see!"

"I don't know what to do," Jack said.

"Again, my friend, you will do nothing. You promised me."

"That I did. I wish I hadn't."

"I am glad you made your promise, and I am glad you are a man of honor and will keep your promise. I don't want to find you dead like the others."

They sat in silence for a long time, sipping their tea.

"Thank you, Fee Lee. I value your friendship. I must go back in case the signal is sounded for the verdict."

"Very well, Jack." They stood and shook hands. "Remember your promise, Jack."

"I will."

Jack slowly walked back to the Lee Street Bridge and then to Main Street. His thoughts focused on Texas Jack, and what, if anything, could be done about him with the complication of his promise to Wong.

He aimlessly walked north down Main Street. Small knots of men stood in the street discussing the trial, and what they thought the outcome would be. As always in Deadwood, most of them had bets on which way the jury would go. Jack was approaching Saloon Number 10.

Jack was about to stop in and check the level of whiskey in his Old Crow bottle when he spotted the makings of a practical joke.

Along the front outside wall of Saloon Number 10 was a rough wooden two-seater bench. Sitting on the bench was one of Deadwood's biggest practical jokers, Johnny the Oyster. Sitting alongside him on the bench was a man Jack had not seen before, probably new to town. Johnny the Oyster was holding a lively conversation with the man about the trial. A small group of men stood around them listening and a few hung in the saloon's doorway, waiting. Unbeknown to the stranger, Carl Mann had drilled a small hole in the bench and had an elaborate setup whereby a long needle lay concealed in a hole in the bench. Mann rigged a weight and a string to the needle. The string led into the saloon and a person within the saloon could pull the string which would then thrust the needle up through the bench hole and into the buttocks of the unsuspecting victim. Before Jack could warn Johnny the Oyster's victim, Johnny winked to one of his co-conspirators, who nodded to the inside man holding the string. The inside man yanked the string. "Yeow!" the victim shouted, leaping up and away from the bench. Johnny the Oyster was laughing so hard tears streamed down his face, and the others all laughed as the victim rubbed his rear and tried to smile.

"Come on, pilgrim!" Johnny the Oyster said as he stood up, still laughing, "Let's go inside where you can buy us a drink!" The man smiled as the others in on the joke pounded him on the back and led him inside to buy them all a drink. Jack shook his head and followed them inside.

Anson Tipple was back behind the bar pouring drinks. Several men were giving him their opinion on the trial proceedings and commiserating with him on Whitehead's badgering while he was on the witness stand. Tipple saw Jack and placed his Old Crow bottle and a glass on the bar in front of him.

"Captain Jones," Tipple said. "What is your take on the trial?" The others in the immediate area stopped their conversations to listen to what Jack had to say.

"Anson, I think you did a good job on the stand today. I'll tell you what I think. Personally, I think Harry thought it was Laughing Sam he was shooting at and I believe he thought Laughing Sam was out to kill him. But I think the jury will find him guilty, and he will hang. I don't think it is right, but that is what I think will happen."

The men around Jack stood silent. "I think you are correct, Captain Jones," Tipple said, and the men murmured their agreement. The conversations began to pick up as Jack listened but did not participate. His mind refocused on Lil. The pit of his stomach was in turmoil. What could he do? How could he make things right?

A commotion arose on the street, louder and louder—men's shouts, barking dogs, and what sounded like wildcats yowling, howling, growling, and hissing.

"If it ain't Old Bedlam itself!" said a begrimed Cornish miner as the noise level increased to mayhem.

Johnny the Oyster ran to the door and looked out "Oh Emma!" he said and laughed. "Lookie at that, would ya!" Several others followed him to the door and began to laugh. Jack downed his whiskey, handed the bottle back to Tipple, and joined the others at the door.

The sight meeting his eyes was probably one of the most unusual he had ever seen on the frontier. A spring wagon pulled by six mules stood in front of Saloon Number 10. Among other items on the wagon bed was a large wooden cage filled with cats. Dogs were leaping at the cage as cats hissed and howled at them. Other cats were clawing and fighting each other. The beaming, rotund driver stood in the driver's box, trying to get the crowd to settle down so he could make an announcement.

Jack stood by Johnny the Oyster and asked, "Do you know who that is?"

Johnny the Oyster glanced over at Jack, "Oh it's you, Captain Jones. Yes, that's William Thompson, but he likes to go by Phatty, and being a reporter, ya should get it right. He spells it with a "Ph", not an "F."

"I'll remember that," Jack said. A crowd was rapidly gathering. The working girls were racing up Main Street to reach the wagon.

"Ladies and gentlemen!" Phatty announced. "Ladies and gentlemen! I have just arrived from Cheyenne with a cage full of feline friends. Those of you desiring a new friend may purchase one of these fine creatures for a mere thirty dollars for the large cats, ranging down to ten dollars for those that might be small and underweight. First come, first served!"

Phatty whipped out a small scale to weigh gold dust and began selling right away. It was quite the process to observe and created lots of entertainment for the denizens of the surrounding saloons.

A cat buyer would point out the cat he or she wished to purchase. Phatty had a young boy along as his assistant. The boy carefully opened the door and attempted to catch the cat being sold. Some were friendly, some were haters of humanity, and it was the haters that provided the greatest entertainment for the onlookers. Many of them were betting as the cats clawed and bit the boy in his attempts to capture the desired cats.

"Phatty!" Johnny the Oyster called. "Where'd ya capture all those cats?"

"Johnny the Oyster, is that you?" Phatty shouted. "I hired young boys in Cheyenne to catch them off the street for me. This here boy, Toby, did the best job and I hired him on to care for the cats."

"How many ya got?"

"Fifty that survived the trip. We had a little accident in Hill City. The wagon turned over and the cage opened up. Toby and me had quite the job capturing these cats and putting them back in the cage."

The cats were selling fast. Phatty was busy weighing out gold dust and Toby had his hands full, grabbing squirming, screaming, clawing cats. Jack wandered over to the cage. A gray striped female came up to him, reached up, and placed her front paws on a wooden bar, and stared at him. Jack reached in and scratched her behind the ears. She began to purr and rubbed her head against his fingers.

"Well, aren't you the friendliest little critter. You will certainly make someone a good pet—a very good pet." He continued to rub her head and then it hit him. "I bet Lil would like you. I bet she would like you very much!" The cat continued to purr.

"I'll take this gray, striped female right here!" Jack shouted to Phatty.

"All right, sir," Phatty responded.

"How much?" Jack asked. Phatty looked over at the cat. "She's midsized and looks to be in good shape. How about twenty dollars?"

"Sounds good," Jack said and handed Phatty a twenty-dollar gold piece.

"Toby!" Phatty shouted. Grab the gray striped cat in front of this gentleman and give it to him."

"Yes sir!" Toby said and had no trouble grabbing the cat and handing her to Jack. She made no attempt to wiggle out of his arms and only purred the whole time. Other cats were not so kind to their benefactors, scratching and clawing until they made their escape, in no mood to be caught again. Some of these escapees led the dogs on a merry chase.

Jack walked up the street to the Deadwood Theater, hoping he might find Lil and give her the cat. He was sure she would love the gift and he would have the opportunity to explain himself. Unfortunately, he was unable to find anyone associated with the theater. He saw Whitehead leaning against the theater and approached him.

"Mr.Whitehead," Jack said. "My name is Jack Jones, reporter for the *Chicago Inter-Ocean.*"

"Nice to meet you, Mr. Jones," Whitehead said. "I'd shake your hand, but it looks like you've got your hands full."

"I do, sir," Jack said. "I wonder if I could ask you a question. It has nothing to do with the trial, and I might add you did a masterful job today."

"Why, thank you, Mr. Jones. I guess we'll see how good of a job I did when the verdict comes in. Still no word from inside the theater. It's been over three hours now."

"I didn't realize that," Jack said. "I've lost track of time."

"What is your question, sir?"

"Oh, yes," Jack said. "Do you happen to know where the members of the Deadwood Theater may be, since they can't be in the theater?"

"I know some of them are waiting in the California Chop House."

"Thank you very much, Mr. Whitehead," Jack said. "I need to track down one of them to give this little gift." The cat was still purring.

"My pleasure, sir," Whitehead said. As Jack started to turn away, he saw Johnny Varnes sitting on a stump across the street, whittling on a stick. Varnes appeared to be staring at them. When he saw Jack look in his direction, he stood and ambled down the street.

"Mr. Whitehead, may I ask you an additional question?"

"Yes."

"What do you know about Johnny Varnes?"

"Johnny Varnes," Whitehead said. "He's an interesting character. As you know, he's a gambler and a poor marksman. You are probably aware of his duel in the streets a few days ago."

"Right, I know about that."

"It's interesting. People say Varnes had run-ins with Wild Bill Hickok in the past. Do you know about them?"

"No, I don't."

"The two of them had been feuding for some time. It's said that they had some sort of dispute in Denver months ago. Shortly before McCall shot Wild Bill to death, Varnes and Wild Bill had a confrontation in the Senate Saloon. Varnes and another man were playing poker and were disputing over the game. Wild Bill drew his pistols and covered Varnes with them while he umpired the game, until friends interfered and ended the encounter."

"So Varnes and Wild Bill had an ongoing feud."

"It would appear so."

"I've interviewed several people who believe Jack McCall was a paid assassin whose job was to kill Wild Bill, because the criminal element in town were worried Wild Bill would be hired by some of the Deadwood merchants to maintain law and order."

"That is a plausible story."

"Again, thank you for the information, Mr. Whitehead."

"You're welcome."

Jack turned and walked back down Main Street to the California Chop House.

So Varnes would stand to benefit with Wild Bill Hickok out of the way, Jack thought. The California Chop House door stood wide open and Jack stepped in. Letting his eyes adjust to the dimmer light, he saw Langrishe, his wife, Banjo Dick Brown, and a woman sitting at a table, but there was no sign of Lil or other members of the troupe.

"Good afternoon, Captain Jones," Langrishe called out.

"Good afternoon, Mr. Langrishe, ladies, sir," Jack said.

"Captain Jones, let me introduce you to my wife, Banjo Dick Brown, and his wife, the incomparable actress Fanny Garrettson."

"Pleased to meet you all. I attended your show last night, and I can say you all gave a first-rate performance," Jack said. All but Mrs. Langrishe smiled and said thank you.

"So Captain Jones, may I ask why you grace our presences with this miniature tigress?" Langrishe asked.

"Well sir, it might be better if we spoke in private."

"Is it about my niece?" Mrs. Langrishe asked.

"Yes it is, ma'am."

"Well, we already know about your blunders, so you can stay here and tell us all," Mrs. Langrishe said.

"Go ahead, Captain," Langrishe said.

"Sir, have you had a chance to explain my story to Lil?" Jack asked.

"Yes, I did. She was still very upset, but said she would ponder your message."

"Will she allow me to speak to her? Can you tell me where she is?"

"I think she needs some time to think about all this. You can't speak to her at this time because she and others in the troupe are on a picnic outside of town."

"Do you think that wise, sir, with the recent Indian trouble outside of town?"

"Don't worry, Captain. The men on the picnic are well armed."

The cat repositioned herself in Jack's arms and purred loudly.

"What a pretty cat," Fanny Garrettson said.

"Yes indeed," Mrs. Langrishe agreed.

"She is my gift to Lil," Jack said.

"You don't say?" Mrs. Langrishe said. "Give her here."

Jack handed the cat over to Mrs. Langrishe, who settled the cat on her lap. It began to purr loudly.

"Please tell Lil that I hope she will like this new little friend," Jack said. "I want..."

Bam! A loud report came from the street.

"That could be the signal," Banjo Dick said. A few seconds later, Bam!

"It is!" he said. Banjo Dick and Langrishe stood to leave.

"Captain Jones, I will make sure this darling cat is taken care of until Lil returns and I will make sure she gets it with your best regards."

"Thank you, Mrs. Langrishe," Jack said as he stepped out the door with the others.

A mob of men was streaming into the theater. Fat Jack stood near the door trying to sell socks. Jack glanced down the street to the ponderosa pine across from Saloon Number 10. Expectant men prepared a rope for the hanging. Someone had already tossed one end over the pine tree's overhanging limb.

Upon entering the theater, Jack found his old seat. This time he beat Merrick and saved his seat for him. Merrick was out of breath when he took his place.

"What do you think, Jones? Guilty or not?"

"I say Harry is not guilty, but I am most certain the jury will find him guilty."

"I agree, only I think he is guilty and the jury will find him as such."

All the officers of the court returned well armed. Keithley placed a pistol on top of his law books, beside his Bible.

The jury took their seats. There was not an empty seat in the audience. It was standing room only, and men lined the walls of the theater on three sides facing the stage. Keithley slammed the hammer down onto the wood block several times before the crowd settled down.

"The court is now in session," Keithley said. "Bring in the prisoner."

Old George and the other guard, each cradling a shotgun, led Harry Young onto the stage.

"The prisoner may take his seat," Keithley said. The other guard began to untie the rope around Young's wrists.

"Leave the prisoner bound until we hear the jury's verdict," Keithley said, then turning to the jury, "Members of the jury, who did you select as your foreman?"

Henry Varnes stood and said, "The jury selected me, Henry Varnes as foreman."

"Very good, Mr. Varnes, and what is the verdict of the jury?"

Henry Varnes paused for dramatic effect and said, "The jury finds Harry Young in the murder of Bummer Dan Myer not guilty!" The crowd began to erupt.

"Order! Order in the court!" Keithley shouted, gaveling the hammer onto the wood block several times. The crowd noise subsided but did not die away. Varnes continued, "The jury finds Harry Young not guilty based on self-defense, and he did not shoot the man he intended to shoot."

"So say you all?" Keithley questioned the jurors.

"Aye," they all responded.

"Very well, thank you, Mr. Varnes and thank you, members of the jury," Keithley said. Then turning to the guards and Young he said, "You may release the prisoner. Mr. Young, you are found not guilty and are hereby set free." Keithley faced the crowd and said, "This concludes this court, and I hereby adjourn it *sine die*." and with that, he gaveled the wood block one last time.

The crowd whooped and hollered. Everyone was talking at once. As the guards were untying Young's wrists, his lawyers pounded him and each other on their backs.

Jack and Merrick sat stunned.

"I thought sure the jury had been rigged to declare Harry guilty," Jack said. "So much for my ideas."

"Hum, well," Merrick said. "After three and a half hours deliberation the jury returns with the usual verdict of not guilty! Bah!" He stood and left.

Jack tried to piece together what had just happened. Young was surrounded by a knot of friends congratulating him. Some jurors were drifting away, others stopped to talk to friends. Henry Varnes was talking with his brother Johnny. Pete Adams continued to sit in his seat staring at Young.

"Well, Mr. Reporter," Texas Jack's voice broke into Jack's thoughts. "What do you think of the verdict?"

Jack took a moment to control himself but felt his voice may have sounded shaky as he said, "Surprised. I'm surprised because I thought sure the verdict would be guilty."

Texas Jack's face broke into its sneer as he said, "We listened to the reading of the law, the evidence, and all concluded it was self-defense. We are law-abiding citizens."

Again, Jack fought to control himself. *Law-abiding!* He thought. *You stand before me and talk about law-abiding after murdering and robbing.* Jack's right hand moved toward where his pistol should be. Then he remembered it was in safekeeping at the Grand Central Hotel. All he could do was grunt, "Humph."

Texas Jack laughed as he sauntered by. Jack was disgusted that he could not think of an appropriate response. Pete was now walking up the aisle and saw Jack.

"Jack!" he said. "Boy, am I glad to see you!"

"I'm happy to see you too, Pete. How did it go on the jury?"

"I wasn't happy with the way things went."

"How so?"

"It's a long story."

"It's suppertime. How about we walk over to the Grand Central Hotel and eat our supper while you fill me in on what happened?"

"That sounds good, Jack."

They stood and made their way through the dispersing crowd and into the hotel. They found an empty table as Stonewall leaped at Jack, whimpering in happiness.

"And how was your day, Stonewall?" Jack said, scratching the hound behind his ears.

"He did quite all right, Captain Jones," Lou said, as she set two plates of ham, sweet potatoes, and carrots before them. "That dog has probably put on a pound or two today," she continued. Stonewall was busy sniffing with interest Jack's coat.

"Must be the cat," Jack said.

"What cat?" Lou asked.

"I bought Lil a cat as a present. I hope she likes it."

"You bought Lil a cat as a present without telling her?"

"Yes."

"What did she say?"

"I don't know, I haven't talked to her yet. I gave it to her aunt to give to her."

Lou scowled at Jack and said, "How do you know she likes cats? For all you know, cats might make her sneeze. Maybe she doesn't want to take care of some old cat. Sometimes I wonder about the way you think, Captain," Lou said as she walked away, shaking her head.

Pete was grinning at Jack and said, "You know, Aunt Lou is right."

Jack wore a troubled expression on his face. "She may be right," he said. "It seemed like a good idea at the time."

"We better eat before this food gets cold," Pete said. "Or Aunt Lou will have something else to scold you about."

They ate in silence and when finished stacked their plates at the end of the table.

"Tell me about the jury," Jack said.

"The first thing we did was elect the foreman," Pete began. "That Texas Jack fellow nominated Henry Varnes. There was a second. No one else was nominated and Mr. Varnes was elected jury foreman. We went over the testimony. Mr. Varnes and Texas Jack were emphatic that Harry Young should be let off since they believed he shot in self-defense. I myself believed Young could have been laying in wait to ambush Laughing Sam, but no one else did. We took several votes and finally it was only me holding out against acquittal."

Pete paused to sip his coffee and continued, "Texas Jack and Mr. Varnes were getting upset with me. I told them all maybe we should compromise, maybe we should say we don't know if it was self-defense or not, and we don't have the authority anyway to try Young. Maybe we should send him to the territorial capital in Yankton to have him tried there. A few of the other jurors liked that idea, but again Texas Jack and Mr. Varnes were against it. They said we need to make a decision here and now. They said we know more about the case than any government officials in Yankton do. I was again the only holdout. The entire jury was against me. I finally gave in, but I feel very bad about giving in. I don't think the verdict is right."

"You did the best you could, Pete," Jack said. "To be honest with you, I side with the jury's decision. I was under the impression the jury was going to convict Harry Young and that he would now be hanging from a tree."

"Why do you say that?"

"Several reasons. First, Henry Varnes and Texas Jack were the two men who originally put a rope around Harry Young's neck to hang him. Second, I believe there is a criminal ring in town controlling most of the crime. I think Henry Varnes and Texas Jack may be a part of that ring, and finally Henry Varnes's brother, Johnny, and a dancehall owner named Al Swearengen, were noticeably helping to select jurors. You were one of those they tried to have rejected, but the judge would not allow it. For some reason, they wanted jurors selected who would vote the way they wanted the outcome to go. I would have bet they wanted Harry convicted, but for some reason, now it seems they wanted Harry to get off."

"They certainly were forceful about it," Pete said, then changing the subject. "What time is it?"

Jack looked at his Elgin pocket watch, "It's ten minutes past eight o'clock."

"It's Friday night. I need to see a little of what Deadwood has to offer," Pete said as he pulled back his coat, removed his wallet from an inside pocket, and began to remove a greenback.

"Pete, put your bills away," Jack said. "Supper is on me. And by the way, didn't I say you should put those greenbacks in the bank?"

'Oh I will, I just haven't gotten around to it and remember, I told you I don't trust banks. I trust my own pistol."

"Just be careful. Don't go flashing those bills about."

"Don't worry, I'll be careful," Pete said as he stood to leave. "Thanks again for supper."

"You're welcome, Pete."

As Pete was leaving, Lou stopped by the table to clear the plates.

"Another cup of coffee, Captain Jones?"

"Yes, thanks, Aunt Lou, and if you could bring my satchel of writing material, I'd appreciate it. I better write my story concerning this trial."

Jack spent the next two hours writing his account of the murder and trial for the paper. It took longer than usual, as his mind wandered to Lil, and then wandered to the string of murders, and then back to why the criminal element in town would want Young to go free. Then he remembered he needed to be riding out of town Sunday. He had lots to do tomorrow to prepare for his search for General Crook.

It was after ten p.m.. Jack had finished the piece for the paper. His mind was still racing back and forth from Lil to the murders to the acquittal.

Deciding he should write down what facts he knew about these murders, Jack took out a blank piece of paper and wrote:

Wild Bill Hickok:
    Jack McCall shot Hickok the day after losing to him in a card game. McCall claimed Hickok had shot his brother. The jury let McCall off. Some businessmen in town wanted to hire Hickok as a peace officer. Varnes and Hickok had one or more confrontations. Colorado

Charlie and California Joe believe others used McCall to assassinate Hickok.

Preacher Smith:

He had over two hundred dollars in gold dust, etc., on him. Someone shot him in the heart at close range. The claim was Indians killed him, but whoever did it did not scalp or otherwise mutilate him. The only thing missing was his money. An Indian was killed near the site of the preacher's murder, but he was making the sign of peace and no evidence of money or anything else from Preacher Smith was found on his body. The man responsible for finding Preacher Smith's body and killing the Indian was Texas Jack, a known killer (known to me).

Bummer Dan:

Harry Young shoots Bummer Dan by mistake thinking he is shooting Laughing Sam. Johnny Varnes and Al Swearengen want Harry Young declared not guilty. Bummer Dan's haversack, with its gold and possibly even more gold from his shanty, which someone ransacked, is missing. Laughing Sam Hartman, who could shed light on all this, is missing.

Poncho and Carlos

Clearly murdered by Texas Jack and he makes the murders look like the mrn killed each other. Their possible bag, with its gold, is missing.

The Criminal Ring:

If there is a criminal ring in Deadwood, the known members are Al Swearengen, Johnny Burns, Johnny Varnes, Henry Varnes, and Texas Jack. There may be others.

Jack reviewed what he had written. It helped him clarify in his mind all the information. He could see how all the murders except the Bummer Dan murder could be attributed to a ring. The only ring connection to Bummer Dan was that ring members worked to get Harry Young off, but why?

Jack was tired. It had been a long day. He closed his books, filed the papers in his satchel, and looked down at Stonewall, who was wagging his tail. "Maybe I'll be able to piece it together better tomorrow, Stonewall."

CHAPTER TWELVE
ℰᴏᴄ℞

Saturday Morning, August 26, 1876—Jack slept later than normal. *It's Saturday,* he reasoned. After breakfast, he and Stonewall stepped out of the hotel into the bright morning sunshine. It was another typical Deadwood Gulch morning. The sights, the sounds, the smells were the same, but one thing was different—people were running toward Lee Street.

Jack called out to one of the runners, "What's going on? Why is everyone running?"

"A body was found in Whitewood Creek under the Lee Street Bridge!" the runner shouted.

Jack joined running with the others. A crowd gathered around the creek as three men stood in the water and pulled a body out from under the bridge. They then carried the body out of the creek and laid it on the bank. As Jack pushed his way through the crowd, one of the men who had recovered the body said, "Anyone know who this young fellow was?"

Jack looked down at the body. His head swam. *This is not happening. This must be some mistake,* Jack's mind roared. The body was Pete Adams.

Jack dropped to his knees alongside the body. Pete's opened, glazed eyes stared at nothing. Tears welled in Jack's eyes. "I know this kid, his name's Pete Adams," he said softly.

"Look there," a second man who had pulled the body from the creek, said. "Look at the back of his head. It looks like he was hit hard." A bad, blood-caked gash ran above Pete's right ear. Jack just stared at the body. Some people began to drift away as others arrived to see what all the commotion was.

"Hey mister," the first man said. "Since you know this fellow, how about you take care of his body from here on out? We got to get back to our claim."

"Thank you," Jack said, "I will take care of him." The three men who had recovered the body stood and left. Jack didn't distinguish what any of the voices around him were saying. He only heard the creek continuing its flow—a false sense of merriment—laughing, tinkling, booming, gurgling.

"Captain Jones!" It was a female voice. "Captain Jones!" It was a female voice he recognized. He looked up. Calamity Jane stood beside him. "Captain Jones, was this here boy a friend?"

"Yes, Calamity, he was."

"All right, me and the girls, we'll take care of him for ya. Get him washed up and presentable for burial."

"Thanks, Calamity, I appreciate that."

Jack stood and began to dig in his pants pocket for some coins. "Put your money away, Captain, we'll settle up some other time."

"Thanks."

Jack decided to check Pete for his money and figure out how to send it to his family. He stooped down to the body and looked at the inside coat pockets. Pete's wallet was missing. He checked all the pockets, but there was no wallet, nothing in any of the pockets. Pete's old pistol was missing too.

Jack stood up and said in a loud voice, "Has anyone seen a leather wallet? It had this man's greenbacks in it. And also has anyone seen an old pistol?"

"I found a pistol along the stream," a mud-splattered miner said and showed Jack the pistol. "That was Pete's," Jack said.

"Do you want it, mister?" the miner asked.

"No, go ahead and keep it."

"A couple of you fellers here help a gal with this body," Calamity ordered. They picked up Pete.

"Where to, Calamity?" one of them asked.

"Take him into the General Custer House Hotel, that's the closest. I'll wash him up in there. If they give ya any guff, tell them they'll have to deal with me!" Turning to Jack, she said, "Captain Jones, what was his name again for the headboard?"

"Pete Adams."

"Any idea what happened here?"

"Pete had a wallet full of greenbacks that's missing. It could have been washed downstream, or someone might have picked it up. But my thinking is based on the blow to his head and the fact that the money is missing—he was killed and robbed. But of course, I can't prove that. We have no witnesses, and we have no idea who did it. Nothing that would hold up in a court of law."

"Sometimes ya have to go beyond the law," Calamity said. "When ya know ya're right, ya got to do the right thing, even if the law won't go there with ya."

"And what law do we really have here in town?"

"I'd say the law is the God-given sense of right and wrong ya have here," as she pointed to her head, "and here," as she pointed to her heart.

"You might be right, Calamity."

"I know I'm right!"

By now the crowd had dissipated. Men carried Pete's body, followed by Calamity, to the nearby General Custer House. Jack walked along the banks of Whitewood Creek looking for the missing wallet but saw nothing.

Jack didn't think it was likely, but maybe, just maybe, Pete put some of his money in the bank. He decided to check it out.

He turned his back on Whitewood Creek and walked to Main Street. It was a short walk south to the small log building with the large sign proclaiming Miners' & Merchants' Bank, Jason M. Woods, Cashier. Jack entered the building. Behind the rough-hewn counter stood Jason M. Woods, Cashier.

"Good morning, Captain Jones," he said.

"Good morning, Jason."

"What can I do for you this fine Saturday morning, sir?"

"The morning is not fine. A friend was murdered last night."

"Goodness! I had not heard!"

"The murder is why I am here. The man's name was Pete Adams. He had a quantity of greenbacks on him and I had suggested to him that he place them here in your bank for safekeeping. Do you know if he did that?"

"I don't recall that name, but let me double-check the books." Woods spent a minute reviewing his ledger book.

"No, no one by that name has deposited anything with us."

"Thank you, Jason, I thought as much, but I wanted to check."

"I'm sorry to hear about your friend, Captain Jones."

"Thank you."

Jack turned and walked out the door. Stoop-shouldered, he stared at the ground. Sensing a presence in front of him, he looked up and saw standing before him a Chinese man, holding a staff in his right hand. He was one of the Cantonese bodyguards who carried Di Lee. The man took two steps forward, tucked the staff under his arm, and bowed. Jack awkwardly followed suit. The man produced an envelope and held it out before him with two hands for Jack to take. Jack took the envelope, the man bowed again, Jack did likewise, and without saying a word, the man grasped his staff and walked down Main Street. Jack watched him leave and then looked at the envelope. There was no writing on it. He tore it open, revealing inside a folded piece of writing paper with a message printed by hand. Jack read the message and then a second time, as his sorrow burned into anger.

Captain Jones,

We are sorry your friend Pete Adams is dead. One of our people saw the murder and robbery. The men who killed Pete Adams are Texas Jack and Johnny Varnes. We are sorry for you.

Your Friends

"Texas Jack and Varnes! You bastards!" Jack spit the words through clenched teeth. "This is it. It's over."

Jack strode up the street to the Grand Central Hotel. He burst through the door. Charlie Wagner was working behind the counter.

"Good morning, Captain..."

"Charlie, get me my pistol and my ammunition!" Jack ordered.

"Yes, sir," a shocked Wagner said. He vanished into the storeroom and quickly returned with Jack's Army Colt, holster and waist belt, and box of cartridges.

"I've been meaning to ask about that holster," Wagner said. "I've not seen one like it."

"A fellow just started making a few of these in Cheyenne, I like the way it holds my pistol," Jack coolly spoke as he checked the Army Colt's cylinders and bore to make sure the pistol was still clean and well oiled. Wagner handed him a rag to wipe it down.

Jack loaded five rounds, leaving one chamber open and set at the firing position. He checked the loops on the waist belt to make sure there was a cartridge in every loop.

"May I ask what's going on?" Wagner said.

"Yes, I'm mad as hell. The young fellow, Pete Adams, who I befriended the other day, is dead and robbed. I know who did it. I'm going to get them. I'm going to do to them what they did to a defenseless kid."

"Who was it? Don't you think we should put a court together and let them decide?"

"Ha!" Jack spat. "The courts in this town are a joke! Where was the justice with Wild Bill? Where was the justice with Bummer Dan? Not to mention Preacher Smith. Indians? I don't think so! Look at Poncho and Carlos, that was a put up job. No, I know who did this and they will pay!"

Jack turned his back on Wagner and stomped out of the hotel, Stonewall trailing behind. His first stop was the Senate Saloon. No one had seen either Varnes or Texas Jack. He then entered the Cricket Saloon. No one he knew was in there except Johnny Burns behind the bar. Before Burns could say a word Jack grabbed the front of Burns's shirt with his left hand and poked the muzzle of his pistol into Burns's left temple.

"Where's Texas Jack and Johnny Varnes!" Jack growled.

Burns's eyes bulged as he blurted and stammered, "I-I don't know. I-I ain't seen them for some time!"

Jack pulled the pistol hammer back to full cock. Burns began to cry. "I'm-I'm tellin' the truth."

Jack slammed him back against the wall and said, "You see them, you tell them I'll kill them for what they did to Pete Adams. You hear?"

"Ye-yes!"

"And don't you try anything or so help me I'll shoot you down like the dog you are."

Jack backed out of the saloon and onto the street. He eased the hammer back from full cock, holstered his Army Colt revolver, and strode over to Saloon Number 10. Several customers stood at the bar. Both Young and Tipple were behind it. Before anyone could say a word or Stonewall could growl at Young, Jack shouted, "Where's Varnes and Texas Jack?"

Everyone stared at him in surprise. "I said, where's those sons of bitches, Varnes and Texas Jack?" Jack repeated.

"No one's seen them since last night," Tipple said. The rest agreed.

"You see them, you tell them I know what they did and I'm coming after them."

The men nodded as Jack left the saloon and headed back up the street. Walking towards Jack was Fat Jack. Jack intercepted him and said, "Fat Jack, I need to buy socks."

"S-Sure thing, C-Captain," Fat Jack said as Jack and Fat Jack exchanged coins for socks.

"Fat Jack, whereabouts in town can I find Johnny Varnes and Texas Jack?"

"You c-can't find them in t-town."

"What do you mean?"

"Th-they're gone."

"What!"

"I h-heard they g-got business in Ch-Cheyenne, and left e-early this m-morning."

"Do you know which trail?"

"I h-heard they were traveling s-straight south through Hill City t-to Custer City. T-That way."

"Thank you, Fat Jack!"

"Y-You're welcome, C-Captain," Fat Jack said as he ran off to find the nearest faro game.

The rage boiled within Jack. *They can't get away. I've got to stop them. But how?* he asked himself. Then it came to him. He could borrow a horse from the livery and ride after them.

He strode up the street, oblivious to his surroundings. He had one goal in mind—to catch and kill Varnes and Texas Jack. He turned right on Gold Street and made his way to the livery stable. Paco nickered as Jack shouted, "Halloo, Old Frenchy!"

Jack spied Old Frenchy in the back of the building. He stopped his work repairing a damaged wheelbarrow and walked toward Jack.

"Good morning, Captain Jones, how may I help you?"

"I need to borrow a horse right away. I'm not sure when I'll be back."

"Is there a problem, Captain? You look upset."

"Old Frenchy, a good young man was murdered last night by Johnny Varnes and Texas Jack. They have left town. I plan to go after them."

"And then what?"

"What do you mean?"

"What will you do when you find them?"

"What will I do? I'm going to kill them."

"Think, my friend, if you do this, do you then become like them?"

"I don't care. I'll think about it later. Right now, I need a horse."

"Take someone with you. Someone who can help you."

"No time, Old Frenchy, every moment I waste gives them more time to get away!"

"If you insist, Captain. The only horse I have available right now is Paco. He is a good horse, but as we all do, he has a few flaws. His big problem is he does not like loud noises, such as guns firing, so if you must shoot, make sure you are not on top of him, or you will be on the ground."

"Thank you for the advice."

Jack waited while Old Frenchy haltered Paco, led him out of the stall, and tied him to a post. He laid a saddle blanket on Paco's back as Jack checked Paco's saddle's stirrup lengths to make sure they were the right length for his legs. The men placed the saddle on Paco's back and cinched him up. Then Old Frenchy picked out Paco's bridle and placed the bit in his mouth and the headstall over his head. Jack checked the cinch again and tightened it. He led Paco around and rechecked the cinch, further tightening it. Jack rubbed Paco's forehead and said, "I need your help, Paco. Let's be partners on this trip. All right?" Jack held the reins and grabbed a bit of mane as he swung up into the saddle and adjusted his seat.

"Old Frenchy, thank you for the advice. I will be careful. I'll think about what you said. These men need to be brought to justice. I'm still bent on killing them, but I will think about your words."

"Captain Jones, here is a canteen full of water and saddle bags with bread in them. Who knows, you may need it if your travels take you longer than you think."

Jack took the canteen and saddlebag and stuck out his hand to Old Frenchy, who took it.

"Thank you, my friend," Jack said.

"I will pray for your safe return, Captain," Old Frenchy said.

"I thank you for that, too," Jack said and then clicked for Paco to move forward. Stonewall trotted alongside.

"Godspeed!" Old Frenchy called after them.

They headed up Main Street to take the road to Lead. Jack didn't expect to catch Varnes and Texas Jack until somewhere between Lead and Hill City, if he was lucky.

Jack wondered if he should stop in the theater to try to talk to Lil. He doubted she would talk to him yet. He better wait until he got back. Then changing his thoughts, he wondered if it would be safer to take someone along with him. If so, who? Bullock and Star? But it would take too long to tell the story, to convince them, then have them find horses and ride along. After all, Old Frenchy said Paco was the last horse at the livery. He decided to push on by himself.

Loud, popping firecrackers interrupted his thoughts. Paco reacted to the noise, bucking and trying to run, but Jack kept his head up and soon had him back under control. Bringing Paco to a stop, Jack dismounted and again tightened the cinch. He stroked Paco's forehead and neck, saying, "Listen, Paco, we may be together for a long time. You need to get over this fear of loud noises."

Jack remounted and they continued south along the road to Lead. Several wagons traveled along the road and Jack had to negotiate around the oxen. Horseback riders rode in both directions. Plenty of prospectors were working their claims along the way, and woodchoppers were on the slopes felling trees for lumber and fuel. After several miles, Jack reached Lead, another expanding, bustling town where miners were working promising hard-rock mines. There were fewer prospectors here, as working hard rock required plenty of capital, something the average miner did not have—and there was no heavy equipment to process the ore.

Jack did not meet anyone he knew well enough to ask for assistance. Several times, he asked familiar faces if they had seen Johnny Varnes and Texas Jack, but no one claimed that they had.

Outside of Lead, he continued south toward Hill City, heading deeper into the Black Hills. The slopes to the ridges became steeper as the narrow valleys and rock walls closed in. Overlapping ponderosa pine and white spruce boughs blocked the sun's rays, creating a false twilight. The road was only a rough-cut trail. Boulders and stumps protruded up through the ungraded surface. Abandoned wagon wrecks, pulled to the side of the trail, had been stripped of anything useful. Wolves and coyotes had scattered bones where oxen, horses, and mules had died of exhaustion.

Jack encountered fewer and fewer miners until they disappeared, as the rock in this area held no gold. Travelers heading out of Lead and Deadwood had disappeared and very few were coming from the opposite direction. Jack asked those few he encountered if they had seen two riders heading south. He described the men. Those who responded said yes, that they had seen two horseback riders who were leading a third horse. This information encouraged Jack to press on.

He stopped by a trickling, gurgling stream to give Paco a rest. Jack, Paco, and Stonewall drank their fill of the ice-cold water. He loosened the cinch, removed Paco's bridle, and tied his lead line to a birch tree growing at the edge of a meadow. There Paco could munch on grass growing in an open spot. Jack sat in the shade on a thick carpet of moss. He ate the bread Old Frenchy had given him and threw chunks of it to Stonewall who wolfed them down without so much as tasting them.

At the end of their break, Jack put the bridle back on Paco and tightened the cinch. He remounted and they continued south.

Time—he had lots of it to think. Most thoughts centered on his hate and disgust for Varnes and Texas Jack. They were done. He would kill them. He had killed before, during the war and afterwards, but always out of self-preservation and never out of revenge. Was revenge right? What would Lil say? Would she be even more disgusted with him if he shot down those two murderers? Maybe he should bring them back to Deadwood after all and let the citizens of Deadwood handle it. But then he knew what would happen. Varnes and Texas Jack would get off, just as Jack McCall and Harry Young had gotten off. Merrick was right. The usual verdict would be not guilty. He had to take matters into his own hands. He knew he was in the right. Those two murdering dogs had snuffed out the life of a boy who appreciated life and wanted to live it to its fullest. Now Pete would never get that opportunity. No. He would do it. He would take care of Varnes and Texas Jack, once and for all.

Jack came to a large rock outcrop on the right that obscured a right-hand bend in the trail from his view. Taking no chances, he pulled his Army Colt and held it at the ready in case he should run into any unforeseen trouble. The Lakota and Cheyenne were not known to venture this far into the Black Hills. They usually stayed on the periphery, but no sense taking any chances. As Jack rounded the outcrop, he came face to face with two outriders and a two-mule team pulling a wagon. A man drove the wagon. A woman sat beside him, and a small girl and a smaller boy peeked from behind the man and woman. One outrider leveled his carbine at Jack and the other ordered in a high voice, "Hold it right there, mister!"

Jack reined Paco to a stop and pointed the barrel of his pistol straight up.

"Good afternoon," Jack said. "I'm just passing by, if you don't mind."

"Trying to catch your friends?" the outrider holding the carbine asked. Both outriders were boys.

"If you mean two riders trailing a horse, they aren't my friends. But I aim to catch up with them."

"What's your business with them, mister?" asked the man sitting on the wagon box, holding the lines to the mules.

"They are bad men. They have murdered several people in Deadwood, and I'm on their trail to catch them."

"Go ahead, mister, holster your pistol then, nice and easy," the older man said. Jack did as he was told. The boy with the carbine continued to aim the barrel towards Jack.

"We ran into those characters about a mile back," the man continued. "We had a nice chat and when we weren't looking, they leveled their pistols at us and demanded all the money we had. While one stood lookout, the other ransacked our wagon, taking valuables they could carry with them. They took all our guns except one that my son Jeb has there. Jeb, you can stop aiming that carbine at this man. They said they would leave us a few cartridges back along the trail to give themselves enough of a head start. Jeb rode back and sure enough, they did leave us a few. Said they didn't want to hear about Indians lifting our scalps."

"I'm sorry to hear of your misfortune, sir," Jack said. "When I catch them, I'll make sure I get your money and possessions back to you. Where do you plan to head to?"

"We want to settle in Deadwood. I was fixing to come by myself, but my missus here wouldn't think of it. She said we need to stay together as a family."

The woman had been looking down until this point but looked up at Jack and said, "That's right, sir! We stick together as a family and I can help our income. I'm a good seamstress and I'm sure those miner boys will need their clothes repaired."

"That they do, ma'am," Jack said. "Some of those fellows look pretty ragged."

"Mister," said the little girl.

"Annie, be quiet," the woman said. "You know it's impolite to speak to a grownup without them speaking to you first."

"It's okay, ma'am," Jack said. "What is it, Annie?"

"Mister, are you a lawman?"

"No, I'm a newspaper reporter, but I am upset about what those bad men are doing to people and I'm going to find them."

"Are you going to take them to the jail?"

"I haven't thought about that."

"Well, if you don't take them to the jail, what else can you do with them?"

Jack looked at the ground. He remembered what Old Frenchy had said, and now this little girl was asking the same thing. His anger subsided, and he knew the right thing was to attempt to capture Varnes and Texas Jack and take them back to Deadwood. There were enough good folks in town who would help him with this. He looked back up at the little girl.

"You know what, Annie?"

"What, mister?"

"I'm going to do what you said, Annie. I'm going to catch those bad men and take them to jail."

Annie beamed. Jack tipped his hat to the family and slowly walked Paco by them.

"Hey, mister!" Jeb said. "What's your name?"

"Jones. Jack Jones."

"Good luck, Mr. Jones."

The family said Varnes and Texas Jack are about a mile back along the trail. Jack thought he might be able to catch up with them soon, and that he'd better be on his guard.

The trail continued under overlapping pine boughs. A squirrel scolded Jack, Paco, and Stonewall as they passed beneath his safe perch atop a white spruce. It was getting late. The sun had dipped behind the western ridges.

In the distance, Jack could make out what appeared to be an abandoned cabin. The roof was partially caved in, but smoke was coming from the chimney. Three unsaddled horses were tied to a rope strung between two trees for a picket line. Jack saw no movement around the cabin. He dismounted, remembering that Paco was not the best around loud noises. He untied the halter's lead line from the saddle ring, and crossing the reins, draped them over Paco's neck. Holding the lead line in his left hand and the Army Colt in his right, he quietly approached the cabin. Stonewall padded silently alongside, huffing and happily looking up at Jack.

He was close enough now he could see the horses. The one belonged to Texas Jack and the other two had belonged to Poncho and Carlos. Three saddles lay on the ground along the front wall of the cabin. On top of one of the saddles lay a black-gummed haversack with white lettering. The two letters were B and D.

Jack quietly and slowly walked closer to the front of the cabin. Paco whinnied. The three other horses looked up and whinnied back. Varnes appeared at the cabin door and stepped outside.

"Hold it right there!" Jack ordered, aiming his pistol at Varnes. Varnes was unarmed. He glanced at a carbine propped by the outside cabin wall to his right and within his reach.

"Don't try it!" Jack ordered. "Put your hands up—now!"

Varnes held his hands up.

"Step forward and to your left, away from the gun," Jack again ordered, and Varnes complied.

"Where's Texas Jack?" Jack asked.

"I don't know," Varnes answered. "He must have gone for a walk."

Jack quickly scanned the area and saw no movement. He knew he probably had little time before Texas Jack returned.

"Keep moving to your left until I tell you to stop," Jack said. Varnes moved left away from the cabin, until Jack said, "Stop!"

Leading Paco, Jack backed over to the picket line while keeping his eye on Varnes. One-handed, he tied Paco's lead line to the picket line, using two half hitches.

"Jones," Varnes said. "You know Texas Jack will return soon. He's armed. If I were you, I'd clear out of here now. I like you. I don't want to see you hurt."

Jack didn't say anything. He slowly moved over to the saddles and haversack, all the while keeping an eye on Varnes and trying to stay aware of his surroundings in case Texas Jack should come back. He reached the saddles and knelt on one knee, all the while not taking his eyes off Varnes. With his left hand, he unfastened the haversack's keeper strap and reached inside. The first item he pulled out and held up to eye level was the possible bag that Carlos and Poncho had owned. It was still heavy with their earnings. Next, he fished out the nugget Bummer Dan had shown him. Jack found two poke bags filled with gold dust. He was pulling out an assortment of gold and silver coins when Varnes spoke.

"Jones, how about we make a deal? We would be willing to give you a cut of the take. Walk away and let us go. No one would be the wiser."

"Do you really believe I would do that?"

"It was worth a try."

Jack's hand reached the last object in the bag. It was rectangular and flat. He pulled it out. It was Pete's wallet, containing his greenbacks.

"You son of a bitch!" Jack snarled.

A click behind Jack's head—the click of a hammer being cocked and then the cold steel of a gun's muzzle pressed against the back of his skull.

Varnes laughed. "You asked where Texas Jack was. Well, I'd say he's right behind you."

"Drop your gun, Jones," Texas Jack ordered. Jack didn't move. "I said drop it or I blow the back of your head off now!" Jack dropped the gun. Varnes walked over to the gun and picked it up. He pointed it at Jack. "Put everything back in the haversack," he ordered. When Jack was done, Texas Jack said, "Can I shoot him now, boss?"

"Not yet," Varnes said. "I want to have a little fun first. Jones, stand up and move over to where I was standing." Jack did as Varnes ordered.

"Texas Jack, make sure everything is back in that haversack and latch the keeper strap. I don't want to lose any of our hard-earned money. You can holster your gun. I've got an eye on Jones here. He can't do us any harm."

"Right, boss," Texas Jack said as he holstered his pistol.

"I'm sure you have plenty of questions, Jones, since you are a reporter. Go ahead, fire away. No pun there at all, ha ha."

Jack was trying to control his anger and trying to figure out how to get out of this situation. He blasted himself for not bringing someone along. He should have known he would not be able to take on two hardened criminals by himself. The only chance he had was to delay the inevitable as long as possible. He thought that when it got dark enough he could dive to the side before they fired, and then run and hide in the dark.

"All right, I want to know if there is a criminal ring in Deadwood. I assume you are both a part of it."

"Ah, a criminal ring in Deadwood. Hum. What do you think, Texas Jack? I never thought of ourselves as a ring, did you?"

"No, Johnny, I didn't," Texas Jack said as he sat down by the saddles, reached over and found his spurs, and started to strap them on his boots.

"But some of us did work together in town," Varnes said.

"What do you mean by the word 'did'?" Jack asked.

"Texas Jack and me figured things were getting a little hot in town, no thanks to the snooping you and your friends were doing. Besides, we felt we had done most of the work to acquire this loot and didn't think we should share it with others who didn't work for it as hard as we did."

"So let me guess, your brother Henry, Swearengen, and Burns are members of your ring," Jack said.

"Very good," Varnes said.

"What about Miller, Harry Young's attorney?"

"Wrong there, Jones, he was just a dupe."

"Who else in town is part of your ring?"

"If you haven't guessed, I'm not going to tell. You can't know everything."

"What about Wild Bill?"

"Wild Bill was a horse's ass!" Varnes snarled. "He thought he could poke his nose into other people's business. He thought he could work for the law, but he was no better than the rest of us. Yes, we had him killed by that buffoon, Jack McCall. If McCall had acted according to plan he wouldn't have gotten caught!"

"What do you mean?"

"We had a horse for him tied to the hitching rack outside Saloon Number 10 so he could make his getaway out of town. We told McCall the cinch would be loose and that he needed to tighten it before he walked in to shoot Hickok. He forgot to tighten the cinch and as you heard, the saddle turned on him. Fortunately, we had our backup plan. We told him if he got caught to tell everyone Hickok had killed his brother. We had to make sure there were enough people on the jury who could sway the verdict to not guilty. We then had to hustle that idiot out of town before Hickok's friends took care of him."

"Preacher Smith," Jack said. "Was he one of your kills?"

"Preacher Smith's death was an unfortunate incident," Varnes said.

"I didn't want to kill him," Texas Jack said as he stood up. "But I had to."

"Why?" Jack asked.

"While me and my *compañeros* was out huntin' for Injuns, I separated myself from them to track down the good parson, knowing that he had just left Deadwood. I spied him walking north. I knew he had quite a heavy poke and I determined I would relieve him of it. I came up behind him. I was real close. I had my bandanna up over my nose so all you could see was my eyes. I told him to deliver up his poke to me. He turned, looked into my eyes, and said, 'I know it's you, Texas Jack. You know the Lord does not condone robbery.' Well, it was his stupidity what got him shot. If he would've kept his mouth shut, I would have let him go, but seeing as how he knew who I was, I had to shoot him. Fortunately, that Injun happened along, I killed him and blamed everything on him. No one was the wiser, until you started your snooping."

"What about Lou Mason, who was killed by the Indian?"

"No, he wasn't in on it, he was just plain stupid."

"What about Carlos and Poncho?" Jack asked.

Texas Jack spat. "Those *hombres* had it coming to them."

Varnes scowled and said, "You were taking too much of a risk by shooting them right in town like that."

"Aw, you're too nervous, boss," Texas Jack said. "I was careful. No one saw me." Jack held his tongue.

"It was still a very stupid move," Varnes said.

"Why did you stack the deck with the jury selection on the Harry Young case?" Jack asked.

"Why? What do you mean?" Varnes asked.

"You already told me Miller was a dupe. Remember? And I saw you and Swearengen passing signals to Miller on who to pick for the jury."

"That was our best scheme yet," Varnes said smiling. "And since you won't be telling anyone, I'll tell you what we did."

"Are you sure you want to tell him this, boss?" Texas Jack said.

"Shut up, it won't hurt. It's nothing compared to the boneheaded moves you've been making!"

Texas Jack spat and growled, "Whatever you say, boss."

"Jones, it was a classic story of greed and retribution," Varnes began. "Bummer Dan was part of your so-called criminal ring. We found out he was withholding a portion of his ill-gotten profits that belonged to us all. We decided to set him up, recover our rightful share, and kill him, making him an example to anyone else who might think of double-crossing us. To do this we set up a fake feud between Laughing Sam and Harry Young."

"A fake feud?" Jack said.

"That's right, Laughing Sam and Harry Young are actually good friends."

"What!"

"That's what I said—good friends," Varnes continued. "Even though they were partners, Laughing Sam was furious that Bummer Dan was skimming off and keeping part of the take for himself. We concocted the fake feud over that Tid Bit whore. Laughing Sam told Bummer Dan he needed to kill Young, so he told Bummer Dan what he wanted to do was divert Young's attention by having Bummer Dan dressing in Laughing Sam's clothes as a distraction. Laughing Sam then told Bummer Dan he would sneak into the saloon and shoot Harry when he was distracted by looking at Bummer Dan wearing Laughing Sam's clothes. We knew Bummer Dan had the nugget in the haversack and that he had his secret stash buried in his shanty. Do you follow me so far?"

"Yes, so I assume Bummer Dan agrees to wear Laughing Sam's hat and coat and trustingly hands Laughing Sam his haversack for safekeeping."

"Right you are, Jones!" Varnes said. "Then after Harry shoots Bummer Dan, Laughing Sam runs back to Bummer Dan's shanty, rummages about the place until he finds the poke sack and has to quickly get out of there before your Celestial friend, what's his name, Wong, runs him off."

"Why would Harry take such a risk?" Jack asked. "He must have known people would come after him and possibly hang him."

"Good point, Jones," Varnes said. "The first reason is money. We paid him very well, and we had our plans set to protect him. When the mob came for Harry, we made sure that my brother Henry and," Varnes turned to Texas Jack.

"And me!" Texas Jack said.

"We made sure they were the ones closest to Harry and were the ones to place any noose around his neck. If you remember, I was the one who did my civic duty to stop the mob and call for law and order. Fortunately, the sheep heeded my call to civility and ended their call for a hanging."

"What if they hadn't?"

"Ah, yes—our backup, we had several men stationed in the dark with rifles. If need be, they would have attempted a rescue of Harry, but again all went well according to plan."

"And then what about the trial?" Jack asked, thinking that the light was beginning to fade. If he could keep delaying them, maybe he could make a break for it when it gets dark. He couldn't think of anything else.

"The trial was almost a masterpiece of deception. I say almost. It would have been perfect if it wasn't for that stupid kid, Adams," Varnes said. Jack fought to keep control of his mouth.

"We were able to select just about everyone we wanted to be on that jury," Varnes continued. "As I said, Miller is not part of our so-called ring. He's new to town. I told him we knew who were reputable Deadwood citizens. We would let him know by nods and shakes of our heads who was a solid citizen and who was not. He bought it. Ha! Ha! That was so much fun. None of those fancy lawyers had a clue that we were controlling what was really going on, and so we got good old Harry off. We're going to have to get him out of town. There's still a few people sore about him shooting Bummer Dan."

"Let's shoot this reporter now, boss," Texas Jack said. "It's getting dark."

"Don't interrupt me!" Varnes growled. "I'm not ready for any shooting just yet." Jack's eyes glanced to the right, then to the left, looking for which direction might give him more cover and a better chance to get away.

"Don't think about trying to escape, Jones," Varnes said. "Step a few feet closer where I can keep a better eye on you."

"Why did you have to kill Pete?" Jack asked, a lump rising in his throat as he slowly moved a few steps forward.

"That was an unfortunate incident," Varnes said. "He died of his own stupidity. He flashed those greenbacks of his during the jury discussions."

"Me and Henry seen that kid's bills ripe for the plucking," Texas Jack said, grinning.

"I walked up to him in the dark and asked him politely to hand over the greenbacks," Varnes said. "Texas Jack snuck up and stood behind him. The kid refused to cooperate and started to go for his gun."

"I whacked him good on the side of the head," Texas Jack said. "Ha! Ha! Too good."

"As I said, it was unfortunate," Varnes said. "If he had only cooperated, he would still be in this world."

"You bastards!" Jack said, taking another step forward.

"Hold it right there, Jones," Varnes growled. "If you know what's good for you."

Jack stopped, his face flushed with rage, his fists balled at his sides.

"It's time to end this part of our little drama," Varnes said, cocking the hammer on Jack's pistol. "Goodbye..." and he swung the pistol to his left, pulling the trigger, firing it into Texas Jack's stomach, "Texas Jack!"

Varnes swiveled back, leveling the pistol at Jack. Texas Jack stood both hands holding his gut, shock and pain etched into his pale face.

Terrified, Paco reared back, snapping the leather lead line. Bucking and kicking, he raced down the trail, back towards Lead.

"You stupid son of a bitch," Varnes said to Texas Jack, not taking his eyes off Jack. "I've had it with your idiocy. You've brought us nothing but trouble and made it too hot for me in Deadwood. If the likes of Jones can start to figure things out, then others smarter than him will also. So now, because of you I have to leave."

Texas Jack dropped to his knees, blood streaming out of the wound, his hands unable to staunch the flow.

"You bastard," Texas Jack cried as he tried to reach for one of his pistols. Varnes turned, kicking Texas Jack's hand while pulling back the hammer on Jack's pistol again. Varnes, aiming at Texas Jack's head, pulled the trigger, blasting a hole through his forehead and out the back. Texas Jack's body slumped to the ground. Jack, shocked, could not move. Varnes swung the pistol back around to Jack, cocking the hammer and barking, "Do not move!"

Jack stood frozen. A little winded from the effort and excitement, Varnes stared at Jack, then not taking his eyes off him, he walked over to Texas Jack's body and removed one of his pistols. He cocked back the hammer, pointed the pistol off into the trees, and shot it twice. He then placed the pistol in Texas Jack's right hand.

"You're probably wondering what I'm doing," Varnes said. "Wondering why I haven't killed you yet. Well, I'm not going to kill you. I like you."

Jack's mouth was dry. He couldn't talk. Stonewall padded over to Texas Jack's body and sniffed it.

"So what am I going to do with you?" Varnes continued. "How am I going to make sure you don't bring your so-called honorable friends after me and my ring? Well, this is what I'm going to do. The news will leak out that you and Texas Jack had this little shootout. He shot at you twice, missing, but you were the better shot, blowing two holes into him. That's why I shot him with your pistol and fired off a couple of rounds from his pistol. A very convenient story for you and me. Don't you think?"

Jack didn't answer. Stonewall walked away from Texas Jack and disappeared behind Jack.

"All right, Jones. If you write about or tell anyone about the truth of this incident or about the so-called Deadwood ring and what we have done, it will not go well for your Deadwood friends. It would be a shame if they found Old Frenchy stomped to death by a horse in one of the stalls. It would be a loss to the Celestials if poor Wong were to slip in Whitewood Creek and crack his head open on a boulder. Oh, what would the poor, famished workers of Deadwood do if Aunt Lou were to be found asphyxiated in her boarding room?"

Jack felt the anger rising in him again and subconsciously moved closer to Varnes who backed up a couple of steps.

"Hold it, Jones! And finally, wouldn't it be a shame if a certain actress was found floating face down in Whitewood Creek? What's her name, Lillian Rochelle?"

"You wouldn't dare!"

"Oh, yes I will!"

Jack glared at Varnes.

"I want you to promise on the life of Lillian Rochelle that you will not tell a soul about me, the ring, the actions of the ring, and what happened here. If you tell anyone, anything about any of this, Lillian Rochelle forfeits her life. There are plenty of people in Deadwood who will carry out my orders. You have guessed one or two, but there are many more, and you do not know who they are. Now promise me on her life!"

Jack's mind was racing. He could not let anything happen to Lil or his friends. If he wrote about his accusations in the paper, it would not lead to anything. If he told the people in Deadwood, nothing would happen. Even if they believed him, there was no law in town. No one would go after Varnes or his ring.

"Come on, Jones," Varnes said. "I don't have all night."

Stonewall growled behind Jack. There was the sound of something striking the hound and a high-pitched yelp. Jack instinctively began to turn.

"Don't move, Jones!" Varnes said. "Promise me, on the life of your sweetheart."

"I promise," Jack said.

Varnes's face broke into a large grin.

"Good, Jones. I like that. I want someone to know the whole story and to have to live with it. It might as well be you. I need to head further down the trail this evening. Any final questions before I leave you?"

Jack thought and decided he might as well ask one last, nagging question.

"Yes, what about Laughing Sam? Where is he?"

"Why, he's right here!" Behind Jack a voice recognizable as Laughing Sam's spoke.

Severe pain and brilliant light flashed through Jack's brain.

CHAPTER THIRTEEN
ॐ

Saturday Night, August 26, to Sunday Afternoon, August 27, 1876—Nothingness.
Wet tongue on face. Dog? Pain in head.
Nothingness.
Soft muzzle on face. Hot horse breath? Pain in head.
Nothingness.
Being lifted? Is that a man? Pain in head.
Nothingness.
Sensation of warm liquid with a pleasant taste in his mouth. Aware of voices, male and female. *Cannot make out what they say,* he thought. *Why can't I understand their words?* Attempt to open eyes. A vision of a beautiful, smiling Asian woman. *Pain in head.*
Nothingness.
Voices... male and female.
"Will he recover?" a female voice asked.
"Yes," a male voice answered. "He has quite a nasty wound on the back of his head."
Both voices sounded familiar.
Sensation of cool, wet cloth on forehead.
"Oh, Jack!" the female voice spoke. "I love you so much! Please stay with me."
He attempted to open his eyes. He saw a beautiful face, a face he knew.

Name? What is her name? Pain in head.

Nothingness.

He felt a cool, wet cloth on his forehead. His mouth felt dry. A throbbing pain coursed through his head. Jack thought this was the worst hangover he'd ever had. He could tell he was lying on his back. He felt covers over him, and realized he was naked and thirsty. "Water," he croaked.

"Ah!" the familiar male voice said. "Miss Lil! Miss Lil! He awakes!"

Jack heard the scrape of a stool on wood flooring and the rush of a human body toward him.

"Jack! Oh, Jack! You're awake!" the familiar female voice said. *That voice is Lil,* Jack thought. *The other is Wong. This is a horrible hangover.* Jack attempted to open his eyes. He was inside a building and even though the natural light was subdued, it still hurt his eyes. But he did not care as he gazed into Lil's smiling, concerned face.

"Jack, I am going to lift you into a sitting position so we can give you something to drink and eat," Wong said. Strong arms lifted him up into a sitting position and laid him back, propped against the wall, with pillows and quilts cushioning him. Lil held a tin cup to his lips as he slowly sipped water. "Would you like to try a little beef broth?" Lil asked. Jack nodded his head.

He stared at her. *She is beautiful,* he thought.

Lil was waiting with a spoon of broth poised in front of his mouth. "Jack, open up." He obeyed, opening his mouth and tasting the warm liquid, then letting it slide down his throat. He allowed her to feed him the entire bowl. The pain in his head was not as great as it had been. Questions formed in his mind and he gave voice to them.

"What has happened? Why am I in bed? Why do I feel so bad?"

Lil looked up at Wong, who was standing beside her.

"We are not certain what happened to you, but we can tell you what we know." Wong said. "What do you remember?"

"I don't remember much of anything right now," Jack said. "Where am I?"

"You are a guest in my house," Wong answered. "It is best you stay here until you are better."

"Why?" Jack asked.

"We will tell you after we piece together what might have happened to you," Wong said.

"Why does my head hurt, why am I weak?"

"Someone hit you on the back of your head. You have been in and out of consciousness for a day."

"I have?"

"Yes," Lil said.

"What happened?"

Lil looked at Wong, who said, "Two Cantonese were bringing a wagon of goods toward Lead Saturday night. As they came to an abandoned cabin, a dog barked and a horse whinnied. They stopped to see what was going on and found you lying on the ground, hurt. They recognized you..."

"Do I know them?" Jack interrupted.

"No, but your good reputation and friendship with me has quickly spread with the Cantonese people in town."

Jack repositioned himself on the bed. "Go on, Fee Lee," he said.

"The men said your horse and Stonewall stood guard over you. Near you lay the body of Texas Jack, with two bullets in him. There was a gun in his hand and a gun in your hand. Both guns had fired two bullets. It appears the two of you had a gunfight and you were the winner. The men placed you in the wagon and brought you to me."

"I see," Jack said. He looked at Lil. Memories flooded back to the forefront. He had hurt her. "Lil, I am so sorry. Please forgive me."

"No, Jack," Lil said. "I'm the one who needs forgiving. I should have trusted what you were trying to tell me. The faro dealer, Dirty Em, explained it all to my aunt and uncle. Let us put all that behind us."

"Those are the most wonderful words I can hear," Jack said.

"More wonderful than the words, I love you?" she said bending over and kissing him on the lips.

"You're right. Those are the most wonderful words, and I love you, Lil."

His head was throbbing. His memory rushed back to him, up to the moment when he must have been struck on his head. He remembered Varnes's threats against Lil and his friends. Then he knew that he couldn't write about any of what had happened. He couldn't tell the law, as there was no law. Who in any authority with the territorial government would believe him? It was his word against all the others who know the truth. And if he did tell the tale, Lil and his friends would be killed. His brow furrowed.

"Jack, what's wrong?" Lil asked.

"Oh, my head hurts," Jack said, which was the truth.

"We should stop talking and let you rest," she said.

"Just a couple more questions. Lil, how did you come to be here at Fee Lee's home?"

"Jack," Fee Lee answered, "you told me about Miss Lil, and while you were out, you repeated her name again and again. I went to the theater and asked for Miss Lil and explained what had happened."

"I came immediately," she said.

"While I was out, I saw the face of a beautiful Chinese woman," he said. Then it dawned on Jack. "It was Di Lee. She was here too."

"Jack, you were delirious at times," Wong said without further comment.

"Jack, you need to rest," Lil said.

"You're right," Jack said. "I need to rest and then head out as soon as I can to find Crook."

"You're not leaving until you are healed up," she said.

We'll see, Jack thought and closed his eyes.

CHAPTER FOURTEEN
ஐ)෬

Tuesday Morning, August 29, 1876—The early morning sun peaked over Hebrew Hill. Deadwood bustled with its internal business—miners extracting gold from the gulch and others extracting the gold from the miners.

Jack stood, a solitary figure in Ingleside Cemetery. He was bareheaded, with his hat held in his left hand at his side. A clean linen bandage wrapped round his head covered his wound.

Jack glanced over at Wild Bill Hickok's headboard, Preacher Smith's cross, the headboards for Carlos, Poncho, and Bummer Dan. His eyes returned to the wooden cross in front of him. Carved in the boards were the words, "Pete Adams, died August 26, 1876, at peace in the arms of the Lord."

A cool, gentle breeze brought the fragrance of pine.

"You shouldn't be here, Pete," Jack said. "You had so much to live for."

As soon as he was done here, he was leaving with California Joe in their quest for General Crook. He reached for his Elgin pocket watch to see what time it was. Then he remembered, his watch was gone. Varnes must have stolen his watch after Laughing Sam knocked him on the head. Varnes did not take anything else, only his watch.

"Pete, I can't tell anyone about what happened to you or the others here," he said. "There are no authorities to tell the tale to. If I did tell people about it, what could they do? And the most important thing is if I told people, Lil, Aunt Lou, and other lives would be in danger."

Jack paused and looked up at the bright blue sky, the pines gently swaying in the breeze.

"But I promise you this, Pete," he said. "This is not over. This is not over by a long shot."

Jack placed his hat back on his head, turned from the grave, and slowly walked down the hill.

CHAPTER FIFTEEN
ℰℭ

A Night in November 1876—The drunk weaved through the empty back alley behind several of Denver's many saloons. He pulled his coat tight against the crisp night air, shoved his hands into his pockets and belched.

Light spilling from a few cracked backdoors or the rare window punctuated the darkness. Laughter and shouting tried to compete with the lively piano music drifting out of the nearest establishment, a rousing rendition of "Camp Town Ladies."

"Frank."

The drunk stopped in his tracks, peering into the dark shadows.

"Who's there?"

"Frank, it's Johnny. Johnny Varnes."

"Oh, Johnny. Ya scared me."

"Frank, I think you got something for me." Varnes stepped out of the shadows. "Don't you?" Varnes asked, inches from Frank's face.

"Johnny, I ain't got your money yet. Give me a couple of days and I'll have it for ya."

"Why, you miserable, drunken idiot! You had enough money to go get yourself soused now, didn't you? I need that money and I need it now!"

"How? I ain't got..."

Varnes's left hand shot out and grabbed Frank by the throat. His right fist smashed into Frank's face. Frank fell to the ground like a sack of potatoes. Varnes gave Frank a swift kick to the ribs, forcing a scream from the injured man, but no one inside the buildings heard over their self-generated racket.

"I want my money and I want it now!" Varnes shouted as he kicked Frank again, this time in the groin. The helpless, sobbing drunk pulled into a fetal position. Varnes bent down and began searching Frank's coat pockets for money.

A dog's snarl a few feet away brought Varnes to a stop.

"What the ..."

"Varnes," a man's voice spoke from the dark.

"What? Who's there?" Varnes said as he stood erect.

"Johnny Varnes."

"What do you want? Show yourself."

The silhouette of a man stepped in front of the meager light spilling from the nearest saloon's backdoor, turned, and faced Varnes.

"It's time you pay up."

"Pay up for what? I don't owe you nothin'. People pay me. I don't pay nothin," Varnes said. His right hand imperceptibly inched toward the grip of his holstered pistol.

"Say, I know you. Get out of here now and I won't hurt you like I hurt this drunk," Varnes sneered.

"It's time to pay up for Wild Bill," the silhouette said.

Varnes's hand reached the pistol grip.

"It's time to pay up for Preacher Smith."

Varnes slipped the pistol from out of the holster.

"It's time to pay up for Carlos, Poncho, Bummer Dan, and the others."

Varnes slowly brought up the pistol's barrel level alongside his holster waist belt.

"But most of all, it's time to pay up for Pete Adams."

Varnes's finger slid to the trigger of his double-action pistol.

"Bummer Dan was a useless fool, and that kid was just as stupid," Varnes sneered, his finger applying pressure to the pistol trigger.

The crack of a pistol shot.

The beat of a heart.

The crack of a pistol shot.

Two blinding muzzle flashes flared the alley into false daylight.

Varnes dropped to the ground, his life ebbing out of a bullet hole through the heart. The silhouetted man stood erect, smoking pistol in hand.

The piano player continued to tickle the ivory keys. The revelers continued to laugh and shout.

The silhouetted man walked over to Varnes. He nudged Varnes with the toe of his boot. No response. The man stooped over the body. The nearest barroom's meager light reflected off a watch fob and chain. The man unfastened the fob from Varnes's vest and pulled out a pocket watch. He found a lucifer in his coat pocket and struck it. The flaring flame revealed the fob bearing the emblem of the Grand Army of the Republic and the watch of Elgin make. The man tripped the button and checked the time— ten p.m. Grunting a "humph," he snapped the cover closed, dropped the watch in his coat pocket, and stood.

The dog sniffed at Frank, who was moaning, oblivious to everything but his own engulfing pain. The dog licked Frank's face, giving a little whimper.

The silhouetted man holstered his pistol. "It's all right, Stonewall. It's all right."

Bill Markley

ACKNOWLEDGEMENTS

In *Deadwood Dead Men*, I wanted to try to get the setting and feel of Deadwood as correct as I could for August, 1876. I read the newspapers and old-timer reminiscences; and asked questions of many folks who have more knowledge than I do. It was fun to put this story together and I want to thank all the people who have helped me along the way. First, thanks to Steven Anderson and all the folks at Goldminds for believing in my story and presenting it to the world. Thank you, Rose Speirs, for checking all aspects of the story and being my Deadwood connection on such things as when does the sun first appear in Deadwood Gulch and when does it disappear over the western ridges in August? Jerry Bryant, thanks for contributing your historical factoids. Nancy Plain, the Comma Queen, thank you for all the help with my grammar; I am a comma minimalist. Mike Pellerzi, Pard, thanks for your help with all things Western! As Mike says, "Keep your power dry and cinch tight!" Sherry Monahan, thank you for guiding me through the game of Faro. Slainte! Lucia Robson, thank you for your Asian advice, Abrazos! Cheryl Stein and Kathy Elijah, thank you for explaining Victorian customs and fashions to this novice on a hot August day along the banks of the Cheyenne River. Richard Bickel and Jim Hatzell, thanks for your help. Joe Nadenicek, thanks for your legal review of the Harry Young trial! King Bennett and the Camptown Shakers, thank you for your musical advice. If anyone wants to hear what the music in Deadwood would have sounded like in August 1876, listen to the Camptown Shakers. Thanks to the folks of the Adams

239

Museum and the South Dakota Archives for all your assistance during my research. I know there have been others who have helped along the way, and if you know me, you know I have a faulty memory, so thanks to all those who have given me support and help during this writing. Thanks to my Mom and brother Doug for their support. Thanks to my wife, Liz, for putting up with my long hours of hogging the laptop and asking, "Hey, how do you spell...?" Thanks to my kids, Chris and Becky, for your support. In all I do, thank you, Lord, for all you have given me. It is a wonderful life! Last but not least, I want to thank you the reader, for time-traveling with me to Deadwood, August, 1876.

OTHER BEST SELLING TITLES FROM

GOLDMINDS

UNBROKE HORSES
By D. B. Jackson

OBLIVION'S ALTAR
By David Marion Wilkinson

MOON OF MADNESS
By Don Coldsmith

THE BITTER ROAD
By Steven Law

THEY RODE GOOD HORSES
By D. B. Jackson

THE TRUE FATHER
By Steven Law

www.goldmindspub.com

ABOUT THE AUTHOR

A member of Western Writers of America (WWA), Bill Markley is a staff writer for WWA's *Roundup Magazine*. He has written three nonfiction books, and also writes for *True West*, *Wild West*, and *South Dakota* magazines. He earned a master's degree in Environmental Engineering, has worked in Antarctica, and currently works for the South Dakota Department of Environment and Natural Resources. Raised on a farm near Valley Forge, Pennsylvania, Bill has always loved history. He reenacts Civil War infantry and frontier cavalry and has participated in movies, including *Dances With Wolves*, *Far and Away*, and *Gettysburg*. Bill and his wife Liz live and work in Pierre, South Dakota, where they have raised two children, now grown. *Deadwood Dead Men* is Markley's first novel.

CPSIA information can be obtained at www.ICGtesting.com
Printed in the USA
LVOW13*0227250414

383225LV00004B/34/P